Anna Mae's BUCKSHOT

A NOVEL ABOUT THE POWER
OF GOD'S LOVE

David R. Kosak

ISBN 978-1-68570-027-0 (paperback)
ISBN 979-8-88685-789-4 (hardcover)
ISBN 978-1-68570-028-7 (digital)

Copyright © 2022 by David R. Kosak

All rights reserved. No part of this publication may be reproduced, distributed, or transmitted in any form or by any means, including photocopying, recording, or other electronic or mechanical methods without the prior written permission of the publisher. For permission requests, solicit the publisher via the address below.

Christian Faith Publishing
832 Park Avenue
Meadville, PA 16335
www.christianfaithpublishing.com

Story contains battle scenes depicted with graphic violence.

Printed in the United States of America

For my granddaughters: Adeline Watts,
Kailey Kosak, and Taryn Kosak

> We look forward to a time when the
> Power of Love will replace the Love of Power.
> Then our world will know the blessings of peace.
>
> —William E. Gladstone

PROLOGUE

> Major, tell my father I died with my face to the enemy.
>
> IE Avery

On July 2, 1863, thirty-four-year-old lieutenant colonel Isaac E. Avery was shot from his horse while leading a Confederate charge on Cemetery Hill. Unable to speak and aware he was about to die, he pulled from his pocket a pencil and a scrap of paper and scrawled those words. He would die the following day.

In the note, sometimes referred as the Letter from the Dead, Avery wanted to convey to his father his honor on the battlefield. Such was the case during the Civil War. The premium for honor and valor was so great he spent his remaining strength galvanizing, with his hand for his father, his honorable end. It is certain that during the most brutal conflict to take place on American soil, his feelings were not unique.

The American Civil War was the deadliest war in its history. More American lives were lost during the Civil War than any other war in which America participated. Not often discussed, however, were horses. It is estimated 1,500,000 horses, mules, and donkeys died by war's end. Many from disease and exhaustion, but countless others from battle wounds. Before armies became mechanized in the twentieth century, horses were indispensable. Moving supplies and artillery for armies numbering in the tens of thousands was impossible without horses and mules. Officers directed men and artillery placement from horseback; and the eyes of the army, North and South, were the cavalry. As a result, infantrymen on both sides would not hesitate to shoot a horse.

A great deal of the story you are about to read involves the Civil War. This, however, will only serve as a backdrop. The story is about a superhero.

A superhero who brings a little girl and a horse together. A living superhero whose name is Jesus. You will not see Jesus directly in this story. You will see him through the eyes of an old woman named Mary. Mary chooses to see Jesus where others don't. For most Christians, it is easy to see Jesus through a life-altering miracle. On the other hand, simple things elude us. We rationalize and dismiss the simple actions of nature as mere happenstance, like, for example, acorns falling from a tree or even a breeze. It is impossible for any of us to fathom the complexity of God's plan and the subtleties that God employs to advance it. Mary chooses to see Jesus and his handiwork even in the simple things around her. Everything except the sinful nature of man. To her, man creates his own problems and misery.

Mary also sees God's greatest superpower. It is the one superpower God gifted man with from the moment of creation and put it on full display when God's Son, Jesus, was crucified. It rests, waiting to be unleashed, in the soul of every man, woman, and child from birth to death. It is the one superpower that can change history, save a troubled world, or salvage a tormented soul. Two thousand years ago, through the crucifixion and resurrection of Jesus, God saved mankind with that superpower.

The superpower is love. You will see as Mary does how God, with a horse, opens the heart of a little girl and unbridle within her the superpower of love. The child is Mary's granddaughter, Anna Mae. The horse, ordinary in every way, will touch all those who come in contact with him. He showed Anna Mae how to see with her heart. He showed her how to love. The horse's name is Buckshot.

CHAPTER 1

Sharpsburg

August 1888

Sharpsburg, Maryland, site of the Battle of Antietam—the deadliest day in American military history—is a small farming community. Founded in 1763 after the French Indian War, Sharpsburg lies within walking distance of the Potomac River. Gettysburg, Pennsylvania, is located fifty miles to the northeast; and Washington DC, lies seventy miles to the southeast.

George Washington briefly considered locating the US Capitol along the Potomac between Shepherdstown, Virginia, and Sharpsburg, Maryland, before settling on its current location. Farmers grew corn, tobacco, and other crops which they would sell throughout the area. In August of 1888, as the nation enjoyed robust growth, Sharpsburg, nestled among patches of wooded areas and soft rolling hills, changed little.

In September 1862, Sharpsburg, Maryland, was at the center of the world stage. Abraham Lincoln wanted to issue his Emancipation Proclamation and free African Americans, including those in the Confederate states, from slavery. At the time, the war was not going well for the North. Several in Lincoln's cabinet felt the Union needed a decisive victory, or the proclamation would be meaningless. Lincoln, taking their advice, put off his proclamation until the Union Army could claim such a victory.

Shortly after the opening shots were fired on Fort Sumter, the Union Army was routed by Confederate forces at Bull Run. It became clear to those in the North that a short war lasting only a few weeks was actually becoming a long-drawn-out struggle. Confederate forces strung together several impressive victories, including the Second Bull Run which was fought between August 28 to August 30, 1862. Like Lincoln, Confederate President Jefferson Davis needed another victory to coax Britain or France to help the Confederate cause. England and France relied heavily on the South's most important export, cotton. However, Britain and France were strongly opposed to the institution of slavery which had been abolished in their respective nations.

On September 17, 1862, along Antietam Creek just outside Sharpsburg, Maryland, Confederate General Robert E. Lee would face off against Union General George McClellan. It would be one of the most pivotal battles of the Civil War and Lee's first venture onto Union soil. Lee was hopeful a victory would cause Maryland, a border state, to join the Confederacy—a hope that would never materialize. The battle in which McClellan eked out a marginal victory over Lee, became known as the Battle of Antietam or Battle of Sharpsburg. After Lee's defeat, both England and France chose to remain neutral. In spite of the weak victory, it was enough for Lincoln to announce his preliminary Emancipation Proclamation on September 22, 1862.

After the Civil War, America was in the golden age of westward expansion that left Sharpsburg behind. On May 10, 1869, the transcontinental railroad was completed at Promontory Summit Utah. The westbound crew of the Union Pacific which originated from Omaha, Nebraska, met the eastbound crew of the Central Pacific which originated from Sacramento California.

Following an opening ceremony, the transcontinental railroad was opened. This allowed the movement of goods and people safely and economically from the east to the west in days instead of months. Nearly eight years earlier, on October 24, 1861, the transcontinental telegraph was completed. Like the railroad, it reached coast-to-coast, allowing information to be communicated at speeds unheard of before. Now even banking transactions could move at near light-speed. Both the railroad and the telegraph intensified the westward expansion well underway since the 1840s.

Westward expansion, sometimes referred to as Manifest Destiny, exasperated existing tensions between native American tribes and settlers seeking to claim the land. Results were fighting and small wars beginning as soon as Europeans started to settle America as early as the 1600s. The increased settling of the West after the Civil War spawned more battles between the native population and settlers moving west of the Mississippi. The ongoing wars between the United States and Native Americans came to a head in the last half of the nineteenth century and early twentieth century. The Posey War, considered by some to be the last Native American uprising, occurred in March 1923.

The American government broke many of its treaties with Native American tribes establishing reservations and an illusion of autonomy. The Fort Laramie Treaty of 1868, for example, created the Great Sioux Reservation which established a large expanse of land west of the Missouri River. The treaty protected the Black Hills of South Dakota and Wyoming from White settlement.

When rumors of gold within the reservation were confirmed by George Custer in 1874, a gold rush was ignited. Mostly White prospectors seeking riches surged into territory set aside in the aforementioned Fort Laramie Treaty. This ultimately led to the Black Hills War or the Great Sioux War, and the annihilation of Lieutenant Colonel George Custer and part of the Seventh Cavalry on June 25, 1876, during the Battle of the Little Big Horn or Custer's Last Stand.

In the end, the United States government prevailed and took the land, leaving the Native American population without the territory originally arranged for in the treaty.

In 1888, Grover Cleveland was president. Elected in 1884, he took office in 1885 and was the first democrat to be elected since James Buchanan in 1856. He had no formal legal education, but while clerking for a prestigious law firm in New York, he studied for the New York Bar and was subsequently admitted in 1858. The burning issue of slavery, however, would ignite a constitutional crisis that only an all-out war could resolve, putting a damper on Cleveland's career in the legal profession.

On April 12, 1861, Confederate forces opened artillery fire on Fort Sumter in Charleston Harbor, marking the start of the Civil War. At the onset of the Civil War, the leadership of the North believed it would be short and relied solely on volunteers who were given an enlistment bounty. With the increased demand for fighting men and the complexity of this system, it was easy for inductees to desert and reenlist elsewhere for additional bounty. This was known as "bounty jumping," and it became necessary to implement a draft.

In March of 1863, the United States Congress passed the Civil War Military Draft Act to fulfill the needs of the Union Army. It was the first draft to actually be put into practice in the history of the United States. The controversial law would allow an exemption for anyone who could find a substitute or pay to the government three hundred dollars, a considerable sum in the 1860s. The Civil War was thought of as the rich man's war and the poor man's fight. In New York City, this inequity increased the already existing resentment Whites felt for free Blacks. They feared free Blacks would take their jobs and, because of this, had sympathies with the South. In July of 1863, as a result of the law, New York City suffered some of the most violent riots in American history to that point. Among draft offices and other government facilities, the African American community suffered much of the violence.

Cleveland, himself, would avoid serving in the army during the Civil War by paying another man three hundred dollars to serve in his stead and thus resume his career. The war ended in April of 1865. In 1870, Cleveland was elected sheriff of Erie County, New York, and his political career began. A career that would take him to the White House when he, after serving as mayor of Buffalo New York, ran for governor. On January 2, 1882, he became governor of New York, paving his way to become president in 1885.

In 1888, however, Lee and McClellan had passed. Only their memories and those who survived the fighting remained. Veterans from the North now lived among those from the South in peace almost as if there never was a war, each telling stories of the war as they saw it. Stories told and retold by aging veterans who, like veterans of wars before and those to come, fought and died for the wills of politicians that often had little interest in fighting themselves. Things like *state's rights* and *slavery* meant little during a battle. Like soldiers in all wars, what the men who fought in the Civil War wanted was to return home.

America's deadliest war and Lincoln's Emancipation Proclamation did nothing to eliminate the oppressive discrimination experienced by free Blacks, both North and South. The abolition of slavery with the ratification of the thirteenth amendment on December 6, 1865, was only the first step in a long journey that would span more than a century and still continues. In 1888, there were many African American intellectuals whose passion for civil rights was forged in slavery. They include Harriet Tubman, Frederick Douglass, and Booker T. Washington.

Harriet Tubman (1820–1913) was born a slave and endured tremendous hardships. She suffered brutal beatings until she managed to escape by way of the Underground Railroad. At great risk to herself, she would return time and again to help other slaves seeking freedom escape. Over time, the Underground Railroad developed into a vast network shuttling slaves from the South, clandestinely, as far north as Canada. She earned the nickname Moses because like Moses, who led the Israelites from Egypt to the Promised Land, she led her people to freedom. During the war, she worked as a nurse and even as a spy and was the first woman to lead an armed expedition. For all this, she received no pay. Later in life, she was granted a small pension and dedicated herself to the suffrage movement.

Frederick Douglass (1818–1895) also born a slave and, like Tubman, endured many beatings. He taught himself to read and write and in turn taught other slaves to read and write. After two attempts, he made good his escape in 1838 and became a writer and orator. He was a famous intellect and wrote several autobiographies throughout his life. He became a committed abolitionist, giving lectures throughout the world. During the Civil War, Douglass advised President Lincoln regarding the treatment of Black soldiers. After the war, he dedicated his efforts toward education and believed that education was the key to Black empowerment and was an advocate for school desegregation.

Booker T. Washington (1856–1915), like Douglass and Tubman, was also born into slavery and, like Douglass, taught himself to read. At sixteen, Washington entered Hampton Normal and Agricultural Institute in Virginia. He covered the cost of his tuition by working as a janitor and studied academics, developing an interest in public speaking. After graduating with honors, he became a teacher. On July 4, 1881, he founded Tuskegee University. He and his students built many of the buildings themselves. At times, Washington was criticized for advocating a slow approach in advancing civil rights like the Atlanta Compromise. Still, Washington was able to raise vast sums of money and political support for his causes and was a tireless advocate for equal rights.

These and countless more would lay the cornerstone upon which racial equality would be built upon in the twentieth century and into the twenty-first century.

The farmers around the small town of Sharpsburg in 1888 cared little about the rapid expansion of the nation, the plight of free Blacks, the fighting between the government and the Native Americans, or the historic Battle of Antietam. What mattered to the farmers in August 1888 were their crops of tobacco and corn. Along the many roads, farmers would move their produce. In August appeared a rising Sirius at dawn to welcome the dog days of summer. The biggest concern for the local farmers was the heat and rain or lack thereof. August 1888 was hot and dry.

CHAPTER 2

Anna Mae Meets Uncle Zeb

"Come on, Lightning. Tarnation, horse. I know it's hot, but don't stop now, ole boy. We're almost tharr," said Zebadiah Ezekiel Abbott, called Zeb by his friends.

Lightning was the name given to the horse due to his slow unhurried nature. If the gentle horse took a notion, he would simply stop, and no amount of cajoling could inspire him to move. Often, in frustration, Zeb would resort to cantankerous outbursts when Lightning became stubborn, but he could never strike the beautiful animal. In fact, one could not even find spurs or a riding crop in his possession. He ran his hand through his horse's sweat-soaked mane then gave it a friendly rub between its ears.

Zeb took meticulous care of the horse that had been at his side since 1862 when he took possession of him after the Battle of Antietam. Lightning's black coat had a shine that, in the light of the morning sun, looked wet. His blaze face matched the white mane, tail, and solid-white belly and legs. The horse was a beautiful, almost gaudy, stallion in spite of his advanced age of twenty-nine years. In the end, Zeb always gave in to the well-meaning horse. He understood horses, and Lightning was special. He never once had seen his ears pinned, and no other being, neither man nor animal, was more dependable. Lightning was the one good thing Zeb got from the war, and in spite of Zeb's frustrations, he loved the horse.

Zeb gently nudged Lightning with his heels. The horse would not budge, showing his displeasure by snorting and blowing. He pulled a handkerchief from his pocket, wiped his brow, and glanced at the August sun that was sinking in a cloudless sky, still high enough to cause considerable misery.

In spite of the heat, Zeb enjoyed the slow ride in the countryside. The freedom of being out on the trail alone and taking in the beauty of the mountains overcame the hardship and hot weather. He was tasked by his sister-in-law, Mary Louise Abbott, to pick up her daughter—Katherine Hill—and granddaughter—Anna Mae—who resided just south of Sharpsburg, Maryland. The trip took him over Catoctin Mountain, a favorite hunting spot for him and his late older brother, John Abbott, Mary's husband. The return journey, however, would take him through the Antietam Battlefield and thus conjure up nightmares of the last battle he took part in during the war. A dread he knew he would have to face.

Zeb realized he pushed his old horse too hard. They were on the last leg of the three-day journey that originated from Mary's farm, ten miles south of Gettysburg. Even though it was August, it seemed hotter than he could remember, and like his horse, Zeb was thirsty, hungry, and ready to rest.

On this journey, he was accompanied by an unwanted companion: a little chihuahua named Caesar after the Roman Emperor Julius Caesar. The small dog weighing less than five pounds was solid-white with a tan patch over his left eye that ran to his left ear. The tip of the dog's tail, which was too big for such a small dog, was also tan. He had large bugged-out brown eyes set in an oddly round head that seemed smushed together by hurried hands.

To Zeb, the dog was ugly and useless. Nevertheless, Mary dearly loved Caesar, a gift given by the pastor of her church, Emerson Giles, for teaching Sunday school. In spite of Mary's feelings, the dog was an annoyance to Zeb. He hated the little dog and had no desire to have it pestering him on this journey. But after several failed attempts to discourage the small animal, Zeb gave up, and much to his chagrin, the dog tagged along.

"Come on, Lightning. Jist a lil' fu'ther. Look see, jist over tharr."

Zeb pleaded with the horse and pointed to his niece's white farmhouse nestled in a grove of large oak trees. Still, he refused to move a muscle. From his saddle, Zeb looked down at Caesar who was standing motionless, enjoying the shade provided by Lightning's shadow, panting and returning a sympathetic gaze. Zeb gave in to the will of his horse and dismounted. Lightning's ears perked straight up, demonstrating the animal's pleasure with Zeb's acquiescence, and his blinking eyes indicated his indifference to his master's wants. Zeb gently tugged on the reins and resumed walking with Caesar, carefully trotting within the confines of the horse's protective shadow.

"Tarnation, horse. Are ya happy now?"

Lightning followed Zeb, and the exhausted trio turned onto a dry and dusty lane lined on either side by overgrown Johnson grass. The spikelet's arcing motionless in the still hot air of August. Heat radiated from Lightning's black sweat-soaked coat. At the end of the lane was their final destination.

"Ole boy, it's plumb hot out here. We been tagether a long time, and ya took me lots of places. I reckon I don't blame ya," said Zeb. He gently patted the horse on the neck and looked at Caesar, still keeping up panting and earning the dog a measure of respect. Zeb said, "Ole boy, we've made it. Look at them tharr shade trees. Jist a few more feet and I'll git ya all the oats and water ya can handle. Sounds good now, don't it?"

A little girl wearing a sky-blue cotton dress trimmed with white lace stood in front of the house like a statue, mesmerized at the sight of Zeb and his two companions headed in her direction. Her bright golden blond hair—which framed a pretty face with large dark brown eyes, high well-defined cheekbones, and small upturned nose—was pulled into a ponytail. She was of normal height and weight for a twelve-year-old girl who was developing into a teenager.

Zeb recognized his great-niece and quickened his pace, and she broke free of her trance and made her way to Zeb. Caesar ran to the child with such speed one would not have known the dog had been walking all day. The two greeted each other as if they were long-lost friends, with Caesar whipping his tail wildly back and forth. She reached down and picked up the friendly little dog as if he were a gift straight from heaven. Caesar expressed his happiness by licking her face with reckless abandon. The little girl laughed with joy, showing no concern over the strange man's intentions.

"What's your dog's name, mister?" asked the girl.

Zeb marveled at the site of the child and her uncanny resemblance to her mother. He said, "Aren't ya a pretty lil' girl. His name's Caesar, named after some Roman king. Why, I hope that tharr king wasn't anythin' like that lil' mutt." A warm smile exposed a single tooth that popped through his beard just below a thin nose which was bent, as if it were dealt a powerful blow. Sweat-soaked black hair with streaks of gray hung below a slouch hat.

The girl cradled the excited dog in her arms. "Caesar. That's a nice name." With an inquisitive look, she asked, "Mister, you have a pretty horse. What's his name? Why are you walking? Is your horse lame?"

At six feet three inches, Zeb towered over the twelve-year-old child. A muslin shirt hung loosely, like his overalls, over a thin frame. A bushy beard covered a disfigurement to his jaw from a wound he received during the Battle of Antietam. Zeb possessed incredible strength acquired from a lifetime of farmwork, and chewing tobacco was his only vice. He was in good shape for his forty-six years.

He looked down at the ground; spit tobacco; then returned his gaze to Lightning, whose nose was in the air smelling water; and replied indignantly, "TARNATION. Lil' lady, ya sure ask a lot a questions. His name's Lightning, and he ain't no more lame than me or you. Why, this here horse is nothin' but a dandy. Forgets he's a horse. Jist plumb lazy's all."

"Are you my uncle Zeb? He's supposed to be here today. Mom and I are waitin' for him."

Zeb ran his fingers through his beard and replied, "Lil' lady, that jist depends."

"Depends on what, mister?"

"Dependin' on if'n ya be Anna Mae Hill. Are ya?"

The girl laughed and said, "Yes, I'm Anna Mae Hill."

"Well then, I be yir ma's uncle Zeb, and that makes me yir great-uncle," replied Zeb with a welcoming grin exposing his lone upper incisor.

ANNA MAE'S BUCKSHOT

Anna Mae, with the dog in her arms, turned and ran to the house, shouting, "I'll tell Mom you're here, Uncle Zeb. She's a 'specting you."

Lightning was standing still with his nose to the air sniffing and his ears rotating in different directions. Zeb asked his horse rhetorically, "Ya smellin' water, ain't ya?" The sight of the shade and the smell of water revived Lightning's remaining energy. The thirsty horse broke free of Zeb's loose grip and trotted to the house and the welcoming shade, leaving Zeb to fend for himself. Zeb laughed as he said, "Tarnation, ole boy, moments ago ya was ready fer the angels, but now ya ready to run that tharr Kentucky Derby." Zeb followed Lightning and made his way to the house. "I'm right behind ya, ole boy."

He found his horse at a water trough among the shade trees. The dense foliage gave welcome relief to the brutal August heat. So hot that robins and blue jays sat silently perched, not wishing to venture into the heat. The only sound he could hear was Lightning feverishly lapping up water. Anna Mae appeared on the porch with her mother, holding her newfound friend Caesar, and said, "Look at Uncle Zeb's dog, Mom. His name's Caesar. Isn't he cute?"

Zeb could not hide the indignation that returned in full to his face. "That lil' mutt ain't mine. He belongs to yir mamaw. Katherine, let me tell ya plainly that whoever give that dog to yir ma knowed what they was a doin'."

With the aim of a skilled marksman, Zeb sent a stream of tobacco juice at a small ant hill not three feet away and, with the sleeve of his shirt, wiped the excess from his chin. He turned to Anna Mae and continued his tirade. "That dog has to be the worst contrivance of man. Who on God's Earth would want a dog like that? Can ya see that dog tryin' to tree a coon? Why hell, I bet he can't even carry a biscuit. Nary a more worthless animal on four legs. I was a hopin' a hawk would a got 'im, but he was smart, never more than five feet from ole Lightning the whole trip." Anna Mae sensed her uncle's protestations were mostly for show and laughed as she pet the happy dog.

Katherine Abbott Hill, Zeb's niece at five feet two inches tall and 110 pounds, was a comely woman of thirty-three who still retained the look of a woman in her twenties. She had large brown eyes and high cheekbones like her daughter and, like her daughter, had her shoulder-length blond hair pulled into a ponytail. Anna Mae looked so much like her mother sometimes they were confused as sisters. An avid reader, Katherine was articulate and often helped teach at Anna Mae's school. Katherine took one look at the man with the bushy beard with one tooth and recognized her Uncle Zeb. Laughing, she ran to him and threw her arms around him, and said, "Uncle Zeb. Why, he's just a little dog. Can't be that bad. No need to fret now. I have beef stew ready. Glad you made it safe. Have any problems?"

Zeb reached up, removed his slouch hat, and wiped his forehead. "No problems, jist hot an' dry. Can't remember it bein' so hot even fer August. Nary even a small breeze. But me an' ole Lightning made it fine. Even that mangy mutt made it."

Katherine said nothing; she just shot a skeptical look at Zeb. His spontaneous smile betrayed his true feelings about the dog as he continued, "I don't reckon the dog's all that bad. Yir ma thinks Jesus sent him to her fer some purpose."

"Yes, Mom is surely full of the Spirit," said Katherine.

Zeb said, "Yeah, ain't nothin' she can touch or see that Jesus don't a plan fer." He pointed at some acorns lying about the ground. "Why, even them acorns on the ground was put tharr by Jesus. She'd tell ya that Jesus hisself piled 'em up with his very hand fer some plan. Can ya jist see Jesus a runnin' aroun' stackin' acorns," said Zeb as he laughed.

Katherine said, "All the good on the Earth that is, Uncle Zeb. As for the wickedness, she'll tell you that's man's doin'. Don't get her going on that now."

Zeb said, "I reckon we all need that woman's faith. Shucks, that dog kept up with me an' ole Lightning an' don't eat much, jist lil' bit a beef jerky. Look at Anna Mae. She's took a shine to 'im. But, Katherine, I don't mind tellin' ya that I'm ready to eat."

With his hat in his right hand, Zeb pointed to the child. "Goodness, last time I saw that child, she was knee-high to a June bug. Tarnation, Katherine. Jist look at her now. By golly, that child looks jist like ya when ya was her age. Why, when she's growed up, I bet she'll be jist as purty too."

Katherine sighed. "Been a while since I've seen any family." Katherine turned her attention to Anna Mae who was holding and petting Caesar, and admonished her daughter, "Anna Mae, mind your manners, put that dog down, and help your uncle Zeb and get some feed for Lightning."

Anna Mae, who could barely contain her excitement over the dog, gently set Caesar down and ran to her uncle, "I'll help ya, Uncle Zeb." She rubbed Lightening between his ears. The horse, still busy drinking water, ignored the child. "He's a pretty horse. Can I ride 'im?" asked Anna Mae.

"Yes, lil' lady, ya can, but not till we git ya to yir mamaw's. She made me promise to git ya back on time. If'n we're one minute late, that woman'll skin me alive. She's plumb excited. Made all kinds of plans. Even got a big dinner planned. Why, I'd rather be struck dead by a lightning bolt than have that woman upset."

Anna Mae ran to the barn with Caesar at her feet, "I'll git some feed for Lightning."

Katherine said, "Uncle Zeb, I'll get dinner ready while you and Anna Mae take care of your horse."

Zeb looked at his horse, still drinking from the trough, and said, "Tarnation, Lightning, yir belly'll split wide open," after a brief pause. "Aw, jist go ahead and git yir fill. Reckon it's good. We've got a long journey tomorrow." The horse was too busy drinking to pay any attention to Zeb as he removed the saddle. "Lightning, even the president don't git that good a treatment. Now don't go a git'n used to it."

Anna Mae returned with feed for Lightning. "He's such a nice horse, Uncle Zeb. I wish I had a horse like that."

"Well, ought not tell ya, but I think yir mamaw has a horse picked out fer ya when ya git tharr," replied Zeb.

Anna Mae's eyes flew open, and she dropped what she was doing and ran into the house shouting, "Mom, I'm git'n a horse. Mamaw is givin' me a horse of my own."

Katherine looked at her daughter and admonished her. "Anna Mae, we got to get there first. We have a long trip. Now get back out there and help your uncle like I told you, or there'll be no horse."

Elated, Anna Mae turned from her mother and joined her uncle with Lightning. "I'll be good, Mom." Zeb was still removing Lightning's saddle when Anna Mae asked, "What kinda horse, Uncle Zeb?"

Zeb already regretted telling the child about the special present. He looked down at her and answered, "Tarnation, lil' lady. No matter. I'm sure yir a git'n a good horse, jist be happy. Shoulda not told ya."

Anna Mae pressed the issue, "Can ya tell me his name?"

Zeb just wanted to put the issue to rest and snapped. "I ain't tellin' ya his name. Yir mamaw'll tell ya when ya git tharr. Now ya jist need to take care of ole Lightning."

Disappointed, Anna Mae said, "I won't say no more, Uncle Zeb," and turned her attention back to Lightning.

"Good. I don't want to hear nary a word about that tharr horse," replied Zeb as he turned and went to the house.

Zeb was greeted by the smell of freshly baked bread as he entered through the front door. He made his way to the kitchen where he found Katherine setting the table. Katherine said, "You can clean up at the sink."

Zeb walked to the sink and worked the pump, "Last time I was here, James jist finished the house. I remember when he put this here pump in. I thought he was plumb crazy, buildin' this house around that well all that work. I got to admit he was right. Sure was a good carpenter he was. Could build jist about anythin'."

"Yes, he built us a nice house. Every winter, I was grateful," said Katherine with a sigh.

Zeb said, "I hate that James passed."

"Yes, I love him and miss him, but the consumption was too much. He was sufferin' so. He's such a good man. Took care of me and Anna Mae, couldn't've asked for a better husband. He had the Spirit like Mom. I bet Mom loved him as much as I loved him. Now he's with the Lord," said Katherine.

"Yes, and a losin' yir pa the same way. I sure miss my brother. Been a tough year fer all of us, but hardest on yir ma. How's Anna Mae holdin' up?"

Katherine said, "She don't understand. She has bad moments. Hard to explain to Anna Mae. I think we're better off together for a while, me and Mom that is. Most our family live around Gettysburg. It'll be good for Anna Mae. She'll get to make new friends."

Anna Mae ran through the front door carrying Caesar. "Took care of Lightning, Mom."

Zeb walked to the dining table and said, "Why, thank ya, lil' lady."

With a beaming smile, Anna Mae replied, "You're welcome, Uncle Zeb. Got to get used to takin' care of horses now that I'm git'n one of my very own. I can't wait. I'll ride him to school every day."

Zeb reminded Anna Mae, "Now don't ya go a tellin' yir mamaw about me lettin' the cat outa the bag. Ya hear me, lil' lady?"

Katherine laughed and said, "Anne Mae, won't say a word till her mamaw does. Now won't you, Anna Mae?"

"Don't you two worry none 'bout me," replied Anna Mae with a devilish grin as she stood petting Caesar.

Katherine said, "Now it's time to eat. You put that dog outside and wash your hands. But first let me bless this meal."

Zeb removed his hat and all bowed their heads as Katherine went to the Lord to ask for the blessing. "Dear heavenly Father, we come before you and ask you to bless this food that we are about to eat. Let it nourish our bodies and sustain us on our long journey. Let us give thanks for all your blessings. Let us also give thanks for Uncle Zeb, as he will guide us. Please grant us safe passage as we unite with our loved ones. It is in the name of your Son, Jesus Christ, we ask. Amen." Zeb and Anna Mae followed with a soft amen.

Zeb returned his hat to his head and said, "Let me have some o' that stew. Those rolls look good, Katherine. I'm a starvin'."

Anna Mae said, "Can't wait to see my horse. What's he look like? Is he a Palomino? I like Palominos."

Katherine snapped. "Now Anna Mae just eat. That horse'll be fine till we get there." Then Katherine turned to Zeb and said,

"Goodness. That child'll think of nothing else till we get there. Now you two eat all you want. I made enough for the trip. I allowed for three days, right, Uncle Zeb?"

Zeb stopped eating and took a long drink of lemonade and said, "Yes, the way I figure it tomorrow, we'll try to git to Rocky Ford. It be more than halfway. It's a good place to make camp tharr's lots a boulders. I like to stop tharr whenever I come this a way. The mountain will slow us some. One thing's fer certain, we can't waste no time."

"I know that spot. Been there once when we come up to visit Mom. Anna Mae was only two," replied Katherine with a smile.

Zeb looked at Anna Mae and said, "We gotta be a goin' as soon as tharr's light. It's goin' to take us near all day to git tharr. We'll need some light to make camp."

Katherine turned to Anna Mae and said, "Ya hear that, Anna Mae? That means to bed early."

Anna Mae protested, "Can't I stay up?"

Katherine said, "After the sun goes down, you're goin' to bed."

Zeb said to Anna Mae as she was wolfing down her stew. "Slow down, lil' lady. Tharr'll be some daylight left enough fer ya to check on Lightning before it gits dark."

Ann Mae, out of breath, looked at her mother and said, "I ate everything. Can I go?"

"Yes," said Katherine. The child bolted from the table.

"That Anna Mae's yir spittin' image, Katherine. Yir like peas in a pod. Tarnation, I remember when ya was that young. Such a sweet lil' girl. I ain't never seen yir ma this happy. All she been a talkin' 'bout fer the last three weeks. How ya was a comin' home an' all. Why, she was a goin' on an' on like to drive me batty," said Zeb.

"Yes, I know. Anna Mae and I are ready to go. She's twelve now, can't hardly believe it. They have a good little school there and a new teacher. She's from our side of the family," said Katherine.

Zeb broke in. "Yup, I know Miss Weatherby." Then he laughed and said, "She's purty near as big as me. Guess why she never got married, the men folk are plumb skeered of her. She'll keep them young'uns in line."

Katherine laughed. "Yes, she's tough but sweet. Pretty too," Katherine explained. "It'll be good for Anna Mae to be with her mamaw. Going to be a while before she gets over losing her father. James loved that little girl. She was always at his feet, helpin' him. I sold the farm and all the animals except those two draft horses and my wagon. I was able to get all our stuff on it. Got fifteen hundred dollars."

Zeb's eyes became big as he swallowed his stew. "Katherine, that's the best stew I ate in a while. Fifteen-hundred dollars, ya say? That's a heap a money. Why, you'll never turn a hand agin. Yir ma has a big place. Plenty a space, an' ya can carve ya out a lil' spot fer a house. Yir pa sure took good care of yir ma." Zeb stabbed his fork in the air at Katherine. "She sure's a feisty ole gal, but she'll still need some help. I'm glad yir a comin'. Worth the trouble to git ya. I live down the road, so I help her some. Why, yir pa would a done the same fer me."

Katherine said, "Now, Zeb, you go out and rest on the porch while I'll finish in here."

Zeb replied, "Let me help ya, Katherine."

"Won't hear of it now, Zeb. You been on that horse all day, and you'll be on that horse all day tomorrow. Just get out there and I'll be there directly," said Katherine.

Zeb got up and made his way to the porch and settled into one of two rocking chairs. He pulled a twist of tobacco from his pocket and cut off a small piece with his pocket knife. As he shoved it to the back of his mouth, he set his gaze upon the setting sun. Its red hue indicated to Zeb fair weather. The pleasant racket of birds finding places to roost for the night filled the air. He watched his grandniece feeding Lightning carrots, as the heat of the day gave way to the coolness of the evening.

Katherine joined him taking the other rocker. As she watched the sun slip below the horizon, she said, "Kinda peaceful here, ain't it? Nice view of the hills. James loved to sit here. Just rock and watch nature. Why, he had designs for us. He did good raising cattle and growin' tobacco. He worked so hard. But now that he's gone, there's nothing holdin' me here."

Zeb said, "Yes, it's nice here, but yir kin is wharr ya need to be. The school's nice. Wish it was tharr when I was lil. Coulda used more book learnin'. Yir pa was the smart one. Always a readin', he was. During the war, he got a fancy commission in the cavalry." The fond memory of his older brother drew a smile and small laugh. "I'd salute him every time I saw him. He'd say, 'Stop it. I'm yir brother'."

Anna Mae finished feeding Lightning and stood gently stroking the horse's mane. Katherine called out, "Anna Mae, time for you to get in bed. We got a considerable way to go tomorrow."

"Can I bring Caesar with me?" asked Anna Mae.

Katherine said, "I don't see any harm."

Anna Mae, with Caesar at her heels, said, "Goodnight, Mom. Goodnight, Uncle Zeb," and went to bed.

Zeb leaned back in his chair and said, "That lil' dog sure took a shine to Anna Mae."

"Yeah, I reckon it's for the best. Keep her occupied during the trip. She's had a rough patch, losing her father," replied Katherine. Then Katherine looked at Zeb, smiled, and said, "It's getting to the point where she's losing interest in everything."

"Well, once we git home, she'll come round," replied Zeb.

Katherine said, "I hope so. Got the wagon loaded. All ready to skedaddle. Want to get this trip over with. I want to see Mom."

CHAPTER 3

A New Life

Katherine rose from a restless sleep and started to prepare breakfast. She stopped and stepped onto the front porch. Stretching, she made her way to the open field and was immersed in the pleasant cool morning air. Overhead, the sky was filled with thousands of stars of varying brightness. Sirius twinkled brightly above the eastern horizon.

A little higher in the twilight sky were the three stars of Orion's belt and the sliver of a new moon. The beauty opened a torrent of pleasant memories. She saw James sitting at the kitchen table eating and making plans for the day as she puttered about the kitchen getting Anna Mae ready for school. The scenes evoked by her mind created a beautiful sorrow. She could only hope the new occupants would fill the house with the kind of love she and James enjoyed. Lightning nickered, breaking the silence and reminding her this was no longer her house and, in a short time, she would leave. Once gone, she knew she would never return. She made her way to the kitchen.

Katherine resumed preparing a breakfast of biscuits and gravy. From the kitchen window, she saw Zeb cinching Lightning's saddle, reinforcing the cold reality that this part of her life was over. A conflict arose between the joy of a new life and leaving her old life and her beloved James to memory. Her sorrow turned into crushing anguish. All of James's hopes and dreams surrounded her in the house and farm.

While she knew James would want her to return home, she felt a sense of betrayal toward James and their love. In spite of this, Katherine remained confident in her decision to leave and knew she was doing the right thing. This, however, did not ease her burden.

When the sun rose, Katherine had the table set, and the smell of fresh-brewed coffee filled the kitchen. Freshly made biscuits were neatly stacked on a plate next to a bowl of gravy at the center of the small table. Along with the biscuits was a plate piled with bacon and scrambled eggs. Places were set for three. Katherine was in no hurry to wake Anna Mae. Zeb entered the house and cheerfully announced, "The wagon's hitched, an' I loaded the charrs. We're ready to go." Zeb looked at Katherine and saw she was fighting emotions and became quiet.

"Better eat. I'll get Anna Mae," replied Katherine. Zeb loaded his plate with eggs, bacon, and fresh biscuits and gravy. After pouring a cup of coffee, he took a seat at the table as Anna Mae entered. Katherine said, "Anna Mae, you need to eat. It'll be near dark before we eat again."

Anna Mae took a plate and, as she was getting her breakfast, asked, "Where's Caesar? Anyone see him?" A rooster crowed like it had every morning. Katherine walked to the front door and looked out. As expected, the rooster was announcing the arrival of the sun as it had every morning. She remembered how James loved the morning. She shut the door and returned to the kitchen. A single tear ran down from her eye. Anna Mae asked, "What's wrong, Mom?"

Zeb looked at Anna Mae and shook his head slowly from side to side. Anna Mae took the gentle suggestion and dropped her inquiry.

As Zeb started to eat, he wanted to lighten Katherine's mood. He looked at Anna Mae and said, "I'll tell ya wharr that lil' mutt is. He's out tharr with Lightning. He was out tharr with me git'n the wagon ready and Lightning's saddle on. We fed the horses, and all the time ya a sleepin'. Ya ain't even brushed yir harr. Lil' lady, ya would scar the divil hisself." Anna Mae shined a guilty smile at her uncle, said nothing, and began to eat.

Zeb realized that he was too firm and laughed. "Ya needed to sleep, lil' lady. We've a long way to go. But ya better eat good 'cause there'll be nothin' to eat. No real meal, no how till dark. Except'n some ole jerky." Zeb worked a biscuit into the gravy with his fork, then pushed it deep into his mouth. As he chewed, he pointed at Katherine with the fork and said, "Now, Katherine, that's the best biscuits and gravy I ever ate."

Katherine flashed a skeptical look and replied, "The best? You better not let Mom hear that."

Zeb laughed and said, "Sure enough, hers is good, but tarnation, I do believe ya got her beat. We just won't talk of it. I've seen that lil' woman mad. She may be small, but she got a heap of fight in dem ole bones a hers. I believe she'd give a full-grown mountain lion a lickin'."

Anna Mae asked, "Uncle Zeb will we run into bears or mountain lions?"

Zeb laughed and reassured Anna Mae, "Why, we jist might, lil' lady. But no need to fret over bears or mountain lions. I have me one a them tharr Henry repeatin' rifles. It cost me near forty dollars. Took me a year to save up. Why, ya just load it on Sunday, and ya keep a shootin' all week. Tarnation, lil' lady, if Custer and his Seventh Cavalry had Henry repeatin' rifles like mine, they would a wupt those Injuns."

Anna Mae asked, "Who's Custer?"

Indignantly Zeb replied, "WHO'S CUSTER? Why, Colonel George Armstrong Custer, that's who. They called him the boy general during the war. They made him a general on account they was a needin' generals. Then when the war was over, they had too many generals and made him a colonel, and then he went to fight Injuns. Yir papaw met him one time."

"OH," said Anna Mae with a yawn.

Zeb continued, "Then he took his Seventh Cavalry out west, and the Injuns slaughtered him at the Little Big Horn. Cut our boys to pieces, they did. Those Injuns had them repeatin' rifles like mine. June 25, 1876."

A look of surprise came over Anna Mae's face. She said, "That's my birthday."

"Sure is, lil' lady, born on that very day. Ain't no bear git'n past that ole Henry rifle a mine. No mountain lion either. No sir. Come to think of it, I wished I had that rifle at Antietam. Might still have my teeth."

With a curious look, Anna Mae asked, "Antietam? That's where war was fought, wasn't it?"

Zeb looked at Katherine and saw the light banter was having its desired effect. He swallowed then answered, "Not the whole war, but a big battle. An' I was in the thick of it. Horrible day it was. Lots of men died on both sides. The worst fight I was ever in and my last."

Anna Mae said, "That's not far from here. Dad took me there one time but didn't talk too much about it."

"Not far at all, just due east a here. We'll go over Burnside's Bridge almost as soon as we git started. I'll tell y'all 'bout it," replied Zeb.

Anna Mae asked, "Is that where you lost your teeth?"

Katherine fixed a plate and joined Zeb and Anna Mae at the table. "Now don't go pesterin' Uncle Zeb about him losin' his teeth. He may not want to talk about it."

Zeb turned to Anna Mae and, smiling he said, "No need to fuss at the child, Katherine. Don't have time now, but when we git tharr, we'll stop an' water the horses. Didn't lose 'em at the bridge though. I fought in that darn cornfield. I don't mind tellin' ya that every time I see a cornfield, I think ole Johnny Reb will be a jumpin' out comin' to git me. I'll tell ya 'bout all that later." Satisfied with Zeb's answer, Anna Mae turned her attention to breakfast.

Katherine stared into her plate and said, "Goin' to miss this ole place. We need to get goin' before I change my mind."

Zeb replied, "Tarnation, woman, ya can't change yir mind now. Yir ma'll kill me." He pushed his hat back. "I'm a bringin' ya and that little varmint back with me even if I have to hog-tie ya, throw ya over my shoulder, and carry ya the whole way."

Anna Mae broke in. "I'm finished, Mom. Can I go out to the wagon?"

Katherine said, "Yeah, go ahead. Me and Uncle Zeb will be out directly." Zeb and Katherine finished breakfast, and cleaned the kitchen.

Zeb said, "I guess it's time to go."

"Yes, go on Uncle Zeb I'll be out. Goin' to walk through this house one last time," replied Katherine. Zeb turned and went outside.

When Zeb reached the door, he looked at Katherine. "It'll be fine. Take yir time."

Zeb let his horse get one last drink of water and walked around the wagon. He marveled at the care and efficiency of its loading. Lighter items were carefully stacked on heavier boxes which were loaded to the front. Odd-shaped boxes turned to maximize the limited space of the wagon. A small space big enough for two to sleep in was left open. Katherine completed her final walk of the house and found Anna Mae in the wagon with Caesar on her lap. Zeb said, "Katherine, we're ready. I like that little contraption ya made to keep the sun off ya. It's lookin' to be a hot day."

Katherine said, "I had an old sheet and some ole tobacco sticks. As long as there's no wind, it should hold." She looked at the house one last time and thought of her late husband James and reminisced. It was the only house Anna Mae knew. All the hard work they put into the farm. It was pleasant work because she and James worked together. Then at the end of a hot day, they would spend time in the shade of the giant oaks watching the sunset. She knew this chapter in her life was behind her.

Katherine turned and headed for the wagon. Zeb and Anna Mae watched. She climbed onto the wagon and, subduing emotion, said, "Let's go. Giddy up." She snapped the reins, and the wagon jerked gently as the horses started to move. It was like ripping a bandage from a wound. It had to be done—the quicker the better. The house began to drift away behind her, and as it did, her sorrow and hesitation were being supplanted with the happy anticipation of being with her mother and a new life.

When she reached the end of the lane, she stopped the wagon and looked at her house one last time. Her life with James was now a pleasant memory. Anna Mae was the last living remnant of her life with James, and as long as Anna Mae was with her, then so too would be James.

CHAPTER 4

The Journey Home

Fear of the looming mountain and weight strengthened Zeb's ability to resist the temptation of riding in the wagon. It was loaded to excess, and the added weight would slow the wagon further. If they encountered problems, they would have to abandon some of the load. Asking Katherine to leave anything on the trail was unfathomable. If on the other hand things went well, he could get in the wagon later—a sort of bargaining chip with Lightning. Pleased with his plan to outsmart his horse, he fell in behind. Holding Caesar, Anna Mae looked at her mother and said, "It'll be good, Mom. Not long we'll be with Mamaw. Think how happy she'll be to see us."

Katherine said, "Anna Mae, it feels like only yesterday you were a baby. Now you're twelve. You're growin' up too fast. Before you know it, you'll be married and movin' off. I want you to stay little a spell longer. Not sure I'm ready."

Zeb worked Lightning next to Katherine. "Tarnation, jist look at that lil' mutt. Caesar, ya be a ridin' like that tharr Roman king today." Zeb wheeled Lightning around and resumed his place in the back. He rubbed Lightning behind the ears and said, "It'll be easy, ole boy. Nice and easy." Zeb took advantage of the cool morning temperatures and easy terrain and pushed the wagon as they passed through gentle rolling hills with patches of wooded areas, cornfields, and tobacco. Once in the mountains, the pace would slow considerably.

Soon the journey would take them through the Antietam battlefield. After the war, Zeb never visited the battlefield, even if passing through would have shortened a trip. On the way down, he was able to avoid it. With the wagon, however, he had to go over Burnside's Bridge, part of the battlefield. He was reconciled to facing the demons of September 17, 1862.

With each step Lightning took, he drew closer, and the horrors of the battle revisited him. The sights, deafening sounds, the smells of burnt gunpowder and rancid flesh came to life in his mind and smothered any pleasant thought. Zeb could not stop it and dreaded the prospect of reliving the nightmare of Antietam. However, the thought of pulling his brother's family together and seeing Katherine, Anna Mae, and Caesar helped him to deal with the mental anguish; but his mind would not let Antietam rest.

Anna Mae turned around and asked, "Can I ride Lightning?"

Zeb replied, "Not today. We got a lot of ground to cover. I promise ya can ride tomorrow. That is if'n we make Rocky Ford." Zeb's answer brought a smile to the child.

Anna Mae said, "Thanks, Uncle Zeb. I need to learn to ride. Bein' that I'm getting a new horse of my own."

The day's journey started uneventful and pleasant. The heat was bearable, and Lightning's pace was strong; and to Zeb's surprise, they made good time even with the wagon. In less than an hour, they entered the Antietam battlefield, and Burnside's Bridge came into view. Little changed since the day of the battle. Upon first inspection, the picturesque limestone bridge gently arching over Antietam Creek showed no evidence of such carnage. It looked more like a place to fish or have a quiet picnic.

The bridge with three distinct arches, a beautiful structure built with local limestone, was easily recognizable. It was one of three bridges constructed in 1836 to ease the movement of produce over Antietam Creek. After construction was completed, it was called Rohrbach's Bridge or simply the Lower Bridge by local famers. After the battle of Antietam, it came to be known as Burnside's Bridge for the Union commander who was tasked with capturing it: Major General Ambrose Burnside.

By whatever name it was called, the bridge had no beauty to Zeb. The sight of the bridge produced within Zeb a Pavlovian response, causing his heart to race and his breathing to become rapid and shallow. The doors to the deepest dungeon of his soul, where he kept Antietam, were flung open. Every horror imaginable was unleashed, and nothing could be done to stop it. But it was not the repressed images, sounds, or smells that tormented him. It was an unkept promise to a friend named Willie that let loose his worst nightmare. He gently tugged on the reins, bringing Lightning to a stop. Zeb stared at the bridge motionless so he could catch his breath, calm himself, and face the dreadful battle.

Zeb joined the Eighty-Eighth Pennsylvania Infantry Regiment shortly after it was formed in September of 1861. Prior to Antietam, the Eighty-Eighth was involved in four battles. His older brother, John, at the urging of his good friend Elon Farnsworth, joined the Eighth Illinois Cavalry regiment. John would see action at Antietam but would come through the battle unscathed.

Up to the day of the battle, Zeb was fortunate not to have been wounded. A prospect frightening soldiers more than death itself. The cornfield would be Zeb's last battle, and it was there he was wounded. Of the more than 620,000 who died in the war, two-thirds were from diseases like typhoid, dysentery, tuberculosis, and measles to name a few. Even taking that into consideration, a staggering number of men would die from battle wounds. Wounds, many of which would have been survivable by the end of the nineteenth century.

At the onset of the Civil War a system of ambulances was put in place to move the dead and wounded. Wounded soldiers were taken from the field of battle to barns converted to makeshift hospitals. Medical science during the Civil War had no understanding of the source of infection. Surgeons would use unclean instruments and probe wounds with unclean fingers. A wound to the gut meant a slow agonizing death. A wound to an arm or leg likely shattered bone and amputation was often the only treatment. A greater understanding of treating diseases like dysentery and treating trauma would be gained by wars end. But advances in medicine involving bacterial infections, that would save countless lives in later wars, were still years away.

Even as late as the 1880s, the work of Joseph Lister concerning the sterilization of operating instruments with carbolic acid was just beginning to be accepted in the United States. On July 2, 1881, the twentieth president of the United States, James Garfield, was shot in two places by Charles Guiteau while waiting on a train. One, a superficial wound to the arm, was not life-threatening. The second wound, imbedded in his abdomen, would take his life. Doctors would insert unclean fingers into the wound or use probes that were not sterilized in a desperate attempt to find the bullet. If Garfield were shot as little as five years later, it is likely he would have survived the shooting. As it was, it would take Garfield eleven agonizing weeks to die while being treated in much the same fashion soldiers were treated on a battlefield during the Civil War.

The American Civil War brought death and disease to the homeland on a scale never seen before or since. Zeb, like many of the soldiers during the war, developed a method of dealing with the brutal carnage. A carnage hidden by daguerreotypes of chivalrous handsome soldiers in crisp uniforms wearing shiny belt buckles and proudly holding muskets and sabers untouched by battle. The chivalry on display during a parade, as the men marched in an orderly procession, eluded them during a battle. Chivalry was replaced by the simple concept of survival. The early bravado, a soldier felt when signing the enlistment papers, was replaced by a brutal fight to stay alive. Each man fighting their individual war of survival.

The cornfield at Antietam became a killing field, changing hands several times throughout the morning. In the wake of battle, was left a wasteland littered with the implements of war. Along with rifles, cannons and sabers were the mangled bodies of the dead and wounded, men crying out in agony. Also, on the battlefield were horses. They, like the men who rode them, died in battle. During the Civil War, like all wars, human loss was an acceptable consequence of fulfilling a military objective, and there was no concern for the horses. Both man and horse, like rifles and cannons and other hardware, were sacrificed.

At Antietam, the Union Army was twice the size of the Confederate Army, prompting General Lee to be near the fighting and making adjustments to his battle plan. The attacking Union Army moved like a wave which started at the cornfield then by midday to the Sunken Road, a readymade trench created from years of wagon traffic. It was at the Sunken Road that Confederate forces lay hunkered down, waiting until advancing Union troops were within range. Then they rose up—aiming at their belt buckles—and opened fire, cutting down the first waves of mostly inexperienced Union troops. Eventually, through superior numbers and as more experienced soldiers reinforced the Union advance, the Confederate forces defending the sunken road were overrun. The sunken road became known as the Bloody Lane. The Union wave would soon find its way to Burnside's Bridge.

Union General Ambrose Burnside was tasked with taking the bridge. The Confederates, while greatly outnumbered, held the high ground which was wooded and strewn with boulders, providing ample protection from Union fire. Making matters worse for the Union was the bridge itself. As well as providing no cover, it was narrow and created a bottleneck, reducing the number of men able to cross. Confederate sharpshooters backed up by cannons had an excellent position to defend themselves and managed to fend off early attempts by the Union Army to capture the bridge.

After two failed attempts, the Confederates, running low on ammunition and wanting to protect their flank, started to withdraw. Finally, on the third attempt, the Union Army prevailed and took the bridge around 1:00 p.m.

Savage fighting continued into the evening after Confederate reinforcements stalled the Union attack on Lee's right flank. The following day, Lee retreated back through Sharpsburg and across the Potomac, ending his first invasion onto Union soil. Casualties for both sides exceeded 22,000, of which 2,108 Union and 1,546 Confederates were killed in action. September 17, 1862, remains the deadliest day in American military history. President Lincoln, seizing on the limited Union victory, issued a preliminary version of the Emancipation Proclamation. Lee would continue to fight for two-

and-a-half years without support from either Britain or France before he surrendered at Appomattox Court House on April 9, 1865.

Meanwhile the civilian population of the North, far removed from the Battle of Antietam, had no idea of the blood bath until Mathew Brady sent Alexander Gardner, along with an assistant, to photograph the battlefield. They returned with photographs of corpses lying silently in formation where they fell. Unlike paintings, photographs, for the first time, captured the gore in minute detail. In October of 1862, Brady opened an exhibit entitled the Dead of Antietam. Americans saw war as it was in photographs of the brutal battle's aftermath. Photographs that captured, in stark uncompromising reality, the final agonizing moments of the fighting men lost. The dead bloated corpses gave a silent reminder to civilians on both sides of the appalling price paid by those who sacrificed everything. With photographs, casualty lists became more than names printed in newspapers. Now they had a human element. Photographs Zeb could never bring himself to look at even when opportunity permitted.

*****

Anna Mae stared at Zeb sitting on Lightning motionlessly looking at the bridge. She turned to Katherine and asked, "Mom, what's wrong with Uncle Zeb? Is he going to be all right?"

Katherine replied, "He'll be fine. Just give 'im a minute."

After a moment, Anna Mae left Caesar with Katherine, jumped from the wagon, and ran to Zeb. She looked at him sitting in the saddle despondent. She rubbed his leg and said, "Uncle Zeb."

He sat motionless.

"Uncle Zeb." Zeb snapped free of the trance and looked at Anna Mae. The worried child asked, "What's wrong?"

He regained his composure, smiled, and answered, "Why, nothin', lil' lady. I'm jist fine. This here's Burnside's Bridge. Let's git to the other side an' water the horses."

Anna Mae, while relieved at Zeb's response, had second thoughts. She wondered to herself if she should push him about the battle. "Uncle Zeb, is this where you fought? I understand if you don't want to talk about it."

Zeb understood the innocence of the child's curiosity. It was hard, however, to explain such carnage to one so young. Even adults could not comprehend the horrors he and many of the veterans saw at Antietam or any battle of the Civil War. Explaining how a man on your left and right, both within arm's reach, fell mortally wounded as a volley of Minie balls ripped through cornstalks was never easy. People, however, had a macabre fascination with the gore. It was the first thing people wanted to hear when they found out he fought at Antietam. Even with the passage of time, Zeb had a hard time talking about it. He gave it some thought and felt it might be a good time to talk. Maybe by seeing the bridge and talking to Anna Mae he could free himself of the demons of Antietam.

Zeb replied, "No, Anna Mae, I fought at the cornfield jist up from the bridge. Yir papaw was here. We was both here that day." Zeb gesticulated with his hand and said, "Katherine, when we git to the other side of that bridge, we can stop an' water the horses."

Katherine replied, "Good idea. I'll stretch my legs."

Zeb guided Katherine and Anna Mae across the bridge. When they reached the other side, Zeb looked back and said, "Let's stop. Looks like this'll be a good place to water the horses an' let 'em rest."

Katherine looked at Anna Mae and said, "Don't wander off, and keep an eye on that dog."

Zeb laughed. "No need to worry. That dog ain't a goin' no wharr."

Anna Mae asked, "Will you take me across the bridge?"

Katherine jumped in and said, "You two go ahead. I'll water the horses."

Zeb tied Lightning's reins around one of the wagon wheels. He tuned to Anna Mae and said, "Let's go." Anna Mae bolted to the center of the bridge, leaving Zeb behind.

"Hold yir taters, lil' lady. Wait fer me," shouted Zeb. Anna Mae gave no response; she obeyed Zeb's friendly command and waited for her uncle. She was enthralled by the beauty. Rocks of varying sizes could be seen through the clear shallow water. She strained to see fish in the gentle slow-moving current.

Hickory and Sycamore trees lined the banks of the creek and provided comforting shade. One such Sycamore known as the Burnside Sycamore or Witness Tree stood beside the bridge like a sentinel. It was small during the battle but survived, growing into a large tree where it stands to this day.

While Anna Mae was looking at the creek, Zeb took in the beauty. He saw the bridge in a different light than his innocent grandniece. To him, it was anguishing, as his mind opened up brutal memories he could never expunge. He said to himself, "Hard to believe so many men died here."

Anna Mae took Zeb's hand and said, "Tell me about the battle." Zeb led the child to a tree, and they sat enjoying the shade.

"Lil' lady, I'll be happy to," replied Zeb.

CHAPTER 5

September 17, 1862

The Cornfield

The Battle of Antietam would be the first time General Robert E. Lee would take the Confederate Army onto Union soil. Lee, the master of the calculated risk, would go up against Union General George McClellan known as Little Mac among his men. The cautious McClellan, who was in a state of perpetual fear of being outnumbered, was emboldened when, on September 13, a copy of Lee's battle plan was found wrapped around three cigars. McClellan moved his men with an uncharacteristic zeal.

Lee, discovering his plans had indeed fallen into Union hands, moved in reinforcements. Nevertheless, McClellan would command a force of eighty-seven thousand, while Lee had only forty-five thousand deployed in defensive positions along Antietam Creek near Sharpsburg, Maryland. The stage was set for what would become the deadliest day in American military history.

As the sun rose, a fierce artillery duel between Union and Confederate forces was taking place. It would be described as artillery hell. A fog that blanketed the battlefield was beginning to lift, and exploding shells were pounding both lines under an otherwise beautiful cloudless September day. McClellan sent word to Union General Joseph Hooker to advance. His objective was Dunker Church, Lee's left flank.

What remained of the light fog had lifted, as Hooker's men emerged from the North Woods. Thus, the Battle of Antietam or, as it was referred to in the South, the Battle of Sharpsburg had begun. The battlefield was open with a patch of woods on the east side referred to as the East Woods. The woods that surrounded Dunker Church were referred to as the West Woods. The Confederate forces defending the church were commanded by Lee's most trusted field commander, the famed Lieutenant General Thomas J. "Stonewall" Jackson.

Later in the war, on May 2, 1863, Jackson would be shot mistakenly by his own pickets while returning from a scouting mission near Chancellorsville, Virginia. His left arm was amputated, and on May 10, he succumbed to his wound. The friendship and respect between Jackson and Lee were so great that while Jackson was dying, Lee said, "He had lost his left arm, but I have lost my right."

While Hooker's forces outnumbered the defending Confederates, the Confederates held strong defensive positions, making matters difficult for the Union General. Furthermore, Hooker's men had to advance in the open, exposed to Confederate artillery. A thirty-acre cornfield stood between them and the church, and it would be there some of the bloodiest fighting of the Civil War would take place. To support the advance, Hooker moved up artillery and fired over the heads of the advancing Union infantry. The cannons fired both solid shell and canister. The latter turning the cannon into a giant shotgun shooting one-inch steel balls. One blast could take out ten men, shredding whoever was unfortunate enough to be the target of the blast.

The Eighty-Eighth Pennsylvania Infantry Regiment fell under the command of Major George W. Gile, who assumed command after Colonel Joseph McLean fell mortally wounded in a previous battle. This regiment, and others, were tasked with taking Dunker Church. The initial push into the cornfield came under heavy fire, and the advancing Union infantry were suffering heavy casualties. The Eighty-Eighth Pennsylvania, for the moment, found themselves in the East Woods and relative safety.

"Hey, Zeb. Hear dat? Bobby Lee's invitin' us to dance," said Private William Johnson—called Willie by his friends—as a shell whistled overhead, exploding harmlessly behind them.

Willie, with the exception of a slight harelip, was perfectly beautiful. He had large pale-blue eyes and a small button nose. Delicate facial features and a fair complexion along with locks of natural curly blond hair made him look younger than his eighteen years and betrayed his innocence. He was the youngest of three boys, and his mother treated him like the daughter she longed for. He looked, to the men in his company, like a fragile doll ready to break at the slightest jar. The war was the first time he had ever traveled more than twenty miles from his home. The other soldiers, skeptical over Willie's ability as a soldier, avoided him. Zeb, out of pity and being two years older, took Willie under his wing and became an older brother, looking out for the green recruit.

Zeb said, "Reckon yir right, Willie. Don't think we'll find any purty girls. Heard we got a git a church out tharr. Ya ain't seen much fightin', but, Willie, that's 'bout to change. I think we're a fixin' to go into a hornet's nest. Our boys got a hand full out tharr."

"Ya think so, Zeb? Maybe dem boys will get dat church widout us a firin' nary a shot," replied Willie with a hopeful tone in his voice. Zeb listened warmly as Willie continued, "I bet dey got canister out dair, Zeb. One blast'll kill a right smart of us. I hate it, I just wished neider of us used it. Ya know, if I get shot, I just as well get kilt. I don't think I want to have an arm or leg took off. Dem ole saw bones kill more of us dan da Rebs. None too quick neider. Just lay dair an suffer, while what's left of ya rots away. No, sir, just a quick bullet to da head is more tolerable."

Zeb laughed as he reassured Willie. "Tarnation, boy, now don't ya go talkin' like that. Ain't like the old days bitin' a bullet. They got gas to put ya to sleep. Don't feel a thing. Then lickety-split, they saw that leg or arm clean off."

Willie considered what Zeb said and replied, "I reckon you're right, Zeb. No matter what, I gotta get back even if I lose my arms an' my legs. Just put me in that knapsack of yours an' carry me to my mama. She'll be happy no matter. Why, Mama had a awful time of it when I left, bein' the youngest an' all. The oldest, Mathew, was twenty-two. An' Mark was twenty-one when dey went to war. Dey both got kilt at Bull Run. Now I'm da only one left."

Zeb shook his head negatively from side to side. "TARNATION Bull Run. Why the war barely started. Everyone thought it'd be over in a couple a weeks. Why folks was a havin' picnics whilst we was a fightin' an a dyin'. Started out great. Then we run into Jackson, an' we run like rabbits, sure did. Lordy, Willie, we even out run some of them hifalutin society folks out watchin' us. Every man fer hisself, I tell ya. We learnt quick jist how hard these Rebs can fight now. Look at us here. They ain't about to give nary a inch. Why, I hear ole Stonewall is jist the other side of that cornfield, waitin' fer us like at Bull Run. Goin' a be tough fightin', Willie."

Astonished, Willie looked at Zeb and asked, "What's all da fuss 'bout anyway, Zeb? I still ain't figured why we're doin' all dis here fightin'. What're we fightin' for?"

With a look of surprise, Zeb answered, "Willie, I keep a tellin' ya we're a fightin' to free the darkies."

"Goodness, Zeb. I know ya keep tellin' me dat, but land sakes dair's a better way if dat's what all da fuss's 'bout. I just can't allow for dat. I'm not all dat smart, but seems to me dat spendin' all dis here money an' all dis killin' ain't da way to go 'bout it. I reckon it'd be easier to buy all dem darkies den turn 'em free." Willie paused as another shell exploded just short of their position. After a brief moment of contemplation, he said, "I knew a darky when I was little. Just as nice as can be, he was. It jist ain't right dem bein' slaves an' all but all dis killin' ain't right neider. You jist let me run dis here war. The darkies would be free, an' we'd be home fishin'."

Zeb gently pushed his forage cap back, looked at Willie, and said, "I remember when a runaway come by our place before the war. Pa hid the poor fella. Hounds a chase 'im an' all. One of them bounty hunters said his dog found his scent. My pa told him if'n he come on his property, he'd blow his head off. Jist wouldn't turn him in even if'n they throwed him in jail fer a hide 'im. Why, that darky told us about them a takin' babies away from their mama's and all. The whoopin' jist ain't right. No, sir, ain't right. But I have to agree with ya, Willie. I allow tharr must be a better way than all this, I tell ya. I wished ya was a runnin' things. Darn good idea ya got, but I reckon the president and all those fellas in Washington figure they know what's best. Besides, we got to git out here so some general gits a big name fer hisself."

Willie sighed. "I swan. Dem generals don't mean a hill a beans to Mama. Why, let me tell ya, she was so upset she just 'bout didn't let me go. Wouldn't even let me outa da house. She just held on to me. I nearly broke her little bony fingers a pryin' 'em off me. Horrible, I tell ya, horrible. Hated to go, but my brudders went. Now it was my turn to do my duty. Everyone was a goin'. I was betwixt a rock and a hard place. I told her not to worry. I'd be home when it was all done."

Willie reached under his shirt and pulled out a cross he wore around his neck and showed it to Zeb. Through the intense sound of exploding shells, Zeb patiently listened to his friend. Willie smiled and said, "Look at dis cross, Zeb. It belongs to my mama, an' before dat, her mama. She knitted me four pair a socks. I don't know how long it took her to knit 'em. Da mornin' I left, she made a big breakfast: biscuits an' gravy. She was cryin' so hard when I walked out dat door. I figured she was about to die right den an' dair. She said da cross would protect me, an' da socks would keep my feet warm. She said, 'Now, Willie, jist ya remember Jesus will be dair wid ya.' I hope she's right. I gotta tell ya, me leaving was like drivin' a spike into dat woman's heart. Can't git da sight of my mama cryin' out a my mind. I put dem socks on last night after we went through dat creek. I hate wet feet. Besides, ain't nothing goin' to happen wearin' dese." Willie slipped off a shoe and lifted his foot in the air and wiggled his toes for Zeb to see.

Zeb could sense his friend was having second thoughts. Willie said, "Ya know, I love Jesus. I got saved five years ago, but to be honest, I don't see Jesus out dair. I reckon if I muster out, it'll be good. I'll be busy lookin' for my brudders up dair in heaven. Don't mind tellin' ya I'd rader git home, see Mama again, an' find me a sweetheart to spark. I reckon I got to make it back, Zeb."

Zeb reached over to Willie and held the cross in his hand and looked it over. He turned his gaze to Willie's eyes and said, "That's a purty cross. But don't go a tryin' to find Jesus in all that mess. Ya just keep 'im in yir heart. You'll find yir way back."

The intensity of the shells exploding about them increased. Zeb looked up as a shell exploded in front of them, falling a tree and sending the shattered limbs through the air like little missiles, and the men scrambled for safety. Zeb took his hat off, scratched his head, and said, "Willie, those shells are git'n close. I'm a thinkin' we're better off out tharr."

A Union officer emerged through the smoke from the open field. Zeb watched the officer run to a colonel shouting and gesticulating frantically. The colonel stood, arms folded and feet anchored to the ground, as he nodded indifferently at the officer's desperate pleas.

An uneasy feeling grew within Willie and he asked, "What do ya think they're jawing on?"

"Not sure, Willie," replied Zeb with a puzzled look. "It's not goin' good out tharr. We better git ready to go." Both Zeb and Willie watched the officer run onto the field. With shells exploding around him, the officer waved his hands, unable to encourage the colonel to move. The colonel instead turned on his heel and ran in the opposite direction, leaving his horse and command behind.

"Why, Zeb, would ya look dair. What a ya make a dat? A jackrabbit couldn't run faster," exclaimed Willie as he and Zeb watched the colonel abscond. "What's goin' on? You reckon dat colonel's a copperhead or jist plain skeered? Which one do we follow?" asked Willie.

"He ain't Major Gile. Willie, ain't sure wharr that colonel come from. We'll just sit here and wait fer the sergeant. If we follow the colonel, we'll be shot or branded a coward," replied Zeb.

Zeb and Willie looked about and noticed other men talking among themselves when another private in their company asked Zeb, "What's goin' on with that colonel? Never seen 'im before."

Zeb laughed as he answered, "Don't reckon I know. I'm a thinkin' he's headed fer Q Company. Hell, don't blame 'im. I wish I could go with 'im."

Major Gile, after watching the panic-stricken colonel, shouted, "Form line."

Their sergeant ran up and shouted, "Attention, form line." The men became quiet and started to form a line as commanded.

Willie looked at Zeb and said, "We're goin' out dair, ain't we, Zeb?"

"'Fraid so, Willie," Zeb replied solemnly. The sounds of exploding artillery shells could not mask the more subtle sounds of clanking canteens and muskets. Sounds that Willie never noticed but added to the surreal feel of the situation. The men readied themselves for battle and were neatly formed into a long line two abreast that Willie or Zeb could see no end. The fear, once distant, gripped Willie tightly. The thought of his mother sobbing uncontrollably replayed in his mind and forced him to face his own mortality; a mortality he was not ready to face. Zeb could see the fear in Willie's eyes as he and Willie stood with the other men in a column, awaiting the next command. Zeb remembered his first battle and knew what his friend was feeling. He looked at Willie and said, "Settle down now, Willie. Settle down. We're all scared. It'll be fine. Jist do as the sergeant tells ya."

"Zeb, promise me I'm goin' home," pleaded Willie.

"Tarnation, Willie, we're not goin' to die out tharr. Yir goin' to be fine. Like I said, jist do as the sergeant tells ya," said Zeb.

Willie pressed his plea with passion. "Promise me, Zeb. Promise me I'll go home. I promise to git ya home. If we promise we'll make it home. Mama has no one. I don't know what she'll do if I get killed. I'm all she's got. She's goin' to need me, Zeb."

As shells exploded about the woods, Zeb looked at the boy. His blond hair was curling up from beneath his forage cap, and blue eyes peering blankly into Zeb's soul, seeking solace. The innocence of Willie's proposal overcame Zeb's annoyance, and in an effort to calm his friend, Zeb agreed to what he thought was a silly promise. "Fer the love of God. Willie, I promise I'll git ya home somehow."

Relieved, Willie said, "Don't ya fret none, Zeb. I promise to git ya home." Willie became quiet.

The sergeant shouted, "WE'RE THE MIGHTY EIGHTY-EIGHTH, AND WE'RE GOIN' TO DO OUR DUTY. DON'T BE SCARED, BOYS, FOLLOW ME. FORWARD MARCH." Zeb, Wille, and the men of the Eighty-Eighth marched to the cornfield, and each man wondered if they would survive the day.

"DOUBLE, QUICK," shouted the sergeant as they emerged from the woods and coming under artillery fire.

"Zeb, if I was home, Mama would have me some biscuits made. Sure miss Mama's biscuits," said Willie, looking at his friend.

Zeb said, "Ya stay close to me." Willie heeded Zeb's advice as the men of the Eighty-Eighth, and the rest of the brigade left the safety of the East Woods and headed to battle. The Union men they were rushing to support appeared as dots of blue peeking through wisps of smoke and broken cornstalks. They were advancing on a well-formed Confederate line.

A sensation of dread washed over Zeb as he entered the open expanse under the beautiful blue cloudless sky. The deafening sounds from a line of Confederate cannons near the church discharging their deadly payload in rapid succession were followed by the explosions of the shells as they crashed all around the advancing column.

The small white church, the objective of the Union advance, was visible in the distance through a cloud of smoke that drifted lazily over the chaotic battlefield. The ground was littered with the dead and wounded to which the men paid little attention. The column of blue rushed forward to support the Union line that was teetering on collapse. Officers on horseback, riding swiftly back and forth, shouted orders in vain which went unheard in the chaos.

The men of the Eighty-Eighth knew what to do as they made their way to the cornfield. They ran a gauntlet of exploding artillery shells and Minie balls that made unnerving buzzing sounds. The former sending plumes of earth, clouds of smoke, and tossing men like ragdolls into the air. Upon reaching the cornfield, the Minie balls began to find their mark with dull thuds and cracks as they struck the men who fell all about. The smoke became thick and the noise so loud they could no longer hear their sergeant. The cold reality of war confronted Zeb and Willie in the harshest of terms as they jumped over men who fell from earlier fighting. Some were dead and others cried out for help, but there was little Zeb and Willie or any of the able-bodied soldiers could do except charge to the fight.

Willie never saw a man die, let alone in battle. The sight of the dead and wounded strewn about caused a great moral conflict within the young boy. A wounded soldier caught Willie's eye, and he stopped motionless over the stricken man and became oblivious to the turmoil about him. The man, lying on his back under Willie's sympathetic gaze, was pleading for water with an outstretched quivering hand. He had been hit in the chest by a Minie ball. His face was ashen and his mustache caked with dry blood. Each beat of his heart pushed blood through the open wound, drenching the dying man's shirt and jacket. The blood formed a puddle in the soil around the man. Willie could not understand how so much blood could come from one man.

More blood ran from the corners of the man's mouth, distorting his pleas with coughs and gasps. Within arm's reach lay the soldier's musket that, had fortunes reversed, would have been used to deliver a similar fate to a Confederate soldier. The moral conflict within Willie intensified. It was one which he could not resolve. The young boy thought of his brothers and wondered if they suffered such as this man. The grizzly sight that Zeb and the other battle-hardened men learned to ignore was new to Willie. His conscience took the form of a mighty hand reaching toward him from the fallen soldier and gripped the boy tightly, holding him in place and refusing to relent.

Zeb moved next to Willie who was frozen with indecision, cupped his hands to his mouth, and shouted directly into Willie's ear, "COME NOW, WILLIE. HE'S GOIN' TO DIE. WE CAN'T HELP HIM. WE GOT TO MOVE FORWARD. THIS A WAY." Willie turned to Zeb.

Swoosh. Crack.

A Minie ball crashed into Willie's head, violently snapping it back, and his forage cap fell to the ground. Zeb's face was showered with a spray of warm blood and small bits of flesh. Willie fell face up, dead, next to the man who was struggling and choking on his own blood. The Minie ball entered through the bridge of his nose, leaving a large hole grotesquely joining the two eyes together. His once beautiful face with childlike features of innocence, now deformed in death, becoming part of a landscape of escalating horror.

Zeb, while grateful his young friend went to the Lord in such a swift and painless manner, thought of Willie's mother and, like Willie, became gripped by conscience.

For a brief moment, silence overtook the noise of battle. The war, even the world, had disappeared from Zeb's conscious thoughts as he looked upon the lifeless form of his friend. He, like his friend Willie, was frozen as he contemplated how not even an inch determined their fate. It could have just as easily been him instead of Willie, who, moments ago, was full of life and worrying about his mother. Zeb, remembering his promise to the young boy, snapped free of his trance and quietly said, "I'll be back fer ya." And before whoever fired the fatal shot could reload, Zeb rejoined the men of the Eighty-Eighth, charging the Confederate forces in the cornfield and ultimately taking Dunker Church.

A surreal scene of unimaginable horror greeted Zeb upon reaching the heart of the battle. Through the blinding smoke and deafening noise, confusion and chaos reigned. A loose line of men standing in the open—shooting, reloading, and shooting. Little was left of the tall cornstalks that hid the fighting men at the start of the fight. Among the trampled corn lay the bodies of men, both Union and Confederate. Men who fell randomly in various positions all about Zeb. Some wounds had hideous disfiguring gashes tearing large swaths of flesh. Other wounds looked as though the stricken soldier had decided to take a nap.

A panicked horse bolted toward Zeb, dragging the body of a Confederate officer. The body was bouncing over broken cornstalks and raising a small cloud of dust. Its foot caught in the stirrup until it was jarred free after colliding with the body of a fallen soldier. The corpse lurched forward, and its eyes stared into Zeb before slumping to the ground.

Under heavy musket fire, Zeb, without any regard to the scene that played out only moments ago with his friend Willie, raised his musket and fired a round at a Confederate soldier. He reached into his ammo pouch and retrieved a paper cartridge that contained a

Minie ball and powder. Placing it between his teeth, he tore out the Minie ball and poured the powder into the musket. After placing the Minie ball into the muzzle, he drove it down the barrel with the rammer until it was firmly seated against the powder. After placing a percussion cap, he raised the musket to his shoulder and fired, falling another Confederate infantryman.

Increased pressure by Union forces caused the Confederate line to break. A Union captain on horseback, wishing to exploit the advantage, ordered his men to advance. Zeb and the other men of the Eighty-Eighth began to chase the retreating Confederates. Their pace increased as the Confederate retreat turned into a rout. Many of the advancing Union soldiers used bayonets to stab, or they swung their rifles, like clubs, to kill the stragglers.

Just as fast, Confederate reinforcements arrived, swarming the battlefield. The retreat was halted, and the tables turned in favor of the Confederates. As more Confederates arrived, they began to advance. Like the Confederate line, only moments ago, the Union line started to falter, and men began to fall back. Zeb heard no call for retreat; he saw the others, and like them, he started back. Now the retreating men found themselves under the Confederate bayonet. They were retreating over the same ground that, only moments ago, they captured. Their goal was to make it to the safety of the woods and reinforcements.

The hasty retreat brought Zeb back to the lifeless form of his friend Willie and the body of the soldier he had stopped to help. The cross Willie, not even thirty minutes ago, was showing him hung loosely about his neck. Zeb grabbed the cross and, with a forceful snap, broke it free placing it in his ammo pouch. Vowing to keep his promise, Zeb struggled and threw Willie's body over his shoulder as the Confederates closed in.

A crushing blow to Zeb's face from a rifle butt swung by a Confederate soldier sent Zeb to the ground, unconscious on top of Willie. The soldier thrust a bayonet into Zeb twice. The war was over for Zeb. The next day found Zeb in a barn that had been converted into a field hospital. He drifted in and out of consciousness, and on the seventh day, he awakened to find a nurse checking his wounds.

"Who are ya? Am I dead?" asked Zeb.

The comely nurse smiled and said, "My name's Clara. Mister, you just don't wanna die. The grim reaper called on you several times. I guess he had a bumper crop this week. I suppose he had more than he could handle. Lucky for you he decided to leave you for another time. You're goin' to make it. Your fever broke this morning. Those two bayonet wounds should've done you in. The surgeon figured you were goin' to die. Told me not to waste my time with you. I figured differently. Judging by the way those stabs didn't hit anything important, the Lord was with you that day."

Zeb struggled to sit up as he asked, "Where's Willie? Last thing I remember is trying to throw him over my shoulder, then I got hit in the face."

"Whoa, slow down. Don't try to sit up. You're not ready. Maybe your friend's here. I can look for him if you want," said Clara.

Zeb ran his right hand over his chest and found Willie's cross. He fell back onto his cot and exclaimed, "TARNATION, I plumb forgot. Won't do no good. Willie's dead. I was a talking to 'im, an' a shot hit 'im in the head. Missed me by nary a inch. This was his cross he was a showin' it to me before he got hit."

Clara, washing Zeb's wounds and replacing the bandages, said, "Sorry to hear that. The cross fell out of your ammo pouch and figured you could use it. It's pretty. Same thing happened to me. A man was shot in my arms. I was tendin' his wounds, and a shot missed me by no more than an inch and killed the poor soul. These wounds look better, but you're not out of the woods. They should heal given time. Your body's strong. It's trying to fight. If you rest, you should make it. Is there anyone you want to try to get word to? I'd be happy to write a letter for you."

"Yes, my brother John Abbott. He's in the Eighth Illinois Cavalry Regiment, H Company. He's somewhere near here. A friend of his, a captain I think. His name's Farnsworth. He's the company commander."

"You think he's here?"

"Yes, ma'am. Could ya check?"

"If he's here, I'll find him for you. Meanwhile, you just need to rest and get well."

The next week, Zeb's brother, with Clara at his side, found Zeb's cot empty. Zeb sauntered up from behind, tapped John on the shoulder, and said, "Tarnation, if it isn't my big brother John. That fancy cavalry uniform ain't got nary a speck a dirt on it. Are ya gon' let me fight this here war all by my lonesome, or are ya goin' to help me wup them Rebs?"

"Howdy, little brother, you sure don't need me. You look good enough to wup Lee on your own," said John as he looked at Clara with a mischievous grin.

Clara laughed. "I believe he's getting better. For a man who had his mouth busted up, he sure can talk up a storm."

John looked at Zeb. "This man couldn't stay quiet to save his life. I reckon that's why they are sending 'im home."

"Send me home?" asked Zeb.

"Yes, little brother, you're goin' home. I hear Little Mack personally signed the papers. He figured you had enough and decided to let you go. When can you leave?"

Zeb looked at Clara and asked, "Is my brother tellin' the truth?"

"Yes, he's tellin' the truth. You're goin' home," replied Clara.

Zeb asked, "When can I leave?"

John handed Zeb the discharge papers bearing McClellan's signature and said, "If you're up to it, now. I have a horse saddled an' ready to go. I was given a thirty-day furlough to take you home. I figure Ma will be glad to see us."

Zeb looked at Clara and asked, "Am I ready? Can I go?"

Clara said, "You can leave now if you want. Just go slow. John tells me you live just outside Gettysburg. You have plenty a time. Your brother promised me he'd go slow. Don't need to let infection set in."

Zeb extended his hand to Clara and said, "Thank ya fer git'n me better. I owe ya my life."

Clara took Zeb's hand, smiled, and with a firm handshake said, "Don't thank me, Zeb. Thank God. The way I figure, he's not through with you. Now get outa here before Little Mack decides he needs you." Zeb and John said their goodbyes to Clara and left.

CHAPTER 6

Lightning

John and Zeb stepped from the barn into a clear blue October sky. A gentle breeze stirred the scent of death as soldiers hurried about their business. "It's goin' to be a good day for a ride, little brother. I got you something. Look, a horse to take you home," said John, and he guided his brother to two horses.

Zeb walked to John's horse, a dapple-gray gelding with a black mane and tail. He ran a hand along the horse's neck, drawing a nicker. Zeb smiled at the animal and, looking into the horse's blue eyes, said, "Howdy, Jim, haven't seen ya in a while," returning his gaze to his brother.

"I see ya still have Jim. He sure's a smart horse. A fine-looking animal."

John walked up to Jim and gently rubbed his horse behind his ears. "We been together a long time. Had him since I joined the cavalry. He's three, a special horse. He's not afraid of anything. Why, he'd charge through the gates of hell. If we make it, I'm goin' to keep 'im."

Zeb looked at the other horse, a beautiful splash overo stallion. His neck, body, and head—except for a white blaze—were solid black. With the exception of random patches of black, his legs and belly—along with his mane and tail—were solid white. The horse appeared as if it had been dipped into a giant vat of white paint up to his belly. Zeb said, "Tarnation, John, where did ya git this dandy?

If'n I ride this horse, a sharp shooter'll think I'm some kind of officer. Maybe even Lil' Mac hisself and shoot me."

John laughed. "Zeb, you worry too much. Lee's retreated back across the Potomac. No Confederates for at least a hundred miles. The Colonel hates that horse. He wanted me to take him out somewhere on the battlefield an' shoot him. I figure you're good with horses. He's well-mannered, but he don't seem to like to do anything useful. He don't like work, an' he don't like to get dirty. He don't even like to get his hooves wet. He don't like to run unless he's chasing a filly. Can't use him as a draft horse, not much use to us. He don't seem to mind a slow walk, but he'll take a notion to stop. I thought I'd give him to you. This, little brother, is just the kinda horse you need to get you home. He minds good and is gentle for a stallion. You just have to show him who's boss. I don't want to shoot the critter."

Zeb ran his fingers through the horse's mane while looking into it's brown eyes and asked, "I can't allow ya to shoot such a purty horse. What's his name?"

John answered, "Beauregard, but the men just call him Lightning on account of him being lazy an' all."

Zeb replied, "Hmm, maybe I can do somethin' with this here horse. How old is he?"

John, relieved at not having to shoot the beautiful animal, answered, "Three. So does this mean you want him?"

Zeb replied sarcastically, "Tarnation, John, ya 'spect me to fly home? Of course, I'll take 'im." Zeb looked at his new horse and asked, "Do I git to keep the saddle?"

"Yes, bridle and blanket too. I was lucky. Got it off a dead Confederate horse."

Zeb laughed. "Lightning, ya may be a dandy, but ya belong to me now." Zeb rubbed Lightning on the neck, and he said to his brother, "Let's git goin'."

John mounted his horse and could see Zeb, still weak, struggling to get on Lightning. He offered to help. "Sorry, Zeb, let me help you up."

Zeb replied indignantly, "TARNATION, JOHN. I can still git on a horse. Don't care how hurt I am." Zeb got on his horse and looked over the battlefield fresh from the recent fight. His gaze fixed upon a small detail of infantrymen trying to coax the bloated carcass of a horse into a large hole as vultures stood, watching a few feet away. They were pulling on the dead animal's legs that were extended and stiffened in death, refusing to yield to the will of the men. They struggled at the task, then stopped and talked among themselves. Zeb could hear voices but could not make out what was being said.

After the discussion, the men stepped back, and one loaded his musket. He took aim at the dead horse and fired. The Minie ball entered the underside of the bloated carcass, releasing a geyser of noxious liquid. The men laughed as the dead horse deflated and, after a brief pause, resumed their task.

The sight made Zeb think of the promise he had made to his friend. Willie was out there and likely already buried. The unkept promise weighed heavily on Zeb. He, like Willie prior to his death, speculated as to what Willie's mother was doing at this moment. No matter what she was doing, Zeb knew Willie was on her mind. John watched his brother staring toward Dunker Church. It had been two weeks since Union forces had dueled with Confederate forces for the strategic position.

"What's on your mind, little brother?" asked John.

Zeb paused for a moment, removing his hat with his right hand. "I didn't keep my promise. Left Willie, told him I'd git 'im home to his mama. I made a promise. I jist didn't keep it."

Zeb made a sweeping motion with his hand toward the open expanse where so many men had fought and died. John, from his horse, listened to his brother. Zeb said, "Willie. He's out tharr somewharr. Didn't git 'im home. What'll I tell his mama? Poor woman, she lost all her boys. She had three, an' Willie was the last one an' the youngest to boot. Need to find her. She lives near Bonneauville. Not far from us."

John said, "What do you say to a woman who's lost everything? Lots of mama's buried out on that field. Every one of them we kill, I reckon we kill a mama. I can't tell you what to say to her. You just can't replace your children. Lord knows I don't understand any of this anymore than you. All I know is our mama's waitin'. Just go home to her. You've done your part. You done all you can."

"Can't do nothin' else here. I've had a belly full of this here war. Let's go," replied Zeb. John gently nudged Jim, and the brothers headed home.

After getting Zeb home safely, his brother John would return to the war. Clara, the woman who nursed Zeb back to health along with countless wounded soldiers, started life as a school teacher. She started her own school in 1853 and briefly worked as a clerk in the patent office.

When the Civil War broke out, she volunteered to help at the Washington infirmary to care for wounded soldiers. She soon realized she could better serve by going directly to the battlefield. There she selflessly dedicated her life to those who fell wounded during the Civil War by bringing supplies and helping the overworked surgeons. She was Clara Barton, referred to as the Angel of the Battlefield. She followed her calling at places like Cedar Mountain, the Second Bull Run, and Antietam among others.

After the war, she would fight for suffrage and civil rights. On May 21, 1881, she founded and became the first president of the American Red Cross. After a life dedicated to service, she died quietly on April 12, 1912, at ninety.

CHAPTER 7

Bear Attack

"So *that's* when you got Lightning," exclaimed Anna Mae.

Zeb said, "Yeah, me and ole Lightning been tagether a long time."

Astounded by Zeb's revelation, Anna Mae asked, "Goodness, he must be old. How old is he?"

Zeb lifted his eyes to the sky and scratched his chin. "I reckon he's twenty-seven." Then, after a short pause, he said, "No, by golly, he's twenty-nine years old."

"Wow, that's old. He's such a pretty horse and in good shape too," said Anna Mae.

Zeb laughed. "Yea, ole Lightning wasn't one to do more than he had to. He knows he's a dandy. I reckon that's why he's in such good shape." Zeb lowered his head and continued, "But I never kept my promise to Willie. I never brought 'im back."

In reassuring tones, Anna Mae said, "It wasn't your fault. You did the best you could."

"I went back tharr and tried to find him after I got better. I reckon he's buried tharr somewharr. Ole Willie was wrong about one thing."

"What's that?" asked the child.

Zeb explained, "Willie told me that he drove a spike into his mama's heart the day he left. Knowin' what I know now, he didn't. I did when I returned that cross."

"If you don't want to talk about it, I understand."

"I need to git it off my chest. I remember when I returned that cross." Zeb paused and collected his thoughts. "It was all I had fer her. Ya know, sometimes I feel like I killed that sweet woman. It was me that took all she had. There are lots of mamas like that, each a sufferin' losing their greatest treasure. I drove a spike into her heart. But she didn't die quick."

"Why do you say that?"

Zeb replied, "Willie died quick, but his mama died a little every day, tormented thinkin' of her boys. Her whole family gone. She never knowed how they died. She had to live with that. I told her how Willie went into battle, brave. How he was shot helpin' a dyin' soldier. That he didn't suffer none. That made her some happy. She asked me if'n I could take her to wharr Willie was buried. I had to tell her that I didn't know wharr he was. Tarnation, Anna Mae, she don't even have a grave to visit. Ya know, up to when Willie got killed, it never occurred to me that I was a killin' mamas too. The Lord took her poor soul a couple of years ago. She's with her boys now. Every now and then she comes to me. Sometimes in a dream. Sometimes while I'm in the field. I tell ya now, God as my witness, I'd rather march into that ole cornfield a thousand times an' git killed myself, as to face a mama like that."

Katherine made her way across the bridge. She paused and watched her uncle talk to Anna Mae as the latter looked on adoringly. She knew how hard it was for Zeb to relive that day in September and shouted, "Hey, you two. We're ready to go."

Zeb looked at Caesar and said, "Enough of this. If'n we're goin' to make Rocky Ford, we better git to movin'." Zeb and Anna Mae, with Caesar close behind, returned to the wagon and resumed their journey home. For the next eight hours, the trio made their way to Rocky Ford. The rolling hills and farmland gave way to denser woods and mountains. Zeb worked his horse next to the wagon and asked, "What time is it?"

Katherine pulled her late husband's watch from her pocket and said, "5:45. Are we about there?"

Zeb recognized the boulders and the woods and said, "Jist a half mile or so around that bend. I reckon about thirty more minutes. We'll find a place to cross and camp."

Anna Mae said, "We did good, didn't we?"

"Yes, we're makin' good time, but we ain't tharr yet," replied Zeb.

"Uncle Zeb, tell me about the horse I'm getting. How old is he?" asked Anna Mae. Zeb kept his head down and pretended he did not hear Anna Mae. "What color is it?" Zeb continued to keep his head down and refused to make eye contact, ignoring the child. Anna Mae continued, "What's its name?"

Anna Mae's unrelenting queries were straining Zeb's patience. He lifted his head, looked her in the eye, and snapped. "TARNATION, CHILD. I ain't goin' to talk about that tharr horse."

Katherine laughed and admonished her daughter. "Just leave Uncle Zeb alone, Anna Mae. It's been a long day. You'll find out soon enough about that horse." She turned to Zeb and admonished him, "You opened a Pandora's box. That horse is all that child's been talking about since we pulled out." Zeb ignored Katherine, kept his head down, and did not say a word.

"Uncle Zeb, is that Rocky Ford?" asked Anna Mae.

Zeb lifted his head and looked about. The boulders appeared as though they had just fallen from the sky. However, as they approached the ford, the boulders became organized as if by design, forming a wall on either side of the trail. A gateway of sorts which would guide them to the other side of the stream.

Laurels and dogwoods lining the edge of the stream enjoyed the shade of the larger chestnut trees and firs which marked the entry point to the larger forest. The ford was a part of the river that became narrow and shallow as the elevation grew. Downstream from the ford was a depression where a pool formed and travelers could fish for trout or swim.

Katherine remembered the spot where her father and Zeb took her and her brother, Nicklaus, camping. Beautiful memories of her childhood flooded her thoughts and further eased her reluctance at leaving to rejoin her mother.

"Uncle Zeb, this is beautiful. Remember you and Dad taught me and Nick to fish here," said Katherine.

Zeb said, "Yes, I remember. Me and yir pa would hunt here after the war."

Anna Mae said, "The shade's cool. Smells good. Are we goin' to camp here?"

"Yes, this's Rocky Ford. We'll take the wagon to the other side an' make camp tharr," said Zeb, and he guided the wagon across the stream.

Katherine said, "Anna Mae, you and Caesar need to gather wood. Get some kindling. Don't wander off too far. Zeb, can you take care of the horses?"

Zeb tied Lightning to a wagon wheel replied, "Didn't think we were goin' to make it. Hope the weather holds. We'll have a slower time tomorrow, going over the mountain and all. The good thing is, we'll be in shade most of the day. Reckon the worst is behind us."

"Come on, Caesar, let's get the wood," said Anna Mae with Caesar tagging along.

Katherine busied herself getting dinner ready, and Zeb began to remove Lightning's saddle. Anna Mae made several short trips piling up kindling. Satisfied with the stack of kindling, Katherine pointed to a fallen tree about fifty yards from their campsite and said, "That's enough kindling. You and Caesar can go over there and get some bigger pieces for the fire."

"Yes, Mom." Anna Mae looked at Caesar and said, "Let's go, ole boy." Anna Mae, with Caesar at her feet, made her way to the fallen tree. Zeb watched the two while placing his saddle in the wagon. Unnoticed by the trio was a black bear calmly walking toward Anna Mae and Caesar.

Katherine was the first to spot the bear and was instantly paralyzed by terror. She shouted, "ZEB, BEAR." Zeb, not hearing her, continued taking care of Lightning. Again she shouted frantically, "ZEB, LOOK! BEAR. SEE IT?" Anne Mae heard her mother and spotted the bear that was between her and the wagon. She dropped the wood, grabbed Caesar, pulled the dog to her chest and clambered onto the fallen tree.

ANNA MAE'S BUCKSHOT

Katherine pointed to the bear and shouted, "Zeb, look. Over there. Do something." Zeb looked at the bear but showed little urgency. It was a simple shot. He calmly pulled his rifle from the scabbard and stepped toward Lightning. The bear, growling, quickened its gate, lumbering toward Anna Mae and Caesar. Katherine shouted, "Anna Mae, stay still. Don't move. Zeb, quick, do something."

Zeb laid the rifle across Lightning's rump and worked the lever to chamber around. The large bear made an easy target at such a short range. "Ya jist hold yir taters. This shot's easy. I'll take care of that bear," said Zeb as he lined the sights of his rifle on the bear and gently squeezed the trigger. *Click.* nothing happened. The bear, gaining speed, closed in on Anna Mae and Caesar. Zeb worked the lever, ejecting the failed round, and chambered another. Again he lined his sights and squeezed the trigger. *Click.* In desperation, Katherine fell to her knees, looked skyward, and shouted, "Jesus, stop the bear."

Caesar twisted uncontrollably and furiously scratched at Anna Mae, freeing himself from her grip. The little dog, without regard to the bear's size, charged fearlessly, yapping and growling. "Stop, Caesar. Uncle Zeb, do something," shouted Anna Mae with her face buried in her hands. The courageous little dog stopped the bear in its tracks with not more than ten yards to spare.

The bear stood menacingly on its hind legs. Caesar snarled and yapped defiantly at the apex predator while darting about, keeping a safe distance with no intention of yielding. Anna Mae and Katherine stared in wonder at the confused bear standing on its hind legs with its upper legs hanging loosely along its side, growling and attempting to intimidate the little dog. Zeb, filled with equal parts fear and astonishment at the two failed shots, chambered another round. He squeezed the trigger, and a shot rang out, missing the bear. It decided it had had enough and ran away with Caesar at its feet yapping.

Zeb stood motionless, amazed at what he had just witnessed. A little dog scaring off a full-grown black bear was one thing. The failure of his rifle, however, was unfathomable. He bent over to retrieve the two unfired rounds. Katherine asked rhetorically, "Well, Uncle Zeb, what happened to that fancy rifle of yours?" Zeb looked at the unfired bullets and studied the dimples left in the primers by the firing pin.

Anne Mae returned holding Caesar and said, "Mom, that bear was about to eat me alive, and Caesar saved my life. I bet it was ten feet tall."

"Caesar's such a good little dog," said Katherine as she took the triumphant dog from her daughter and gently stroked the excited animal. She looked at Anna Mae and, talking to Zeb, said, "It's a good thing Caesar was here."

Zeb, in disbelief, tried to understand what he saw and broke his silence. "Tarnation. In all my born days, I can't count the number a times I fired this here rifle. Never, nary a single time had I ever seen that happen. I ain't never seen a factory-made cartridge misfire like that in any rifle. Not one time, let alone two times. I jist ain't never seen that happen anytime. If'n I tell this here story, folks will think I'm as crazy as a loon." Zeb showed the two unfired rounds to Katherine and exclaimed, "See that? Look how that tharr firing pin struck that primer. See the dent? Shoulda went off."

Katherine took the unfired bullets from Zeb and scrutinized them. She saw the small dimples made by the firing pin, then she handed them back and said, "I see. Kinda peculiar."

"Kinda peculiar? Why, it's plumb impossible," protested Zeb as he took the unfired bullets from Katherine and pushed them into the rifle. He worked the lever and chambered a round, aiming at the fallen tree that Anna Mae and Caesar had just returned from. He squeezed the trigger and the round went off with a loud bang, and the bullet struck a small branch, sending it to the ground. He chambered the second round and again squeezed the trigger, and like before, it went off. He worked the lever and ejected the second casing and reached down to retrieve both casings.

He examined them and looked at the second dimple created by the firing pin, slightly offset from the first dimple. He shook his head in utter disbelief. He turned to Katherine who was holding Caesar as Anna Mae was petting the dog that had just saved her life. He said, "This here is the strangest thing I ever saw."

Zeb remembered how Caesar persistently followed him during the journey, even after all the attempts he made to dissuade the dog. What Anna Mae's grandmother, Mary, said of the dog. That in spite of the dog's apparent uselessness, Zeb thought maybe Mary was right: God did indeed have a purpose for Caesar. Zeb put the empty casings in his pocket and said, "I'll have to save these. No one will ever believe this."

CHAPTER 8

Buster

"Hey, Buster, it's ole Slop Jar. Why don't ya try out that slingshot ya just made? Bet ya can't hit 'im," said William Mason. Twelve-year-old William Mason went by Lil' Bill because of his small size and childlike appearance.

His friend, fourteen-year-old Tucker Watson Haywood, noticed the horse quietly grazing and had already determined it would indeed make a nice target. Tucker Watson Haywood, more commonly known as Buster, was already five feet ten inches tall and 170 pounds with several years of growing still ahead of him. Buster was developing into a sinewy good-looking man like his father. His thick shaggy black hair, square jaw, and hazel eyes drew the flirtations of many of the teenage girls at school. He was the youngest of seven boys, and along with his size and looks came a cruel streak that grew from constant fighting with his brothers.

Buster's mother passed away when he was five from typhoid fever, and his father let the boys look after him. They had a reputation among local citizens, a reputation Buster would acquire along with a false sense of entitlement. Even the older boys rarely challenged him out of fear of retribution from his older siblings. The brothers had no wants. When things got out of hand and the boys, including Buster, caused problems, their father used his wealth to buy their way out of trouble.

Two years earlier, Lil' Bill met Buster, and the two became friends. The relationship was mutually beneficial. Lil' Bill enjoyed the protection of his older friend, and Buster enjoyed having his own toady to order about. Lil' Bill and Buster fed off each other, and a third personality that bordered on evil emerged when they were together. Buster, emboldened by Lil' Bill's adoration, enjoyed bullying the younger children.

Buster drew the slingshot from his overall pocket and found a small rock and, after securing the rock in the sling, stretched it back as far as it would allow. He aimed it at Lil' Bill and laughed. "Lil' Bill, why don't I just try it out on you?"

Lil' Bill had never witnessed Buster physically injure anyone beyond bruises. However, he never knew for sure how far his friend would go when he was in this state of mind. Lil' Bill, not wishing to be hurt, was troubled. The small boy, scared, pointed to a fence post he felt was far enough away to render the projectile harmless and said, "At least let me stand over there."

Buster laughed hysterically, "I ain't goin' to shoot ya, Lil' Bill. Hell, just wanted to scare ya is all."

The relieved child pointed to the horse twenty-five yards away and repeated his appeal, "Ya better hurry before ole Slop Jar takes a notion to leave."

Buster walked up to the fence and rested his right elbow on a post and stretched the sling with his left hand as far as it would go. He was patient taking care to adjust the slingshot, allowing for the downward trajectory of the small rock. Lil' Bill whispered, "Ya got it, Buster."

"Quiet. Can't ya see I'm concentratin' here?" replied Buster.

Buster let loose, and the rock bounced off of the horse's rump with a loud smack and it fell harmlessly to the ground. The horse did not move. In fact, to the frustration of the boys, the horse, unimpressed by the assault, continued to graze. "*Wow*. Look at that. It works good. Try a bigger rock," said Lil' Bill. Both boys searched feverishly for another rock. One which would be large enough to stir the horse to excitement.

Buster said, "Here, this'll do." He stooped over and picked up the rock then flashed it at his friend.

"Yeah, that's better. Perfect," said Lil' Bill. Again, Buster launched the rock at the horse. Like before, it hit the horse on the rump with a loud smack. Still, the horse did nothing. "What do ya make of that, Buster? Had to sting," exclaimed Lil' Bill.

Buster laughed. "Hell, not only is ole Slop Jar ugly but I reckon he's stupid too." The old flea-bitten gray nag had a sway back. Along the left side of the horse, extending from the base of its neck to its rump, appeared circular silver dollar-size faded patches that, to the boys, were the likely remnants of some disease. Where its left ear should have been was a small lump of flesh. Its left eye was missing as a result of injury, and the lids had been sutured together long ago. However, the decrepit old horse's faded black mane and tail were meticulously brushed and groomed, and its hooves neatly trimmed, indicating a great deal of love by its owner. When seen from the right side, with the exception of the sway back, the horse looked normal.

Without further prompting, the horse casually turned and approached the boys. They stood frozen as the old flea-bitten gray nag, with a sway back and missing both its left eye and left ear, came close. The horse stopped short of the fence and looked Lil' Bill in the eye. Just standing, the tired old animal showed neither anger nor curiosity, staring at the boy, occasionally blinking its good eye, and rotating his one ear slowly. Lil' Bill returned the gaze and they became locked in a test of will. The wretched old horse affected Lil' Bill as the remnants of his conscience were dredged up from the depths of his soul.

As they silently stared at each other, Lil' Bill saw, for the first time, the cruelty he so often meted out at the expense of others. The sight he saw of himself through the horse was unsettling, and he lost his nerve.

Buster laughed. "Aw, look, ole Slop Jar likes ya. That horse is asking for it. Maybe I should put out his other eye. That stupid horse is so close now I think I can hit it."

For the first time, Lil' Bill questioned himself and his older friend. He said, "I don't know, Buster. Why don't we let it be? The slingshot works good."

Buster, surprised by his friend's sudden reluctance to follow him, replied, "Are ya turnin' yella? That horse ain't fit for nothin'. It should've been shot a long time ago. It'll be funny to watch that worthless horse stumble around."

Lil' Bill looked back at the horse who continued to stare at the boy. Harassing the younger kids or scaring a horse to make it run was one thing, but blinding it reached deep into Lil' Bill and tore at his heart. This was the first time he'd seen Buster's cruelty go this far. He silently asked himself, "How could one derive enjoyment by permanently blinding such a gentle animal going about its business, causing problems for no one?" The cruelty suggested by Buster was too much for Lil' Bill. At his limit, he made one last plea to his friend. "Don't do it, Buster. Let's just leave."

Buster mocked his friend. "Chicken. Just go. I'll catch up with ya later." Lil' Bill, upset, said nothing else; he turned on his heel and left.

*****

Witnessing the drama unfold was the horse's owner, Mary Louise Abbott. A small wiry woman who barely stood five feet tall and weighed ninety pounds. Her fifty-six years and hardworking life seemed to have little effect on her sun-darkened skin which displayed few wrinkles. She had possession of her teeth, which were as white and straight as someone half her age. Her large deep-set indigo eyes gave her beautiful oval face a more vibrant and determined look. In spite of her years, Mary retained her beauty.

She enjoyed her role of homemaker and always had a cheery smile even when she had no reason. She loved to cook and spent a lifetime helping her late husband John on the farm. Above all, Mary had an unshakable faith in the risen Savior, Jesus Christ. If she entertained any doubts about her God, she never confessed it, and no one saw it. She saw the Lord in everything about her. Even when the most devout Christian saw practical explanations, Mary chose to see Jesus. No matter how trivial the occurrence, Mary had not the slightest doubt it was part of a grand plan orchestrated by God through Jesus Christ.

At first inspection, she appeared frail, wearing a light-pink ankle-length dress adorned with yellow daisies. Like all her dresses, she designed and sewed it herself. She also made the matching yellow bonnet trimmed with light-pink daisies that covered the once golden hair of her youth, now white. Only within the confines of her house did she not wear her bonnet, and only in her bedroom did she let her hair down. Each morning, she carefully brushed her hair then pinned it into a bun and, after covering it with one of the many bonnets she kept, started her day. Her frail outward appearance masked a strong willful personality. When it came to her family and loved ones, she never backed down from a fight.

Moments ago, she was preparing a big dinner in anticipation of the return of her brother-in-law, Zeb, along with her daughter, Katherine, and granddaughter, Anna Mae. It was nearly five in the evening, and she expected them at any moment. The commotion created by the boys caused her to stop and investigate. Mary knew Buster and his father, Elijah, as well as the boys and their reputation. She and her late husband, John, grew up with Elijah who, like John, fought in the Civil War. Both John Abbot and Elijah Haywood were successful, but Elijah lost interest in his family after his wife passed, concentrating instead on his business interests which included cattle and lumber. The wealth created by his business skills provided the boys with everything and fueled their sense of entitlement.

Mary watched Buster patiently. It was time, however, to put an end to his cruel game before he could do real harm to her horse. While searching for a rock, Buster forgot about Lil' Bill and his surroundings, and Mary quietly slipped behind him. She stood over Buster like a coiled snake ready to strike, and for a brief moment, she did nothing. She watched the determined boy crawl about on his hands and knees, rummaging through the dirt looking for the perfect rock to launch at her horse.

Mary suddenly seized the initiative, catching Buster by surprise. She moved swiftly, grabbing his left ear with her left hand while simultaneously grabbing his right arm with the other. She twisted the ear without consideration for the child's anguish and forced Buster on his belly with his face in the dry dirt of the road while drawing the strong boy's arm around his back in a hammerlock. She fell in on top of him, driving her knee into his back. The slingshot fell from Buster's hand. The more the boy resisted, the greater force she used on the arm. Mary let go of the ear and now her left arm was wrapped around his neck with her left elbow under Buster's chin. She pushed on his arm until his hand reached between his shoulders in order to maximize the intense pain. She screamed into his ear, "I had brothers growin' up too. They taught me to fight. I'll break that arm a yirs, Buster."

"Stop. Stop, let me go. I had enough," cried the defeated child.

Mary let the boy go and, as she got to her feet gasping for air, said, "Ya ain't so big now, are ya? Ya shoulda listened to yir pal. At least he had some sense 'bout 'im. Ya shoulda left while ya was ahead." As Buster got to his feet; Mary adjusted her bonnet and brushed dry dirt from her dress. Only his brothers had ever bested him. He stood staring at Mary in utter disbelief that such a small woman handled him so easily.

"YA THINK THAT HORSE IS AFRAID A YA, BOY? WHY, THAT HORSE FACED A LOT WORSE THAN THAT CONTRAPTION," shouted Mary, looking up into his eyes. Buster stood humiliated and shamed as the seemingly meek old woman berated him. Even Buster knew better than to touch a woman, especially one as old as Mary. He was in no position to say anything.

Mary continued her tirade. "Yeah, I know yir pa's rich, but that won't mean nothin' when word gits out that an old woman jist wupt yir ass." Buster stood silently staring as Mary stepped into his space, glaring at the man-sized boy that towered over her. She said, "What? Ya got nothing to say, do ya? Ya were looking pretty big a minute ago."

Mary pointed to the wagon road on which they were standing. First to the north then to the south. She said, "There ain't nothin' I can do as long as you are on this here road. But God as my witness, *boy*, I see ya a messin' with anything on my land, I'll make ya regret it. Now pick that thing up and git outa here."

Buster said nothing, he retrieved his slingshot and left. Mary stood defiantly with her arms akimbo, watching the defeated and humiliated boy leave, staring him down until he was out of sight. She approached the horse at the center of the controversy. The horse slowly walked to Mary and broke his silence with a friendly nicker. Mary pulled a carrot from her pocket and held it out to the animal.

She said, "Buckshot. Don't you fret none, hear? God as my witness, ain't no one goin' a hurt ya." Mary rubbed Buckshot's nose as he ate the carrot. She said in a reassuring voice, "They keep a talkin' about that Montrose, how great and handsome he is. How he won that Kentucky Derby. He ain't got nothin' on ya, Buckshot. I wouldn't take a thousand Montroses fer nary one of ya. Why, yir the most handsome an' greatest horse I knowed. I have a surprise fer ya too. My Anna Mae's a comin'. She'll brush yir mane and tail just the way ya like it. She'll feed ya apples, take ya ridin', and love ya. Jist like Katherine done when she was little." Mary returned to the house with Buckshot following her along the fence as far as he could. He stared at Mary, his good ear perked up and his tail gently swaying. Mary paused, looked at Buckshot, and smiled.

CHAPTER 9

Reunion

The distant sound of an approaching wagon caused Mary's heart to race with anticipation. She turned her head, looking south down the road, and strained to listen. She saw Anna Mae proudly mounted on Lightning, and behind her was Zeb and Katherine riding in the wagon; and to her surprise, Caesar was between them. Anna Mae nudged the horse gently with her heels, and Lightning, recognizing Mary, broke into an energetic trot.

Anna Mae reined up short of Mary. "Mamaw, Mamaw, you won't believe it. Caesar saved my life," said Anna Mae.

Mary laughed and said, "Git off ole Lightning and come over here so I can see ya, child." Anna Mae jumped off Lightning and ran into Mary's waiting arms, and Lightning headed for the water trough by the barn behind the house.

"Child, yir a growin' like a weed, ya are. Can't pick ya up like the last time I saw ya. I see ya found Caesar. I was looking all over fer that ole dog. Sure a hawk snatched him, and here ya tell me he saved yir life. Jist tell me about it," said Mary overcome with joy as she held her granddaughter tight.

"Whoa," said Zeb to the horses while pulling on the reins, and before the wagon came to a stop, Katherine began to climb out.

Mary said, "Anna Mae says that Caesar saved her life." Tired, Zeb said nothing climbing off the wagon.

Katherine joined Anna Mae, and the three exchanged hugs. Katherine said, "Yeah, Mom, he sure did. Chased a big ole black bear away. Good thing too 'cause that fancy gun of Zeb's misfired twice. Why, not for Caesar, no tellin' where Anna Mae would be now." Zeb remained silent, rolling his eyes which Mary acknowledged with a quiet laugh.

In the excitement, Anna Mae shouted, "Yeah, Mamaw, Uncle Zeb's gun didn't work. I was a goner for sure. Just as that bear was about to eat me alive, Caesar attacked him and run 'im off. That bear stood on his legs and was ten feet tall. Caesar made that bear turn tail and run."

Zeb, still in disbelief at the scene he witnessed, said, "Craziest thing I ever did see. That lil' mutt run that bear off as fast as it come. TARNATION. When I left here, I tried everythin' to chase that lil' mutt off. But he wouldn't have none of it. Why, that lil' mutt was determined come with me. He jist kept a comin' the whole way. Hate to admit kinda glad he did."

"Well, no need a frettin'. I told ya that Jesus had a plan fer that dog. Ya never doubt the Lord," replied Mary with a degree of pride in her voice.

Katherine looked at her mother and said, "That's sure a pretty dress, Mom. Looks like you been wrestling a bear yourself."

Mary snapped, "More like the divil."

"What's goin' on, Mom?" asked Katherine.

Mary said, "Buster. He was a causin' trouble. I had to straighten 'im out."

"Elijah Haywood's youngest boy? Why, that man prit near owns everything in this neck of the woods," said Katherine somewhat surprised.

Mary said sarcastically, "Yeah, he does. Everythin' except in that boy's heart. Satan owns that. I'm a feared the child's lost. Him and his brothers think they own the whole county an' can do as they please. I've said more prayers for that child than I can count. I ain't a goin' a give up. No needin' me a tellin' ya. Now let's go inside. I got dinner ready."

ANNA MAE'S BUCKSHOT

Zeb saw Caesar in the wagon. The dog, anxious to join the gathering, stood trembling on the seat, looking over the edge ready to jump but restrained by fear. "Now look at this here mutt. One day he's a fightin' a bear, the next he's afraid of a lil' jump," said Zeb.

Anna Mae ran to the wagon and reached for the little dog and said, "Here, Caesar, I'll get ya down." Caesar eagerly jumped into Anna Mae's arms, and she took him to Mary. "Here, Mamaw, you can have your dog back," said Anna Mae as she handed the excited dog to her grandmother.

Mary replied, "Looks like the two of ya git'n on fine. Why don't ya jist keep 'im?"

"Are you giving me Caesar?" asked Anna Mae.

Mary said, "I sure am, child."

"Thanks, Mamaw. Caesar, ya hear that? You're my dog now," said Anna Mae.

Anna Mae caught sight of a horse with its neck stretched over the fence. She put Caesar on the ground and ran to the horse, shouting, "What a beautiful horse. What's his name?" Mary looked to the spot where she left Buckshot and was shocked to find he was gone. In his place stood a beautiful large stallion, sixteen hands, with a shiny black coat, black mane, black tail, and a white-blaze face.

Mary scolded Zeb. "Goodness, Zeb, ya need to fix that fence a yirs. Storm got into my pasture agin and run off Buckshot."

Katherine looked at Zeb and laughed. "You know how Mom feels about Buckshot."

Zeb answered, "Yes, I'll git to it in the morning. Promise."

Mary watched Anna Mae running her hand through Storm's mane with Caesar at her feet, and walked up to Zeb and hugged him. "I'm sorry, Zeb, I shouldn't be so mean. No need to fret over that. Now let's have a nice dinner an' visit. Thank ya fer bringing my family back. I don't know what I'd a done without ya. Ya helped so much since my John got sick," said Mary.

Zeb understood the feelings Mary had for Buckshot and said, "It's fine. I know how ya feel. Ole Buckshot's a special horse."

Anna Mae returned to the informal gathering with Caesar at her feet. "Mamaw, you got some carrots so I can feed 'im?" asked Anna Mae.

Mary had one carrot in her pocket and gave it to Anna Mae and said, "Here, ya can give this to Storm."

"Storm. That's a nice name. Thanks, Mamaw," said Anna Mae as she ran back to Storm with Caesar close behind.

Mary turned to Katherine and said, "That dog ain't goin' to leave that child's side. Let's go in the house. Ya can rest while I finish dinner."

"Sounds good. I'll move the wagon to the barn an' take care of the horses first," replied Zeb as Mary and Katherine went inside the house.

Katherine turned back to Zeb and said, "Let me help."

"No, ya jist help yir ma. Anna Mae can help me out here." Zeb looked at Anna Mae and said, "Soon as ya feed Storm that carrot, ya need to bring Lightning to the barn an' git his saddle off an' feed 'im."

"I'll take care a Lightning," replied Anna Mae. She looked at the beautiful horse and said, "You're the prettiest horse I ever laid eyes on. Such beautiful green eyes. You reckon you goin' a be my horse, boy? I'm sure of it." She turned to take care of Lightning.

*****

Katherine stepped onto the porch, and a flood of pleasant memories transported her back in time with images of her when she was Anna Mae's age. She and her brother Nicklaus played under a shroud of large black walnut trees, oaks, and hickories and gathered walnuts for their mother to make pies. The larger hardwoods provided ample shade for the smaller dogwood trees and the large white Victorian house in the summer. She glanced at the pasture and saw herself on Buckshot, learning to ride the gentle horse. Her father rocking on the porch when James asked him for her hand and when she gave birth to Anna Mae. And when she, James, and Anna Mae left to start a life of their own.

Following her mother, she stepped inside and found, to her relief, little had changed. Upon entry, the outward simplicity of the house gave way to a more sophisticated elegance adorned with knickknacks acquired between a husband and wife over a long life together. The parlor was directly to the left of the front door, and a reading room to the right. Two large windows on the exterior walls of each room ensured ample sunlight. Portraits hung neatly on the walls of a small hall that led from the front door to a staircase that led to four bedrooms. The fourth smaller bedroom was converted into a sewing room after Katherine moved out. At the base of the staircase, to the right, opened into the kitchen. The left side was the dining room. It was joined to the kitchen beneath the staircase to ease conveyance meals for gatherings, formal and informal. The house was the reflection of a man and wife of modest means who together made it into a warm and loving Christian home.

Katherine stepped into the dining room where she found the table set. "I don't know how you do it, Mom. Making clothes and cooking all this. I'm so glad to be home."

"Child, it's the will of the Lord. He knowed how bad I wanted ya here." Mary sighed as she continued, "Jist don't know what I'd've done without Zeb. He pitched in when yir pa got sick, knowing ya had yir hands full carin' fer James an' all. Zeb an' his brother was real close."

Katherine said, "We had a good trip. Uncle Zeb took good care of us. He was upset over the rifle not firing like it should. I have to admit that was strange. I told him not to worry."

"Child, ya jist have to trust Jesus. The Lord used that little dog. There's a plan. Ya jist have to have faith," said Mary.

*****

Anna Mae found Lightning and the two draft horses at the trough lapping water, while Zeb was working the pump. Anna Mae began to remove the saddle from Lightning and asked, "Uncle Zeb, who does Storm belong to?"

Zeb realized where Anna Mae was going with her question and answered, "Lil' lady, that horse belongs to yir mamaw, an' she wants me to sell it fer her. Don't ya be a git'n any ideas 'bout that tharr horse. The horse's a stallion. Ya have to have experience to handle them horses. Yir Papaw was a workin' on Storm before he got sick, an' he couldn't do nothin' with 'im. Yir mamaw wants to sell it. She said if'n I had to, I could give 'im away."

"I could train Storm. Maybe you could help me," said Anna Mae.

Zeb replied, "Tarnation, I ain't a goin' a help ya. Got 'nuff to do as it is. Besides, yir mamaw has a nice horse fer ya to ride. It's trained an' real gentle like. Ya ain't ready fer a horse like Storm. I ain't a sayin' no more. Been on the road all day, an' I'm hungry. All I want to do is eat."

Anna Mae shrugged her shoulders and sighed. "I won't say nothing else." However, Anna Mae's mind was made up, and she remained convinced in the notion that Storm was the horse her Mamaw would give her.

*****

Katherine's mind was on Buckshot as she helped her mother. She grew up with the horse, took care of him, went riding, fed him apples and other treats, and remembered how she loved to brush the horse's mane and tail. Buckshot was Katherine's first horse given to her by her father. She saw her father in Buckshot, and the horse's presence conjured up warm memories of her father and how he patiently taught her to ride. Katherine asked, "Mom, where's Buckshot?"

Mary was looking out of the kitchen window, watching Anna Mae and Zeb talk, while the horses were at the water trough. Mary said, "Buckshot's a git'n old. I reckon he's out in the pasture. I was with him before ya pulled up. Storm chased 'im off. I reckon horses are like people. Storm is a handsome horse, but he thinks he's a bit a somethin'. Kinda like Lightning, but Lightning's a sweet horse. That horse is plumb ornery, he is. Seen his ears pinned more than once. Yir pa couldn't do a thing with 'im. Zeb's supposed to take 'im off an' find 'im a home. Wish I could keep 'im in the pasture, but Storm an' Buckshot don't seem to git along. Buckshot's too old, can't fight like he used to. Maybe yir uncle Zeb'll take Storm. He's so good with horses."

Katherine said, "Buckshot's such a sweet horse. So smart too. Are you goin' to give Buckshot to Anna Mae?"

"What makes ya think I'm a givin' Anna Mae a horse?" replied Mary with a probing look.

"Well, Mom, don't tell Zeb I told you, but he kinda spilled the beans. He didn't tell Anna Mae she was get'n Buckshot, but she knows she's gettin' a horse."

Mary laughed. "I love yir uncle to death, but bless his heart, he can't keep a secret to save his life." Mary fixed her gaze back on Anna Mae and said, "Aw, it'll be all right. But yes, child, I am givin' Buckshot to Anna Mae."

"I figured you would. I'm sure Anna Mae'll be happy. She was only one when we left and doesn't have any memories of Buckshot," replied Katherine.

Zeb bounced through the front door with Anna Mae and Caesar close behind. He took off his hat and declared, "Tarnation. I'm done an' ready to eat."

Katherine smiled at her mother and said, "Yes, Uncle Zeb, you're done. You did a good job."

"Yes, ya did, Zeb. Now jist ya sit down, an' I'll take it from here," said Mary.

Zeb looked at Anna Mae and said, "Ya here that, lil' lady? Let's wash up and eat. If'n I had shot that bear, I believe I could eat the whole thing."

Anna Mae, overcome with excitement, hugged her uncle and said, "Thank you, Uncle Zeb, for takin' care a me."

"Tarnation, Mary, look. Ya went all out the whole kit and caboodle. My favorite fried chicken, mashed taters, okra, and fresh rolls," exclaimed Zeb as they all gathered around the table.

Anna Mae asked, "Mamaw, can I say the blessing?"

"Yes, child, go ahead," replied Mary.

"Dear Jesus, thank you for this food and Mamaw and Uncle Zeb and Mom and Caesar. AMEN."

Katherine said, "Amen."

"Mamaw," said Anna Mae as they filled their plates.

Mary asked, "What, child?"

"Are you going to sell Storm?" asked Anna Mae.

Katherine looked at her mother. They knew where Anna Mae was going with her query. Mary had no intentions of giving Anna Mae the horse, even though she knew Anna Mae wanted Storm. The events of the day raced through Mary's mind. She saw the manifestation of God's love emerge. She thought of her encounter, Lil' Bill, and saw firsthand the softening of his hard heart. She wondered if Buster's cold heart could be reached as well.

Mary was certain God's hand was involved in weaving a complex tapestry of which Anna Mae, Storm, and Buckshot were all threads. She saw a grand plan in which all would witness God's love through Buckshot.

Before Zeb could say a word, Mary said, "Well, child, not sure. I did tell yir uncle to sell the horse, but I ain't decided. He's a purty horse, child, but he's a stallion. An' they can be hard to handle. Yir papaw couldn't do nary a thing with 'im. Why do ya ask?" Zeb shot a curious look at Mary as he ate.

"Oh, nothing, Mamaw. I was just wondering," replied Anna Mae.

"Wonderin' 'bout what, child?" asked Mary.

Zeb, unaware Mary knew he had revealed her plan to give Anna Mae a horse, stopped eating and said, "I think I got a buyer fer Storm."

Surprised by Zeb's comment, Mary said, "Zeb, let's discuss this later. Anna Mae, jist as well tell ya," said Mary while she looked at Katherine.

Katherine said, "Your mamaw has a surprise for you."

Anna Mae knew what her mamaw was going to say. She asked, "What kind of surprise, Mamaw?"

"It seems everyone knows, so I may as well jist tell ya. I got ya a horse, but ya can't git it till tomorrow," said Mary.

The confirmation put a smile on Anna Mae's face. Excited, she said, "Tell me about the horse, Mamaw."

"One thing I'll tell ya," replied Mary to her granddaughter, "ya ain't a git'n Storm. Ya ain't ready fer a horse like that."

"That's good, Mamaw. Is he a pretty horse like Storm?" asked Anna Mae.

"Anna Mae," replied Mary, "yir a git'n a very special horse."

"Mom, do you know the horse? Can you tell me about 'im?" asked Anna Mae as she looked at her mother.

Katherine said, "Anna Mae you're get'n a special horse. You'll find out in the morning."

Anna Mae turned to Zeb and asked, "Tell me about the horse, Uncle Zeb."

Zeb replied, "Lil' lady, I done said enough, an' I ain't goin' to say nary another word 'bout that horse."

Mary smiled at Anna Mae and said, "Child, that horse'll make ya very happy."

"Well," replied Anna Mae, "can you tell me his name?"

Mary said, "Why, I see no harm in that. His name's Buckshot."

CHAPTER 10

Anna Mae's Disappointment

The morning sun shined brightly into Anna Mae's eyes, rousing her from a restless sleep. Too excited to sleep, she felt as though she hadn't slept at all. Ready to meet Buckshot, she stretched out her hands, shielding her eyes from the sun. Without further thought, she jumped out of bed; threw on her clothes; and rushed down the stairs, flying by her grandmother who was sipping coffee.

"Whoa. Slow down, child. Ya don't have time to say good mornin'," said Mary as Anna Mae reached the front door.

"Good morning, Mamaw," said Anna Mae as she disappeared.

Katherine, with a cup of coffee, joined her mother. "I see Anna Mae's up and about."

Mary, lowering her coffee cup, laughed. "Yeah, she didn't even comb her hair. She's out tharr a lookin' fer Buckshot. Won't have to look far 'cause he's right where I left 'im yesterday."

"Mom, I hope she don't get disappointed with Buckshot after seeing Storm," said Katherine.

Mary said, "Child, don't go a borrow'n trouble. I couldn't blame her none, I reckon. Poor ole Buckshot seen better days."

Katherine leaned back in her chair. "Buckshot's the right horse for her."

Mary replied, "It'll be fine. I remember how ya loved Buckshot."

Anna Mae rushed into to house and said, "Mamaw, I can't find Buckshot."

Mary replied, "Child, did ya look good? Why, I jist saw him out tharr this mornin'."

Anna Mae shot back, "Yes, Mamaw, I did. All I saw was a old lame horse. It must be one of Uncle Zeb's horses."

Katherine smiled at her mother, anticipating her response. "Anna Mae," replied Mary, "that's Buckshot. He's yir horse."

Katherine said, "Buckshot used to be my horse when I was your age. You're getting a very special horse."

Anna Mae stood speechless, frozen in disbelief. The joy of getting a magnificent horse she could proudly ride to school was dashed into the depths of despair. The child's face was contorted to such an extent by shock and disappointment, little room was left for doubt in Mary's mind as to Anna Mae's feelings about the horse. Mary, expecting the reaction, said, "Let me take ya down tharr, child, and introduce ya to Buckshot."

Katherine said, "I'll go with you."

Dejected and looking at her feet, Anna Mae said, "Yes, Mamaw, let's go." The three went to see the horse. Buckshot, with his ear erect, eagerly greeted the trio with repeated nickers. Then he stepped against the fence and stretched his neck in anticipation of a treat.

Mary pulled half an apple from her pocket and said, "Here, child, give 'im this. That's what he's a lookin' fer." Anna Mae took the apple and halfheartedly gave it to Buckshot. The horse gently pulled the apple from the child's hand into his mouth with his lips and began to chew.

Mary looked at Katherine and said, "Would ya look at that? Buckshot thinks Anna Mae's you. Remember how ya took care of 'im when ya was little?"

Katherine replied, "He was my first horse. I spent a lot of time with 'im. I don't think Anna Mae is warming up to Buckshot. Are you going to tell Anna Mae about 'im?"

Mary answered, "In time, child. In time, when she's ready, we'll tell her."

CHAPTER 11

Zeb's Lost Sweetheart

The following morning, Katherine found her daughter with Caesar on her lap, rocking and staring coldly at Buckshot. The horse, seeking attention, was staring back at the child, snorting and scratching at the dirt. Nothing Buckshot did roused any affection from the child. She had no desire to be with the horse. Her hatred for Buckshot did not go unnoticed by Katherine. She took a seat in the rocker next to her daughter. "What's troubling you?"

"Why can't I have Storm? Mamaw's goin' to sell 'im anyway. I don't see why I can't have 'im."

Katherine gently ran her fingers through the child's hair. "Anna Mae, Buckshot's a special horse to Mamaw and me. He was Papaw's horse. He's a very sweet and gentle horse, and is perfect for you to learn to ride. Buckshot was my first horse. He taught me to ride. I know you don't see it now, but one day he'll be special to you too."

Anna Mae snapped back, "I don't understand. What makes that horse so special? He's old and ugly, and his back is caved in. Can't I have Storm and Buckshot? I'll take care of 'em, Mom."

"You're not ready for a horse like Storm. For now, you'll just have to trust us," said Katherine as she looked at Buckshot. "Look, he's wanting you to say hello. Let's go down and say hello to Buckshot. I have a brush. He likes his mane and tail brushed. I used to do that when I was your age. I'll show you how he likes it."

ANNA MAE'S BUCKSHOT

Anna Mae looked at her feet and remained silent. Katherine got up, turned to Anna Mae, and said, "Come now." Reluctantly, Anna Mae joined her mother. Katherine handed Anna Mae the brush, three carrots, and said, "He loves you. I can tell. Put these in your pocket. You can give Buckshot a treat."

Buckshot perked up at the sight of Anna Mae carrying the brush. He stretched his neck as far as he could over the fence. The child, however, had not the slightest interest in the old horse. Her heart was set on Storm. Katherine took the brush from her daughter and gently worked it through Buckshot's mane and turned to Anna Mae and said, "Here, you give it a try." Katherine held out the brush for Anna Mae.

"Yes, Mom, I'll do it," said Anna Mae with a mild tone of irritation. She took the brush and halfheartedly worked it through the horse's mane. Buckshot nickered and took a step closer to the child. Anna Mae asked, "Can I go to Uncle Zeb's house?"

Katherine felt helpless and forlorn. The empathy she felt provided little comfort for her daughter. Katherine said, "If that's what you want, Anna Mae, you can go. Just be back by lunch." Happy, Anna Mae handed the brush back to her mother. She turned and ambled down the road to her uncle's house. Buckshot ignored Katherine and followed Anna Mae along the fence. Katherine smiled as she watched the determined horse seek the child's affection.

Snorts and trotting hooves broke the silence. Anna Mae turned, looked, and found Backshot standing, staring her in the eye. Angry, she shouted, "Quit following me, you stupid horse." Anna Mae picked up a small rock and hurled it at the animal, hitting him in the chest, and resumed her trip. Undeterred, Buckshot continued to follow Anna Mae. She made a vain attempt to shake the resolute animal by running as fast as her legs would carry her, but Buckshot broke into a gallop and kept up.

Exasperated, Anna Mae stopped in her tracks and walked to the horse that continued to stare at her, craning its neck over the fence and nickering. Out of breath, Anna Mae cried out, "I hate you. You're ugly and old. You're a worthless horse. Don't follow me. Just die." Anna Mae resumed running, and again Buckshot broke into a gallop until a fence that divided Zeb's property from Mary's stopped the horse. Still, Buckshot stood and stared at the child as she walked down the road. Buckshot beckoned Anna Mae to return with loud neighs, causing her to stop and look back. Buckshot's pleas, along with repeated snorts and nickers, left Anna Mae unmoved. She turned away and resumed her trip to her uncle's house and Storm.

The wagon road which ran in front of Mary's house also ran in front of Zeb's house and several small farms beyond. Zeb's small house that he and his older brother John built after the war came into view. Like Mary, Zeb kept horses and a few head of cattle in a pasture on the other side of the road across from his house. Along with the cows, Anna Mae spotted Storm grazing in the distance. She climbed on the fence and called out to the horse, "Here, Storm. Come here, ole boy." But the horse, unimpressed with Anna Mae's calls, continued to graze. Zeb, hearing Anna Mae, emerged from his house and joined his grandniece at the fence.

"What're ya lookin' fer, lil' lady?" asked Zeb.

"Oh nothin', Uncle Zeb."

Zeb looked into the pasture at Storm, grazing as he scratched his chin. "I see Storm out tharr. Ya wouldn't be a wantin' to see 'im now, would ya?"

"Well, maybe," replied Anna Mae.

"I'll git 'im fer ya," said Zeb, and he called out at the horse.

Anna Mae's smile confirmed her desire for the horse. "Here he comes. He sure listens to you," said the child.

Zeb reached in his pocket and pulled out a carrot and handed it to Anna Mae. "Why, that horse thinks he's the biggest toad in the pond. He can be plumb ornery, but he still knows wharr his bread is buttered. Here, ya goin' to need this," Zeb handed Anna Mae a carrot.

"I got carrots." She held out the three carrots meant for Buckshot and gave one to Storm. The child lit up feeding the beautiful horse, forgetting—for the moment—the horse she had left behind.

"Ya like Storm, don't ya?" asked Zeb.

"He's a beautiful horse," said Anna Mae.

ANNA MAE'S BUCKSHOT

Zeb thought of Buckshot and his brother. "Yeah, I reckon he is. Ya know, Anna Mae, every horse has its own personality, kinda like folks. Storm's a high-falutin horse. A dandy. He thinks he's a cut above the rest of us."

"Mamaw gave me Buckshot. Everyone tells me how special he is."

"Ya don't think so, do ya?"

"I love Mamaw, but Buckshot's just an old horse. I can't ride him to school. I'll be laughed at."

Zeb removed his hat and wiped his forehead with his sleeve. "Goin' to be hot today." He returned his hat and scratched his chin. "Yeah, I reckon ole Buckshot has seen better days."

"How old is he, Uncle Zeb?"

"'Bout the same age as Lightning, I reckon."

"Why does Lightning look so much better?"

Zeb said, "Well, Anna Mae, I'll let yir mamaw 'splain all that to ya. But remember the old saying, 'Ya can't judge a book by its cover.'"

A puzzled look came over the child. "What do you mean?"

"Let's jist say that outside beauty ain't the same as inside beauty."

Anna Mae, sensing what her uncle was about to say, changed the subject. She asked, "Why don't you have a wife and children?"

Zeb, unprepared to answer such a question, realized this was a good time to help Anna Mae understand Buckshot.

He leaned against a fence post and said, "Well, I guess it won't hurt to tell ya, lil' lady. Fact is, I did have a sweetheart. Why she was the purtiest gal in the county. Had the purtiest golden hair like yir mamaw did when she was yir ma's age. She loved me too. We was even goin' to git married, then the war come along. I done told ya what happened in the cornfield. Guess when I got home, she saw me. I was a pitiful sight. S'pose she jist couldn't handle it. Just cut and left."

Zeb paused for a moment. "Tarnation, didn't even say goodbye. I reckon don't blame her none. I looked bad with my face busted up an' all. That's when I decided to grow this here beard, maybe hide some of it. I waited fer nearly five years a hopin' she would come back. Never did gave up. I had to git on with my life. Still, I always hope that she'll just come wandering up that road to see me some day."

"But, Uncle Zeb, it wasn't your fault."

"No, don't reckon it was, lil' lady, but none of that means a hill a beans now. Still love her. Jist couldn't bring myself to find another 'un. Besides, what woman would have me. It all worked out. Yir papaw shared his family with me. Had yir ma, an' she was like my own daughter. Now look, I got you." Zeb pushed his hat back as he continued, "Ya know, the Lord blessed me, sure did. I know lots of folks worse off than me. Why, poor ole Willie never left that ole cornfield. An' his ma, she lost everythin'. No, Anna Mae, I'm happy the way things are."

Anna Mae looked at the ground and said, "I miss Dad and Papaw."

Zeb said, "Yeah, I miss 'em too. Yir papaw thought the sun rose an' set on ya, lil' lady. Me an' my brother was close. He looked after me, an' I looked after 'im."

Zeb changed the subject. "Enough of that. Ya ready fer school? Yir mamaw been a talkin' to the school marm. She got ya all fixed up. Ya need book learnin', or ya will end up like me. Besides, you'll meet young'uns yir age."

Anna Mae smiled and asked, "Can you teach me about horses and how to ride?"

"Sure can, lil' lady."

"Can you show me how to ride Storm?"

Zeb realized the child did not grasp what he was trying to tell her. Not wanting to let her down, he put her off. "Let's jist let ya git settled in first. Then I'll teach ya. Whatever horse ya end up with. We got a deal, lil' lady?"

"Yes, Uncle Zeb, we got a deal," replied Anna Mae. She held out her hand.

Zeb shook it gently and said, "Deal."

"I reckon I'll head back," said Anna Mae, and she turned and left for home.

CHAPTER 12

Anna Mae's New Friend

Mary stepped onto the porch and saw Katherine standing by the fence, and she shouted, "Come up here, child, an' set with me." Katherine made her way to the porch. "It's such a nice mornin'," said Mary as they settled into their rockers.

Mary asked, "Wharr's that little varmint a yirs?"

Katherine replied, "Just had no interest in Buckshot. She went to Uncle Zeb's? Poor ole Buckshot lit out after her."

Mary let out a breath, "That child has her heart set on Storm."

"Sorry, Mom. I allowed she would love Buckshot, and she just don't care for 'im at all. I reckon I was just looking at it from my seat. I don't know what to do. She's still upset about losing her father and papaw," said Katherine.

Mary replied, "Katherine, it's goin' to take her a spell. Real hard fer a child to deal with all that."

"Mom, I've never seen her act this way before," said Katherine.

Mary said, "Goodness, I don't reckon I blame her. Losin' her pa an' papaw. Jist look at ole Buckshot. He's ugly next to Storm. Like askin' her to wear a burlap sack after bein' shown a fine silk gown. She don't understand. She's a lookin' with her eyes, not her heart. We're a askin' a heap of Anna Mae. Remember, she's a turnin' into a woman, but she's jist a child. I remember when you was that age. She won't be a child much longer."

"Don't remind me, Mom. I reckon you're right. But I was hopin'," said Katherine.

Mary's eyes softened, "Child, this here's the Lord's work. Jist be patient an' let it be. Ya can't force love. Need to let her see things fer herself. She'll come 'round in time."

"Goodness, Mom, I know you're right. I just wish I had your faith. I reckon we need to just to go ahead and tell her about Buckshot. Maybe she'll understand," said Katherine.

Mary said, "No, child, that's the last thing to do. She's jist not ready. It'll have no meaning to her. No need to go a pokin' in the Lord's work. As fer faith, jist be patient. We all struggle with faith, child."

Mary leaned back in her rocker and explained, "Like I told ya, it's God's work. His hand is in everythin'. Jist look at the Pharaoh. The Pharaoh was a runnin' roughshod over the Israelites. He didn't believe in the same God as Moses and the Israelites. The Israelites was his slaves. God chose Moses to lead the Israelites outa Egypt, slavery, an' to the land a milk and honey. Why, ya know that even Moses wasn't keen on bein' God's prophet at first even after God commanded him. Moses stuttered an' was a skeered he couldn't speak. So, God sent Moses's brother, Aaron, with 'im to convince the Pharaoh to free God's people."

"Yes, Mom, I read Exodus. I know all about that," said Katherine.

Mary said, "Now, child, this is the important part. The Lord hardened the Pharaoh's heart, an' the Pharaoh refused to let the Israelites go. Then the Lord turned loose on the Pharaoh all kinds of plagues. He turned the water into blood, sent frogs, gnats, locusts, flies. Ya jist name it, an' the Lord sent it. Every time, the Lord would harden the Pharaoh's heart, an' the Pharaoh wouldn't let the Israelites go. Why, child, the Lord even struck down the firstborn son of every Egyptian. Struck 'em dead, he did. The Lord did this so that the Pharaoh an' the Israelites would know the one true God. Even after Moses escaped with the Lord's people, the Egyptians chased 'em. Ya know what I'm a talkin' about, child. God even gave ole Moses the power to part the Red Sea. God meant fer the Israelites to see all the signs an' believe he's their God an' the God of the Egyptians. Above all to let them know ya can't lick God."

"Mom, I'm sorry I don't understand," said Katherine.

Mary said, "Then you'll understand when I tell ya that God is a hardenin' Anna Mae's heart. God wants to teach that child to know love an' that God's love is everywharr. Why, God's jist a git'n started. All this's a sign. You'll see, she'll be fine. Land sakes, when all this is done, Anna Mae will learn what real love is, an' yir faith'll grow. Why, I see it as sure as the nose on yir face."

"Mom, you're so smart with these things. Maybe if Anna Mae had friends, that would help," sighed Katherine.

Mary reached over to her daughter and held her hand. "Ya only been here a couple days. School starts the first week in September. That's next week. I already went down to the school an' told Miss Weatherby 'bout Anna Mae. I got everythin' set up. She'll meet some friends. Don't cha worry none. Before long, everythin'll be jist fine."

"Yes, Mom," replied Katherine. "It's hard. I miss James and Dad too, you know. I wish they were here."

Mary's eyes became big, "Yir pa and James are jist fine. They're with the Lord. As long as ya keep 'em in yir heart, they're with ya. Jist like Jesus. Yir faith'll grow. Ya jist have to keep a workin' on it." Mary saw Anna Mae with Buckshot following along the fence. She said, "Speak of the divil, here comes that varmint now with Buckshot. Lookin' like she found the morbs." Katherine directed her gaze to the road and saw her daughter's crestfallen face, slowly walking toward them. Mary exclaimed, "She looks like she's a totin' a heap a misery."

Caesar saw Anna Mae and ran toward the child. As Anna Mae bent over to pick up the dog, Katherine laughed. "She may not a took a shine to Buckshot, but the sun rises and sets on that little dog."

Anna Mae slowly made her way to the house. When she reached the porch, Mary said, "Cheer up, child. Can't be all that bad. What's got cha so down?"

Anna Mae set Caesar down and answered, "Mamaw, I love Buckshot, but he keeps following me an' never stops lookin' at me."

Mary answered, "Anna Mae, all Buckshot's a wantin' is ya to pay attention to him's all. If'n ya pet him, he'll leave ya be."

A boy carrying a fishing pole caught Katherine's eye. He was making his way toward the trio from the same direction Anna Mae came. Katherine looked at her mother and asked, "Mom, you see that boy? Who is he?"

Mary stood up and studied the boy with the confident stride. He bounded up the road without a care. In spite of his small size, he was a fine-looking boy with a shock of thick, unkempt sandy blond hair. Mary answered, "Why, that's William Mason. Ever one calls 'im Lil' Bill. Stephen Mason's boy. Stephen bought the Brewer farm some years back. Jist come here a few years ago from yir neck a the woods. Sharpsburg, ya don't know 'im."

Mary pointed down the road and said, "If'n ya go down the road a little beyond yir uncle Zeb's place, you'll find it. I reckon he's headed to the gristmill next to the church. Lots of the young'uns fish an' swim tharr."

Anna Mae studied the boy carefully. When he reached Buckshot, he stopped and gently ran his hands through the horse's mane, showing great affection. Anna Mae, anxious to make a new friend, looked at her mother and asked hesitantly, "Who's with Buckshot? Should I go down and say hello?"

Seeking reassurance, Katherine glanced at her mother. Mary quietly nodded her approval. Mary said, "Yes, child, he's a good boy. Go down tharr an' say hello." Anna Mae suddenly acquired a fondness for Buckshot—albeit insincere—and, seizing the opportunity to meet a new friend, bolted from the porch running as fast as she could. In her excitement, she tripped, drawing laughter from Katherine and Mary.

Katherine said, "That's one way to get her interested in Buckshot."

"Lord's work, child. I'm a tellin' ya it's the Lord's work," said Mary beaming. She leaned back in her rocker and watched Anna Mae regain her dignity then make her way to Buckshot and Lil' Bill.

Buckshot nickered as she approached. The horse stepped away from Lil' Bill to be near Anna Mae. The boy, who's childlike face was

ANNA MAE'S BUCKSHOT

giving way to that of a young man, turned to Anna Mae and flashed a welcoming smile of straight white teeth. She was smitten by the good-looking boy with the cleft chin and square jaw, blond hair, and blue eyes. Anna Mae began to notice things she had never noticed before in a boy. His hair and eyes, but most of all his smile. She said, "You like my horse? His name's Buckshot."

The sudden appearance of the striking young girl caught Lil' Bill by surprise. "This is your horse? I know this ole horse. Everyone calls him Slop Jar." Before Anna Mae could say anything, Lil' Bill caught himself. "Well, I don't. I mean, I used to. But I don't anymore."

Innocently, Anna Mae asked, "Why do they call him Slop Jar?"

"I guess 'cause of what he looks like. How'd he get the name Buckshot?" asked Lil' Bill.

Anna Mae said, "Don't know. Everyone tells me how special he is, but no one wants to tell me why."

"He don't seem special. I see him here all the time, just an old worn-out horse," said Lil' Bill.

"Yeah, he was my papaw's horse before he died," said Anna Mae.

"I knew your papaw, Mr. John. He was a nice old guy. I would see him with Buckshot. Sorry he passed," said Lil' Bill. Then Lil' Bill stopped rubbing the horse and stepped to the other side of the animal. He said, "You know what? If you look at Buckshot from this side, he don't look so bad."

Anna Mae stepped around and stood next to Lil' Bill and studied Buckshot. She said, "Yeah, I guess he don't look so bad this way." Anna Mae smiled and announced, "My name is Anna Mae Hill. I got here Friday evening."

Lil' Bill, eager to get to know the pretty girl, replied, "My name's William Mason, but my friends just call me Lil' Bill." He pointed south down the wagon road where he came and said, "I live down that way a piece."

Anna Mae said, "My uncle Zeb lives that way too. He has the first place."

"I know, Mr. Zeb. Him and my dad are friends," replied Lil' Bill.

Lil' Bill returned his attention to Buckshot and thought of his last encounter with the animal. He said, "Before you came, I guess I was mean to ole Buckshot, and I got to thinkin', *Why was I bein' so mean?* He just minds his own business and don't hurt no one. I don't know why I was mean, but something suddenly came over me and just felt I needed to leave 'im alone. Even if he's an ugly old nag."

Anna Mae looked at Buckshot and said, "I reckon I've been mean to 'im too." Then Anna Mae found the last carrot in her pocket and fed it to Buckshot.

Mary and Katherine were watching Lil' Bill and Anna Mae. Mary said, "See, child, everthin's a goin' to be fine." Katherine said nothing; she just watched her daughter while she listened to her mother. Mary asked, "Ya remember when ya come?"

"Yes, Mom. When I saw you, you said you had a fight with the devil," replied Katherine.

"Well," said Mary as she continued, "I fought the divil an' me, an' the Lord won."

Katherine said, "Do tell, Mom."

Mary said, "Jist before ya pulled up, Lil' Bill an' Buster was a causin' trouble fer Buckshot. Well, jist as Buster was 'bout to try an' shoot Buckshot's good eye out with his slingshot, Lil' Bill had enough. The Lord took his heart right then an' tharr. That child jist up and skedaddled, an' left Buster a standin' tharr. I was jist watchin' 'em. They never knowed I was tharr. Before Buster had a chance to hurt Buckshot, I got so riled that I thought I was possessed with the divil myself. I weren't. I was possessed with the Holy Spirit. I'll tell ya what, ole Buster found out quick I was tharr. I jumped 'im good."

Katherine laughed. "If he's like his brothers, he's a good-sized boy. Weren't you scared?"

"Land sakes, child, no. He's a big 'un, but nothin' to fear when ya have Jesus on yir side," replied Mary.

"Mom, you're something," said Katherine laughing as she looked at Lil' Bill.

Lil' Bill wanted to get to know Anna Mae. He said, "Hey, you wanna go fishin'? There's a good spot at the mill next to the church.

Rainbow Cascades: not far, just down the road. That's where I was goin' when I stopped to see Buckshot."

"I like to fish, but I don't have a fishin' pole," said Anna Mae with a shrug of her shoulders.

Lil' Bill smiled and said, "It's okay. I'll let you use mine. We can take turns."

Anna Mae pointed at Caesar and asked, "Do you mind if my dog comes along? His name's Caesar. He won't be any trouble."

Lil' Bill reached down to pet the excited dog. He answered, "Sure. He's a friendly little guy."

Anna Mae said, "He'll protect us. On the way here, a big black bear was about to eat me alive. Uncle Zeb tried to shoot it, but his gun didn't work. Caesar must a thought he was a bear and went after that bear like he was goin' to eat 'im alive, and saved my life."

Lil' Bill laughed and asked rhetorically, "That little dog?"

"*Yes*, that little dog. Just ask my uncle Zeb. He'll tell you. His gun jammed. His fancy rifle, and not for Caesar, that bear woulda eat me alive. That bear was ten feet tall, and Caesar saved me," said Anna Mae indignantly.

"I believe you. I didn't mean anything. It's just funny's all. Was it his Henry rifle?"

Anna Mae replied, "Yes, that one."

"He let me shoot it one time. It's a real nice rifle. Hard to believe it misfired," said Lil' Bill.

"Yes, it did. Wouldn't fire a shot. But after Caesar saved me, it worked just fine." Anna Mae shouted up to her mother, "Mom, can I go fishin' with Lil' Bill? It's just down the road."

Katherine remembered how she and Nicklaus often played at Rainbow Cascades when they were young. "Yes, Anna Mae. Be back before supper."

"Yes, Mom," shouted Anna Mae as she and Lil' Bill headed down the road with Caesar at their feet.

Mary looked at her daughter, grabbed her hand, and said, "Lord's work, child. Lord's work. Tharr's a reason fer everythin'. Part of God's plan."

CHAPTER 13

The Fish Fry

The road upon which Anna Mae and Lil' Bill were walking was sunken from years of wagon traffic. The lack of trees left no escape from the bright sun. The absence of rain and heavy wagon traffic left a covering of fine dust over the hard road. A wagon loaded to excess with sacks of freshly ground cornmeal pulled by two large Clydesdales passed in the opposite direction. The driver acknowledged the children with a friendly nod.

Anna Mae and Lil' Bill stepped to one side, allowing the driver to pass. Lil' Bill looked at Anna Mae, who was wiping sweat from her brow, then pointed to their destination: a small wooded oasis within which lay the gristmill and cascades. "Look, we've not far to go," said Lil' Bill. Anna Mae returned Lil' Bill's comment with a quiet smile; her excitement at meeting a new friend and the fishing excursion overcame the discomfort of the heat.

The welcoming sound of rushing water and a grove of tall firs, hickories, and pin oaks signaled their destination was near. On the right side of the road was a gristmill, and across from the gristmill was Antioch Baptist Church, a small white clapboard structure fifty feet square.

At the height of the Civil War, the church elders, wishing to provide a good education for their children, agreed to establish a school. The underutilized church building was the least expensive solution, and a teacher was hired to teach grades one through twelve. Anna

Mae's mother, Katherine, was among the first to attend. Katherine excelled in school and later would help the teacher with the younger children.

The church and the gristmill were dwarfed by tall hardwoods that formed a canopy and provided cool shade. Farmers dropping off wheat and corn, to be ground, were standing about. The playful shouts and laughter of children enjoying the cascades that fed the sluice from above the slow-moving creaking waterwheel went unnoticed to the farmers as they exchanged pleasantries.

Upon entering the shade of the dense woods, Anna Mae and Lil' Bill were overtaken by a pleasant drop in temperature which chilled their damp shirts and intensified their senses. As her eyes adjusted to the darkness, Anna Mae admired the beauty. With each breath of cool air she took in, her problems with Buckshot grew more distant. Except for the cascades, Rainbow Creek was lined with laurel trees and rhododendrons that benefitted from the shade of the larger hardwoods. The locals used the glabrous leaves of the laurels as a folk remedy for things like minor burns and poison ivy. Below the gristmill, the water collected into a pool of still water.

"I can't believe how cool it is," said Anna Mae.

Lil' Bill said, "Yes, it's nice. I come here all the time." The boy pointed to the cascades above the mill. "In a little while, we'll see a rainbow."

Lil' Bill pointed to a wagon with two draft horses. He said, "That's my dad's wagon. All the farmers bring their corn here. He had our corn ground into meal, and he's taking it to Sharpsburg tomorrow to sell." Lil' Bill turned to Anna Mae and said, "He should be back in a week. I helped him, and he'll pay me when he gets back." He pointed to the church and said, "That's where we go to school. Miss Weatherby's our teacher. You'll like her, but make sure you mind. She's as tough as nails and bigger than my dad."

Anna Mae said, "I'm from Sharpsburg. We had a nice school there too. Moved back here after my dad died. We're goin' to live with my mamaw till we get our own place." A curious look came over Anna Mae's face. "How big is your dad?"

Lil' Bill said, "Sorry to hear about your dad. How'd he die?"

"Consumption like Papaw," said Anna Mae.

Lil' Bill said, "I remember when your papaw died. Mr. John and Mr. Zeb were the first people we met. Come this way." Anna Mae followed Lil' Bill down a small footpath between small boulders to the fishing hole. The path opened to a circular pool of still clearwater shrouded in shade about five feet deep and one hundred feet in diameter. Toward the center protruded a boulder the children used as a diving platform. Upon close inspection, schools of small fish could be seen darting about the rocky bottom. Lil' Bill said, "This is a great spot to catch fish. I've caught trout here, but it's a good place to catch brim. Some folks calls 'em blue gills."

Fixated on the size of her teacher, Anna Mae asked, "You said the teacher's big. Is she really bigger than your dad?"

Lil' Bill said, "Dad's big, but Miss Weatherby is bigger. No foolin', and she don't take no guff neither. So you better be good."

Anna Mae's senses overflowed. Along with the gentle sound of the waterwheel emptying into the pool and the coolness of the shade came the fresh scent of the trees. She looked upstream past the gristmill, at the cascades, and was captivated by the beauty. She said, "This is the most beautiful place I've ever seen."

Lil' Bill, wishing to impress Anna Mae with kindness, handed her the pole and said, "You're new here. You go first." He pulled a large lively earthworm from a bag and said, "I dug these up last night. Let me bait your hook."

Anna Mae proclaimed with confidence, "Hand it here. I can bait my own hook." Without a word, Lil' Bill handed Anna Mae the worm and watched as she ran the hook through the worm and swung the line into the still pool.

As the cork bobber settled on the surface, Lil' Bill said, "Not bad for a girl. Bet cha can't clean 'em."

"Yes, I can. Dad taught me how to fish and to clean 'em too," said Anna Mae.

Within moments, the bobber started bouncing on the water. Excited, Lil' Bill shouted, "LOOK. YOU GOT ONE BITING ALREADY. Now watch it. Be ready."

Anna Mae said nothing as she glanced at Lil' Bill, her furrowed brow giving indication at her displeasure at being told the obvious. She said, "I told you I know how to fish." Suddenly the float disappeared from the surface. Anna Mae gave the pole a quick snap, setting the hook. The fish swam in circles, tugging mightily, trying to escape, bending the pole noticeably, and seeking the safety of deeper water. Anna Mae shouted, "I GOT A BIG ONE."

Lil' Bill replied, "Look at 'im. He's pulling your line everywhere. Swing your pole this way, and I'll pull 'im in." Anna Mae did as Lil' Bill suggested, and he grabbed the line, struggling with the fish that was wildly flopping about. "You got a brim, a big one. Maybe even a pound. They put up a good fight for a little fish," said Lil' Bill. Anna Mae smiled, and Lil' Bill finally freed the fish from the line and put it on his stringer. He said, "Good eatin' fish too."

Anna Mae acknowledged his proclamation with a smile. She handed the poll to Lil' Bill. "Your turn. You think you can catch one?" As he reached for the pole, Anna Mae asked smugly, "Do you want me to bait it for you?"

Lil' Bill laughed at Anna Mae's sarcastic joke. "No, I'll get it. But thanks anyway."

The two settled in and spent a happy afternoon fishing, each taking turns with the pole. Neither were aware that, like the summer of 1888, their childhood innocence was fading. Soon they would enter adolescence on their own terms. For now the cool shade, sound of rushing water, the gentle creaking of the waterwheel, and fishing would allow them to enjoy the remnants of childhood a little longer.

"Look, Anna Mae," said Lil' Bill, pointing to the cascades. Anna Mae looked up from the bobber at the cascades. A small brilliant multicolored rainbow arched into the sky. Hoping to impress Anna Mae, Lil' Bill said, "Yeah, every day, 'bout this time if the sun's out, you'll see a rainbow."

Anna Mae said, "Out of nowhere. I've never seen anything like that. Well, except after a rain. It's so beautiful."

A deep voice from nowhere asked, "Will, who's your new friend?" The voice belonged to Lil' Bill's father, Stephen Mason—a tall big-boned man of six feet in his early forties. The clean-shaved man wore denim bib overalls and a plaid shirt with the sleeves rolled up to his elbows, exposing large forearms. He was mostly bald, save for remnants of graying black hair protruding from under a straw hat. Everything about him was big, solid, and evenly proportioned.

Lil' Bill turned and said, "Anna Mae, this is my dad. Dad, Mr. Zeb is Anna Mae's uncle." Lil' Bill's father reached out to Anna Mae with huge calloused dark hands that swallowed hers.

Anna Mae remembered what Lil' Bill said about Miss Weatherby as she greeted Lil' Bill's father and was amazed at the idea of a woman that big. She said, "Hello, Mr. Mason. I'm Anna Mae Hill. We just moved here from Sharpsburg."

"Nice to meet you, Anna Mae. We're from Sharpsburg too. I see you got Caesar with you. Your grandmother was worried that something got that little dog. I know your uncle Zeb. He helps me on the farm now and then. He told me he was goin' to bring you and your mother back," said Lil' Bill's father.

"That little dog saved Anna Mae's life, Dad. He chased off a big black bear," said Lil' Bill.

Lil' Bill's father laughed and said, "I'm not surprised. Some dogs don't know they're small. Sure is a feisty little pup." Lil' Bill's father turned his gaze to Anna Mae. "Did you show my son how to fish?"

Lil' Bill said, "Dad, she can fish better than any girl I ever saw. Even Mom."

Lil' Bill's father laughed. "She must be pretty dang good then." Anna Mae flashed a confident smile and raised the stringer filled with fish twisting about for close examination. Lil' Bill's father said, "Looks like you two got 'em all." He pulled a pocket watch out and, after giving it a quick glance, said, "Anna Mae, nice meeting you. I'm about to head back. It's nearly four. Do you two want a ride back?"

Lil' Bill, wishing to spend more time with Anna Mae, looked at her, seeking approval. She acknowledged her desire with a smile and an affirmative nod. "No, Dad, I'll walk Anna Mae home," said Lil' Bill. He opened his bait bag and said to his father, "We're out of worms. We're ready to go. We won't be far behind." Lil' Bill took the pole and the stringer and said to Anna Mae, "We better git. We don't have all that far to go. But I have a lot of fish to clean."

ANNA MAE'S BUCKSHOT

Lil' Bill's father turned and walked away. Anna Mae, still absorbed with her teacher, asked Lil' Bill, "Miss Weatherby's as big as your dad?"

Lil' Bill laughed and said, "Well, maybe not quite as big, but just about. You don't want to make her mad." Anna Mae listened as Lil' Bill continued, "Like I said, she don't take any guff, not even from Buster."

Anna Mae asked, "Who's Buster?"

"Why, he's the meanest and biggest boy at school. He has six brothers, and all of 'em are mean. Buster used to be my friend," replied Lil' Bill.

Anna Mae asked, "Why aren't you friends now?"

Lil' Bill, not wanting to talk about what happened with Buckshot, said, "I reckon he just got too mean."

The two made their way to the road and headed home with Caesar at their feet. Lil' Bill, captivated by Anna Mae's emerging beauty, said, "I can walk you to school if you want. I walk by your house."

Anna Mae, with no hesitation, welcomed Lil' Bill's offer and said, "That'll be nice."

Unsure of himself, Lil' Bill qualified his offer, "At least till you make friends." While walking, the children forgot about the afternoon heat and time as they made small talk, getting to know each other. Buckshot saw the two children approach, stopped grazing, and broke into a trot toward the road. Lil' Bill looked at Anna Mae and said, "Look, here comes Buckshot."

Anna Mae made no attempt to hide the contempt she had for the horse. She replied, "I know. He won't leave me alone." Buckshot stopped at the fence line and nickered as Lil' Bill greeted the horse with a pat on the neck. Anna Mae ignored Buckshot and continued to her house. Buckshot followed Anna Mae from the fence, leaving Lil' Bill alone watching the horse walk after Anna Mae.

The boy ran to Anna Mae and said, "He sure likes you."

"Yes, I know. He won't leave me alone," snapped Anna Mae.

The sight of Anna Mae's displeasure prompted Lil' Bill. "He's not such a bad horse."

Anna Mae said, "You wouldn't say that if he were your horse. You don't have to ride 'im. Following you everywhere. Never leaving you alone."

Anna Mae's cutting remarks made it clear to Lil' Bill she loathed the horse. He said nothing and looked at the pitiful horse and, like the past Friday with Buster, felt a sense of compassion and sorrow for the animal. Lil' Bill followed Anna Mae, leaving Buckshot standing alone staring like a lonely child in search of a friend. Holding up the stringer full of fish, he said, "We're almost at your house." Wishing to prolong their time together, Lil' Bill added, "Maybe I can clean these here. Half of 'em are yours anyway."

Mary, Katherine, and Zeb watched Lil' Bill and Anna Mae from the porch. Zeb greeted the two children, "Is that Lil' Bill? Tarnation, look at all them tharr fish ya got. Been a while since we had a fish fry." Zeb's warm greeting buoyed Lil' Bill's hopes of spending the evening with Anna Mae.

Mary said, "Hello, Lil' Bill. Yir pa just passed here twenty minutes ago. He had a big load of corn meal."

Lil' Bill replied, "Yes, Miss Mary, we had a good crop of corn this year. He had it ground today. He has a buyer in Sharpsburg. Tomorrow he's takin' it there to sell it."

Katherine noticed Lil' Bill's desire to spend time with Anna Mae and asked, "What're you goin' to do with all the fish you caught?"

Anna Mae said, "I caught half of 'em, Mom."

Lil' Bill said, "She sure did. Why, she can fish better than most boys I know. Even baited her own hook."

Zeb said, "Looks like those two caught enough fer everyone to eat today. I jist wonder what're they goin' to do with them fish."

"If you cook 'em, I'll clean 'em, Mr. Zeb," said Lil' Bill.

Katherine said, "Sure, Lil' Bill, sounds good. What about it, Uncle Zeb? Can you cook 'em?"

Zeb spit tobacco and looked at Anna Mae and said, "I reckon that depends on Anna Mae. What 'bout it, lil' lady?"

Anna Mae, excited over the impromptu dinner party, said, "I'll help Lil' Bill."

Mary looked at Katherine and said, "Good thing I made a pie this morning. I reckon we better git busy."

Katherine said, "You're right. We got a lot to do. I've missed your pies, Mom."

Mary said, "I made an apple pie. Yir pa's favorite." All were soon immersed in their tasks. Anna Mae and Lil' Bill cleaned the fish. Zeb prepared a fire. Mary and Katherine made biscuits and coleslaw.

Anna Mae's spirits soared as she helped Lil' Bill clean fish. The misery Buckshot brought to her was, for the moment, forgotten. Lil' Bill was her first friend at her new home, and Monday, school would start. Anna Mae finally found a bright spot for the first time since her arrival. Her mood swung from utter despair to the apex of joy.

Time flew by for Lil' Bill and Anna Mae as the afternoon surrendered to evening. Katherine and Mary had the table set, and Zeb, with the children, brought up the freshly fried fish. Zeb set the fish on the table and said, "I love brim. It's a good eatin' fish. Mary, would you hurry and ask the blessing so we can eat?"

Mary said, "Yes, Zeb." Everyone gathered around the table and bowed their heads, and Zeb removed his hat. She asked for the blessing, "Dear heavenly Father, we ask that ya bless the food we're 'bout to eat an' those a eatin' it. Let it nourish our bodies an' give us the strength to follow yir will. Bless those who are less fortunate than us. We ask fer yir guidance during our troubles, an' that the light of yir saving grace enter the hearts of those lost an' find yir love an' mercy so they may have eternal life. In the name of yir Son who died on the cross, Jesus, we ask these things. Amen."

Everyone began to move about chaotically as they filled their plates and take seats around the table. Lil' Bill quietly positioned himself next to Anna Mae which did not go unnoticed by Katherine, bringing a smile. Zeb declared, "That's a good spot fer fishin'. Me an' Anna Mae's papaw fished there before the war. In fact, we fished there before the mill was built."

Anna Mae said, "There was a pretty rainbow, Uncle Zeb. Did you see it when you and papaw went fishing?"

Zeb replied, "Sure did, lil' lady."

Katherine said, "Uncle Zeb, this fish is good."

Mary looked at Anna Mae and said, "Yir uncle Zeb knows how to cook fish."

Zeb took another biscuit and said, "Thank ya. Been a cookin' fish since I learned to walk." He turned to Lil' Bill and said, "Yir pa's a goin' to Spartanburg to sell his meal. I asked if'n he wanted me to ride with 'im. He said he would be all right. To be honest, I'm glad. This last trip plumb wore me out."

Lil' Bill flashed a big smile and said, "Yeah, when he sells the meal, he's goin' to pay me for helping him."

Mary asked, "Good, Lil' Bill. What cha goin' to do with all that money?"

Lil' Bill, with a prideful smile, said, "My dad said I could do what I wanted. It was my money, and I earned it. So I'm goin' to get a horse."

Anna Mae asked, "What kinda horse are you getting?"

Lil' Bill looked at Zeb and said, "Mr. Zeb, you know that horse you tried to sell my dad?"

Zeb knew the horse Lil' Bill was talking about and asked rhetorically, "Ya talkin' 'bout Storm?"

"Yes. Storm. When Dad gets back, I'll have the money to buy him," snapped Lil' Bill.

Everyone stopped, and a deathly silence fell over the dinner party. Katherine looked at Anna Mae and saw the color drain from the child's face, and her body become tense. A sense of betrayal by her mother and grandmother overwhelmed Anna Mae and drove away all her joy. Instantly she found herself in a worse state than when she had awoken that morning and seethed with rage. Zeb looked at Mary, who had a guilty smile, as Anna Mae stood and glared at her grandmother. She angerly declared, "Mamaw, you can't let Zeb sell Storm to Lil' Bill. You just can't."

Before Mary could respond, Katherine looked at Anna Mae and said with a reassuring voice, "Sweetheart, your mamaw knows what's best."

ANNA MAE'S BUCKSHOT

Lil' Bill, unaware of Anna Mae's feelings for Storm, was unprepared for the scene unfolding before his eyes. He looked at Zeb and asked, "Did I say something wrong?"

"I don't understand, Mamaw. Why can't you sell Buckshot to Lil' Bill and let me have Storm? He likes Buckshot. It's not fair," cried Anna Mae. Without acknowledging Lil' Bill, Anna Mae stormed upstairs to her room crying.

Attempting to make things right with his new friend, Lil' Bill turned to Zeb and said, "Mr. Zeb, I don't need that horse. I'll take Buckshot."

Mary said, "Child, Buckshot's not fer sale. If'n ya want, ya can buy Storm."

Like Anna Mae, Lil' Bill's heart came crashing down. "I'm sorry, Miss Mary, I didn't mean to upset Anna Mae. I guess I better go," said Lil' Bill.

Katherine reassured Lil' Bill, "You did nothing wrong. Ya can stay if you want."

The joyful party turned into a funeral procession. Lil' Bill replied, "No, I think I'll go."

Disappointed, Lil' Bill got up to leave. Mary retrieved a napkin and gathered some fish and a few biscuits. She said, "Here, take some of this fish with ya. We can't eat all this. Yir pa can eat this later." She gave the napkin and handed it to Lil' Bill as he left.

"Tarnation. I forgot about Lil' Bill's pa wantin' to buy Storm," said Zeb.

Katherine, upset at her daughter's behavior, said, "I have a mind to take a switch to that child."

"You'll do no such a thing, Katherine. I told ya this is God's doin'. Ya need to let it be. Have patience. It'll all work out. Ya just have to have faith," said Mary.

Zeb got up and said, "I reckon I caused enough trouble fer one day. I better go." He grabbed a couple pieces of fish and left.

Katherine looked at her mother and said, "We need to explain Buckshot to Anna Mae. I grew up with Buckshot, so it was easier for me. I saw 'im with Dad, but Anna Mae was too little when we left."

Mary gently held her daughter's hand and explained, "Now, child, be patient. Anna Mae's heart ain't ready. She jist won't understand. She starts school Monday. It'll work out. Have faith. I see it. This is the Lord's doin', an' we don't need to be a pokin' in his work. Trust the Lord's plan."

CHAPTER 14

Buckshot Goes to School

Katherine stepped onto the porch and joined Mary who was gently rocking with coffee in hand. The coolness of the morning air indicated fall. Mary asked, as she sipped coffee, "Did ya git ya some coffee? Come an' join me, child. Nice, this morning." Katherine looked, through the haze of the thinning fog, at Buckshot quietly grazing, and settled into the rocker next to her mother.

"Yes, Mom. It's beautiful, this morning. I feel fall comin'," said Katherine.

The faint sound of honking geese caught Mary's attention. "Shush. Hear that?" asked Mary. Both women became quiet. Mary said, "Geese." As they passed, overhead, air that pulsed from the beating of hundreds of wings could be heard through the honking. Katherine looked up and saw the geese in a giant V formation that stretched across the clear blue sky.

Katherine said, "I forgot about the geese. They're so pretty." Katherine and Mary silently watched until the honking grew faint and the large line grew smaller until it was lost in the horizon.

Mary leaned back in her rocker and said, "Fall was yir pa's favorite time of year. When he saw them geese, he'd say, 'Time to go a hunting,' an' him an' Zeb would disappear fer two or three weeks. Them geese's a good omen. Somethin's goin' to change fer the better."

Katherine said, "I remember Dad saying it was a sign of good luck. After Nicklaus and I got old enough, he let us go with 'em one time. I sure enjoyed it. You know, Dad enjoyed the simple things."

Mary said, "He was happy with what the Lord blessed 'im. Why, he had everythin' he wanted. I reckon that made 'im as rich as that tharr Carnegie fella."

Katherine said, "I miss 'im, Mom. I miss James."

Mary took on a reassuring tone and said, "I miss 'em too. Both fine Christian men, they are indeed. Why, child, death's our destiny. Jist the way it is. This past winter was jist too much fer 'em. We'll see 'em again."

Katherine asked, "Have you heard anything from Nicklaus?"

Mary answered, "Not fer a while. I did git a letter last Christmas. Said he was in St. Louis. Doin' good in the dry goods business. He said he was a make'n plans to come home. But he had to settle affairs before he could leave."

Katherine said, "I miss Nick Mom. Why Anna Mae never even seen 'im."

Mary said, "Yes, I do too. I remember when he left a talkin' about all the money to be made out west. Said he wanted adventure. That one day there'd be nothin' left. He wanted to see it befir it was gone. He joined the cavalry like yir pa an' made it out okay. I was worried with all them Injun wars an' all. He made it, an' he'll be back this way someday. I jist knowed it. I keep a prayin'."

"Mom, I admire your faith. Sometimes I question things. I just don't understand," said Katherine.

Mary said, "Only natural. We all question God at some point. He ain't a goin' to come out of the sky and say, 'Here I am.' But if'n ya look hard enough, ya can see God. Why, he's all around us, ya know. After a while, ya don't have to look hard at all. Don't really need to understand him neither. Jist know he's here. Ya can see his hand in everythin' if'n ya jist let yourself. If'n I find myself a doubtin' God, I jist look around."

Katherine said, "Zeb said that you believed Caesar was sent to you by the Lord. I think, after seeing that little dog chase off that bear and that gun of his not firing, that convinced him you were right.

You should have seen it. There was nothing we could do. I called out for Jesus, and that little dog went crazy mad."

Mary laughed as she said, "Yeah, ole Zeb sure hated that little dog. Land sakes I was a lookin' all over fer 'im after Zeb left. I didn't even know the dog lit out after him till y'all come back."

"He picked up those bullets and put 'em in his rifle, and they went off like nothing was wrong. I got to admit that was a trifle queer. I mean, the very same bullets two of 'em. I think Zeb and I both saw God then," said Katherine with an astonished look.

Mary smiled at her daughter and explained, "I'm not a bit surprised, child. Ya jist gotta have faith. Look at Peter. Why, there was Jesus a walkin' on the water, an' the wind a blowin' their boat everywharr. At first Peter asked Jesus to tell him to come. Jesus said, 'Come this way, Peter.' An' Peter got outa that boat an' commenced to walkin' on the water. He headed straight to Jesus. But then he got to thinkin' 'bout the wind an' the waves, an' he got plumb skeered. He started to sink, he did. Then he cried out to Jesus, 'Save me.' An' then Jesus snatched him before he went under. Jesus said, 'Ye of lil' faith. Why did ya doubt me?'"

Mary glanced into her coffee cup and continued, "Ya see, Katherine, it's our nature to doubt. Still, Peter doubted God, and there was God a standin' right smack-dab in front of 'im. An' even after all them miracles, like a feedin' all them folks an' raising Lazarus after bein' dead, Peter would deny Jesus three times. So don't go a feelin' poorly about yir doubts, child. But ya need to learn to find ways to see God instead of a not seein' 'im. Ya start a doin' that, yir faith'll grow."

Katherine returned her gaze to Buckshot who was grazing and asked, "What about Buckshot? Where does he fit in God's grand plan you keep talking about?"

Mary took her daughter's hand and, with a warm smile, answered, "Don't rightly know fer sure, child. All I know is, he's part of God's plan. He was from the very beginning even before you was born. See, Buckshot is a teachin' horse. He won't teach Anna Mae about horse things. He'll a teach that child love. That's what

God wants. Why, we may even learn a thing or two before he settles accounts with Anna Mae."

Katherine said, "Mom, I'm afraid. She hates that horse, but it's more than that. I am not sure she feels anything now."

"Oh, child, she's a goin' through a heap a heartache. That child has plenty of love. You'll see. It'll come as sudden as a clap of thunder. Tharr'll be no doubt," said Mary reassuringly. Anna Mae suddenly joined them on the porch. Mary greeted the child, "Look what the cat dragged in. Ya ready fer school?"

Anna Mae answered, "Yeah, Mamaw, I'm ready." At the sound of Anna Mae's voice, Buckshot quit grazing and trotted to the fence, drawing an exasperated sigh from the child. Each time she saw the horse, her hatred for the animal that was ruining her new life intensified.

Katherine said, "You need to eat something before you go."

They went inside, and Mary said, "I got some fresh biscuits fer ya an' some jam. It'll only take a lil' bit to fry up some bacon an' a couple a eggs. Ya got a long day ahead a ya, child."

"No, Mamaw, the jam'll be good. I need to get going before Lil' Bill gets here," said Anna Mae as she spread jam on her biscuits.

Katherine asked, "Why aren't you goin' to wait for Lil' Bill? He's a good boy."

Anna Mae snapped, "I just don't want to, Mom. I just want to get this over with."

Mary could see Katherine getting upset and intervened. "Child, eat befir ya go."

Anna Mae ate the biscuits and drank a glass of milk and started for the door. Mary wrapped two biscuits in a napkin and said, "Here, take these with ya. Ya may git hungry later." Anna Mae took the offering and headed to school. Katherine and her mother returned to their rocking chairs on the porch. They watched Anna Mae walk by Buckshot. The horse stood by the fence, seeking acknowledgment from the child with repeated snorts, which Anna Mae ignored. She quickened her pace, refusing to look back.

"Mom, I just don't know what to do with her. I've never seen her act this way before," said Katherine.

Mary replied, "You'll do nothin' is what you'll do."

Click, click, click. Pause. *Click, click, click.* Pause. *Click, click, click.*

The two women were drawn to the sound of the clicking. "What's that?" asked Katherine. She looked at the fence and saw Buckshot working on the gate. "Mom. What's that horse up to?" asked Katherine, unable to hide a chuckle.

Mary broke into a loud laugh as she answered, "You'll see. He's a crafty horse. Buckshot may not look like much, but he's crafty."

Katherine said, "I remember now. He's letting himself out. He wants to go after Anna Mae."

Tears poured from Mary's eyes from laughter. She said, "One time, ole Buckshot followed yir pa clean to town an' 'im not even a knowin' it."

"You think Buckshot'll be okay?" asked Katherine.

Laughing, Mary answered, "Yes, child, that horse'll do jist fine. You'll see."

Katherine's mood changed and, like her mother, began to laugh hysterically at the smart horse. She said, "That horse is as determined as Anna Mae to get his way."

Buckshot worked on the latch and, with persistence, worked it free. After gently nudging the gate with his muzzle, it swung open. Buckshot, without a care, walked through the opening and trotted after Anna Mae to the delight of Katherine and her mother. Still laughing, Katherine said, "I wish I could be there when she sees 'im." Katherine, not over the sight of Buckshot following her daughter, spotted Lil' Bill headed their way. She said, "Look, Mom, here comes Lil' Bill."

Mary shouted, "Hello. Ya off to school, are ya?"

Lil' Bill made his way to the women. "Where's Anna Mae? I was goin' to walk her to school."

Katherine answered, "She left. If you hurry, you can catch her."

Lil' Bill said, "I reckon it's for the best. I don't think she wants to see me now."

Mary asked, "Child, what makes ya say that?"

Lil' Bill answered, "I didn't know she wanted Storm. She's really upset."

Mary said, "She sure was, but she'll git over it. Don't ya fret none."

"I'm not sure, Miss Mary. She hates Buckshot. I'd be happy to buy Buckshot if that would make her happy," said Lil' Bill.

Mary barely able to contain her laugh said, "Child, I ain't a sellin' Buckshot. I done told ya no need to fret. She'll git over it."

Lil' Bill looked at the open gate and asked, "Where's Buckshot, Miss Mary?"

Katherine said, "He went to school with Anna Mae."

Lil' Bill asked, "How'd he get out?"

Mary smiled at Lil' Bill and said, "I reckon he wanted to go to school an' let hisself out."

Lil' Bill thought of the encounter he and Buster had with Buckshot and said, "I gotta go," and took off running.

Mary said, "See ya later." She looked at Katherine and said, "It's the Lord's plan, I tell ya. The Lord's plan."

CHAPTER 15

Anna Mae Learns Love

Anna Mae, alone on the road, could see the gristmill and the church building. Several children varying in age were milling about, unaware of her presence. Thoughts raced through her mind. Should she have waited for Lil' Bill to talk to him. If he could buy Buckshot, all her problems would be solved. After all, was not Buckshot the source of her misery? Her thoughts turned to regrets, and the regrets to anxiety that grew with each step she took. "I'll just get this over with," said Anna Mae under her breath, and she picked up her pace.

Clop, clop, clop.

She stopped and listened as dread overtook her. The sound stopped and, refusing to look back, resumed walking to school.

Clop, clop, clop.

She stopped and listened, and again the sound stopped. The same dread held her in place and prevented her from looking back, and she resumed walking.

Clop, clop, clop.

The sound was getting louder, and the pace increased. Again she stopped, and like before, the sound stopped. Under her breath, she muttered, "It can't be. It just can't be. Please, God, don't let it be Buckshot."

She stood frozen, contemplating the unthinkable and refusing to look back. Nor could she look at the other children. She just stood and stared at her feet. Then Buckshot's muzzle drifted over her shoulder followed by an intense snort, confirming her greatest fear. Seeking the attention of the child, Buckshot nickered and gently nudged her head and snorted into the child's ear. Anna Mae's fear turned to rage as Buckshot made his presence known. She turned and shouted, "BUCKSHOT."

Anna Mae took two steps back from the animal and again shouted, "WHY CAN'T YOU JUST LEAVE ME ALONE!? CAN'T YOU SEE I HATE YOU? YOU'RE NOTHING BUT AN OLD BROKEN-DOWN WORTHLESS HORSE. I DON'T WANT YOU AROUND. JUST GET OUTA HERE. YOU'RE RUINING MY LIFE." Buckshot, indifferent to her rage, silently stared at Anna Mae with his eye blinking and ear rotating about, seeking a kind sound as his tail gently swayed. The children stopped playing and watched the horse and girl they had never seen before. She turned on her heel and ran to school with Buckshot trotting behind. The odd spectacle of the new girl trying to escape the determined horse caused some of the children to laugh.

In front of the gristmill was Buster who welcomed the opportunity to torment the decrepit old horse. Buster stepped toward Anna Mae and Buckshot, and shouted, "Hey, look, it's Slop Jar. Little girl, your horse thinks it's a dog," drawing more laughter from the children. Tense with fear, humiliated, and nowhere to hide, Anna Mae said nothing; she just looked at the man-sized boy.

Buster said, "If I knew ole Slop Jar was coming, I woulda brought my slingshot." He picked up a rock and tossed it gently in the air, catching it in his hand several times to gauge its weight. Buster said, "I guess this'll have to do for today." He hurled the rock with all his might at Buckshot, bouncing it off the horse's head with a loud crack, barely missing his bad eye. "That horse is just as stupid as the last time I saw him. Don't worry, little girl, that eye's bad anyway," said Buster laughing.

Anna Mae cast her gaze upon Buckshot as the horse stood, unflinchingly, looking at her. The site of the calm horse softened her, and for the first time, she felt empathy for the animal. Buster reached down for another rock and threw it, bouncing the rock off his neck with a loud smack. Buckshot took two steps back and snorted.

ANNA MAE'S BUCKSHOT

Now some of the older children scattered about, searching for rocks to throw. Anna Mae watched the children as they threw rocks, which bounced off Buckshot, making loud smacks and thuds as they struck him and fell to the ground at the horse's hooves. Buckshot began a slow walk toward Anna Mae, his eye fixed on the child with no regard to the rocks that were hitting him.

The children laughed and shouted, "SLOP JAR! SLOP JAR!" The sight of the rocks bouncing off her horse turned humiliation into horror. In the children, she saw herself. She saw she was no different than those she was watching as they heaped misery on the defenseless animal. The sight of the old flea-bitten gray nag with the sway back, one eye, and one ear enduring the torment that even she inflicted unleashed her forgotten conscience buried deep within her heart.

Anna Mae replayed the conversation she had with Zeb at Burnside's Bridge and later at his house. Anna Mae, through Buckshot, felt the heartbreak Zeb felt over the sweetheart that left him. Was not Zeb the same person after the war as before? If his sweetheart loved him before the war, why not after? Her mamaw did not leave her papaw; she loved him. The only woman Zeb ever loved left him for reasons out of his control. The ugly scars carved into his face by the brutality of war were his constant reminder of his lost love. These contemplations fueled the empathy which was growing within her. She understood her uncle's pain, and that pain was coursing deep into her soul.

As the children threw rocks and shouted insults, she looked at Buckshot, and the pain rolled over her like an emotional tsunami. She began to wonder how Buckshot became the way he was. But did it matter how or why? To Anna Mae, she was no different than the woman who abandoned her uncle years ago. She could no longer bear the cruelty of the children toward her horse and ran to Buckshot, throwing her arms around his neck sobbing. Anna Mae found love for a horse that, only moments ago, she loathed with her entire being.

"HIS NAME ISN'T SLOP JAR. IT'S BUCKSHOT. HE'S MY HORSE. LEAVE 'IM ALONE," Anna Mae cried out through heaving sobs.

The children, unmoved by Anna Mae's pleas, continued to hurl insults and throw rocks. Some of the rocks hit Buckshot, and some hit Anna Mae. The crowd of children became an unruly mob, a hideous entity. As the rocks and insults came her way, Anna Mae pulled one of the biscuits Mary gave her and held it out for Buckshot. She said, "Here, ole boy, have this. Come on, Buckshot, let's go home." Under a hail of small rocks, she turned away with Buckshot following.

Headed her way was Lil' Bill. He had a good idea what had happened and asked, "What's wrong? What happened?"

Distraught, Anna Mae, with Buckshot, walked by Lil' Bill sobbing without saying a word.

Buster saw Lil' Bill and mocked his former friend. "Look, it's Lil' Bill. Slop Jar's his horse."

Lil' Bill, who was overcome with a rage that drove away the fear he had of his former friend, ran to meet Buster and shouted, "LEAVE 'EM ALONE." Buster, wishing to mete out justice to the boy, he felt turned against him, charged to meet Lil' Bill. They met on the road between the gristmill and the church. Without warning, Buster delivered a right uppercut into the boy's solar plexus. The blow drove Lil' Bill to the ground, leaving him doubled over, paralyzed with pain, and gasping for air. Buster said nothing; he just stood over Lil' Bill, basking in his dominance.

The other children saw the encounter. They, who moments ago were sharing in Buster's torment, found a new respect for Lil' Bill who stood up to Buster. Not long ago it was Lil' Bill standing with Buster tormenting them. He was now one of them, and the children began to drop their rocks and turned away from Buster.

Miss Weatherby ran out of the church to investigate the commotion and saw Anna Mae with Buckshot walking away. The sight of Buckshot, a horse she knew, reminded the teacher of Gettysburg. She remembered, as a child of ten, the frightening sounds of artillery and musket fire that were easily heard from her house. After the battle, she helped her mother tend to the wounded and saw death on an unimaginable scale. The memory rekindled a horror of the wounded and dead bodies left in the wake of the battle, both man and horse. Also left in the wake of battle was the hideous stench of death. The smell of thousands of dead soldiers and horses, rotting in the sun, hung over the town. The memory unleashed a rage from deep within the teacher.

Miss June Weatherby, thirty-five, stood six feet tall and weighed one hundred and eighty pounds. She wore her bright red hair pulled into a bun which accentuated her green eyes. A faint smattering of freckles covered her cheeks. She was a comely woman and was unmarried. Not for lack of suitors, but because she wished to remain single. She loved to teach and took her profession seriously. Unlike most women of the day, she dressed in denim and boots and appeared more ready to ride than to teach. She was tough and a paddle hung from her desk in plain view. She was not afraid to use it but preferred not to. It was only a matter of time before she and Buster would square off, and today was that day. Lil' Bill was on the ground with Buster walking toward her defiantly, as if nothing had happened.

Not anticipating a challenge, Buster locked eyes with the teacher as their paths crossed. The children, who moments ago were caught up in Buster's cruelty, began to quietly scatter. She looked down at Lil' Bill who was gasping for breath. The teacher was surprised. She remembered not long ago the boy had stood alongside Buster tormenting the others. She asked, "Are you all right?"

Through coughs, he said, "I'm all right, Miss Weatherby. This's my fight." Her rage reached its boiling point and required all the patience she could muster to remain calm. She told the children to get in the school.

"Go on in with everyone else," said Miss Weatherby as she helped Lil' Bill to his feet.

The children were silent when Miss Weatherby entered. She said, "You little ones can leave." She pointed them out, and they left. The four remaining students, all boys, watched Miss Weatherby pace in front of them like a caged lion as she tapped a yardstick on the floor. Lil' Bill took his seat, and Buster, showing no sign of humility, leaned back in his chair wearing a smug smile. Like so many times before, he was confident nothing would come of this episode, daring the teacher to do something. Miss Weatherby decided now was the time to take this boy down. She walked to the boy and brought the yardstick down on his head with such force it snapped in two. Then the large woman, with all her might, dragged him to the front of the class and threw him on a stool.

She was determined to make an example of Buster. "Do you have any idea just who that horse is? Do you?" shouted the teacher. The boys sat quietly, shocked, and motionless looking at Buster, waiting to see what he was going to do. No one had ever seen Buster manhandled in such a manner.

Buster got up and headed for the door and said, "I'm goin' home, and ya can't stop me." Miss Weatherby grabbed him and again threw him onto the stool. Again he got up, and she backhanded him across the face as hard as she could. He got up again, and she made a fist and hit him in the nose with a loud crack. Blood started to flow freely, and a torrent of water flowed from his eyes. He retreated to the stool.

Buster said, "Miss Weatherby, you broke my nose."

Miss Weatherby squeezed his nose which increased the flow of blood and felt it pop. Buster let out a scream appropriate for the level of extreme pain he experienced. She said, "It'll be fine. I broke my nose once falling off a horse when I was your age." She got a handkerchief from her desk and handed it to Buster. She shouted at the defeated boy, "You try to get up again, I'll break more than your nose. God as my witness, you're going nowhere. I don't care who your pa is." Defeated and humiliated, Buster sat slumped on the stool.

The boy made no further attempt to leave. Satisfied she had established control, Miss Weatherby said, "I wasn't going to get into this. I wanted to wait until after Christmas, but after I saw the horrible way you boys were acting this morning, I decided today we are going to learn about the Battle of Gettysburg and a special horse."

Miss Weatherby began, "We have a lot of ground to cover, so let's get started. The Battle of Gettysburg started on July 1, 1863."

CHAPTER 16

Gettysburg: July 1–3, 1863

Prelude: May 6, 1863–June 30, 1863

Early in June 1863, after a dramatic victory at Chancellorsville, Confederate General Robert E. Lee started his march north from Fredericksburg, Virginia, through the Shenandoah Valley in the shadow of the Blue Ridge Mountains. He decided to take the war to Pennsylvania, which was untouched by battle. The rich farmlands of Pennsylvania would provide Lee's army, seventy-five thousand men with food and supplies. To this point, the Civil War had claimed over two hundred thousand Confederate and Union lives. Lee knew that a large group of Peace Democrats in the North, sometimes referred to as Copperheads, was gaining influence. Lee was convinced a Confederate victory on Northern soil would add to the growing sentiment for peace in the North and force Lincoln to negotiate. Also, Lee felt it would help with the ongoing struggle at Vicksburg, Mississippi, considered the Gibraltar of the South, which was under a brutal siege.

Union General Joseph Hooker—commander of the Army of the Potomac—still recovering from his humiliating defeat at Chancellorsville, wanted to pursue the failed objective of capturing Richmond, Virginia. President Lincoln thought otherwise and insisted that Lee's army, not Richmond, be the objective of the Union Army. Reluctantly, Hooker would pursue Lee, keeping the Army of the Potomac, around one hundred thousand men, between Lee and Washington, DC.

On June 9, Confederate cavalry under the command of Major General J. E. B. Stuart was caught by surprise by a determined Union cavalry under the command of Major General Alfred Pleasanton at Brandy Station in Culpeper County, Virginia. While the battle was relatively small in comparison to earlier engagements, it was the largest cavalry battle of the Civil War. The battle, which proved inconclusive, demonstrated for the first time Union cavalry could fight on equal terms with Confederate cavalry.

On June 13, the Second Corps of the Army of Northern Virginia, under the command of Lieutenant General Richard Ewell, appeared outside the Union Garrison at Winchester, Virginia, eighty miles north of Chancellorsville, Virginia. The next morning, the Confederates attacked. The battle sent Union forces, commanded by General Robert H. Milroy, reeling under a Confederate juggernaut. Left in the wake of the hasty Union retreat was much-needed war material, which fell into Confederate hands including horses, cannons, and hundreds of wagons loaded with stores vital to the war effort. On June 15, Ewell and his men began to cross the Potomac. After slicing through Maryland and entering Pennsylvania, the rest of Lee's army followed and scattered around Gettysburg, foraging for much needed supplies.

Gettysburg—in spite of its small size with a population of less than 2,500—boasted a thriving economy which included a college, a Lutheran seminary, several newspapers, carriage manufacturers, gaslit streets, piped water, and the Gettysburg Railroad that ran to nearby Hanover. With ten roads that entered Gettysburg, like the spokes of a wagon wheel, it was an excellent point of convergence for any large modern army.

Lee, perhaps remembering the looting of Fredericksburg by Union forces several months earlier, issued an order for the officers and enlisted men to behave and only acquire the needed supplies through proper channels. Lee's generals—James Longstreet, A. P. Hill, and Richard Ewell—offered up worthless Confederate script to pay for the large quantity of supplies—like bacon, flour, sugar, and shoes—leaving the local farmers and businessmen feeling as if they had been looted nonetheless. But further down the command, it descended into actual looting, as hungry Confederate soldiers simply ignored Lee's orders and took as they pleased. Even worse, runaway slaves were found and rounded up to be returned south. Among these were actual free Blacks who were kidnapped. The extent of the looting was too great for Lee, with limited resources, to control. More often than not, he ignored the pleas of local citizens.

Meanwhile, President Lincoln was still frustrated with generals that seemed unwilling to pursue Lee. The latest being Joseph Hooker. Hopes were initially high when Hooker was given command of the Army of the Potomac in January of 1863. Those hopes were dashed after Lee's stunning victory at Chancellorsville in early May of that year.

After Chancellorsville, neither Lincoln nor his staff were able to motivate Hooker to be more aggressive, and it became apparent, from Lincoln's point of view, that Hooker adopted the same timid approach to battle as McClellan. Like McClellan, Hooker constantly complained he was outnumbered and would ask for reinforcements, which Lincoln would not release to his command. Hooker soon understood he had not only lost the confidence of his generals, but Lincoln as well.

To salvage his command, Hooker developed a plan to attack the Army of Northern Virginia. After Lincoln refused to support this battle plan, Hooker asked to be relieved of command which Lincoln granted on June 28, 1863, days before the Battle of Gettysburg. Lincoln replaced Hooker with Major General George Meade.

When Meade was handed the dispatch from General Henry Halleck, General-in-Chief of all Union armies, Meade thought he was being arrested due to Hooker's dissatisfaction over the Union debacle at Chancellorsville. After reading the dispatch, he learned he was given command of the Army of the Potomac. A reluctant Meade accepted the command with a return dispatch to Halleck that simply read, "The order placing me in command of the army had been received and that, as a soldier, I obey it."

Lincoln tasked Meade with defending Washington and engaging Lee in battle. Meade's strategy was simple. Since Lee and the

Confederate Army were the invading force, it would be Lee who must initiate the battle. Meade would concentrate his army in a defensive position of his choosing near Pipe Creek, Maryland (south of the Pennsylvania state line), and wait.

Meanwhile on June 28, through a spy by the name of Henry Thomas Harrison, Lee learned the Union Army was within a day's march of his position. He ordered his army, that at the time was foraging for supplies, to concentrate at Cashtown just west of Gettysburg. Upon hearing that Union troops were actually spotted in Gettysburg, Lee made plans to move his forces to Gettysburg.

July 1, 1863

On June 30, a Confederate foraging detail spotted Union cavalry gathering around Gettysburg, which they chose not to engage. When word reached General A. P. Hill, he was skeptical. Hill did not believe these soldiers were from the Army of the Potomac. Instead he believed they were local militia. On the morning of July 1, Hill sent General Henry "Harry" Heth to lead a reconnaissance mission and thus gain a better understanding of the situation.

On Chambersburg Pike, just west of Gettysburg, leading elements of Heth's infantry were spotted by Union videttes of the Eighth Illinois Cavalry under the command of Brigadier General John Buford. Shortly after 7:00 a.m., upon seeing the Confederate infantry advancing, Lieutenant Marcellus Jones took a single shot that failed to hit anything. The shot, scarcely noticed by the advancing Confederate column, was the first shot of the Battle of Gettysburg.

Perched in the cupola above the Lutheran seminary, the highest point in Gettysburg, General Buford was able to observe the Confederate advance from the north and northwest of Gettysburg. If there was any doubt of the seriousness of the deteriorating situation, the distant boom of artillery removed it from Buford's mind. Confederate forces were just three miles from Gettysburg. Buford knew he could not stop the enemy advance without infantry support. He only had a few hours before his line would break. Buford hastily organized a delaying action to buy time for his own infantry support to arrive.

In the early fighting, breech-loading carbines used by Union cavalry—while lacking the range and accuracy of infantry muzzle-loading rifled muskets—were able to be fired more rapidly. The carbines were also able to be loaded from a crouching position unlike the muzzle-loading muskets. This would aid Buford's cavalry who offered a stiff defense against a superior force of Confederate infantry that was advancing from the northwest along Chambersburg Pike toward Gettysburg.

Earlier, around 6:00 a.m., Union Major General John Reynolds made the decision to move his men to Gettysburg. Reynolds rode ahead of his men to appraise the situation. As Reynold's column marched north toward Gettysburg, they were met by the sobering sight of streaming refugees. Southbound women, children, and old men escaping war passed Union soldiers who were heading north to the boom of cannons and the popping of rifles.

As fighting intensified, General Heth began to shift his men from a marching column into a firing line, a complicated and time-consuming process. The first nebulous movements were rapidly evolving into a major battle delineated by distinct, if not crudely formed fronts, on the north and northwest sides of Gettysburg in the form of a semi-circle. Union cavalry would keep Heth's infantry at bay as long as possible along Seminary Ridge, McPherson Ridge, and Barlow's Knoll to the north, anxiously waiting for Reynolds to relieve them.

Upon arrival, Reynolds was greeted by a chaotic scene of desperate fighting. He was now the highest-ranking Union officer on the field and took command. As his men began to arrive, he sent a message to General Meade advising him of the deteriorating situation. Soon after the message was sent, Reynolds was shot from his horse while directing the placement of men and artillery. He died instantly.

Adding to the chaotic situation was more Confederate infantry, under the command of General Richard Ewell, arriving north of Gettysburg. In spite of the arrival of Reynold's infantry, Heth's infantry was pushing the Union Army south and east toward Gettysburg. Under increasing pressure, the Union line collapsed and was forced to retreat south through Gettysburg to Cemetery Hill.

Meade did not want to fight at Gettysburg and was still determined to fight at Pipe Creek. The momentum of the developing battle would determine Meade's plan. When Meade received word of Reynolds's death and Buford's desperate plea for help, Meade sent General Winfield Scott Hancock to take command and report on the situation.

When Hancock arrived on the battlefield, he met with Major General Otis Howard, Reynolds's second-in-command. After seeing the strong defensive potential of Cemetery Hill and surveying the situation, Hancock advised Howard, "I think this is the strongest position by nature upon which to fight a battle that I ever saw, and if it meets your approbation, I select this as the battlefield," to which Howard agreed.

With that, the die was cast. Gettysburg, a site neither Lee nor Meade had intended to fight, would be the site of a three-day battle which would be the bloodiest engagement of the Civil War and the largest battle ever on the North American continent.

Lee arrived on the battlefield that afternoon. At the start of the day, he was reluctant to fight. Lee did not wish to attack until all his men were in place. In the early hours, Confederate attacks were not well-coordinated, and General Longstreet and his corps were hours away. Upon arrival, Lee realized that Ewell, after a slow start, had gained the initiative. Ewell was pursuing the retreating Union Army south, and Lee had a change of heart. When he came to the understanding that most of the Union Army would soon be there and the importance of the ground, Lee decided to press the attack.

Wishing for Ewell to capitalize on his advantage, Lee ordered Ewell to take Cemetery Hill if practicable. The wording "if practicable" would have serious repercussions on the battle's outcome and be debated by historians to this day. Because after the brutal fighting and heavy losses earlier, Ewell felt his men had had enough. He chose to stop fighting, allowing Culp's Hill and Cemetery Hill to remain in Union hands.

While Lee's army won the day, the Union Army held a nearly impregnable defensive position. That night, Union forces would dig in on Cemetery Hill, and Meade moved the remainder of his army from Pipe Creek, bringing his strength to a hundred thousand men, along with artillery. Lee had the battle he was looking for. He was still confident of victory and the opportunity to capitalize on the growing descent and weariness of war among Northerners. In Lee's words, "If the enemy is there tomorrow, we will attack him."

July 2, 1863

As the sun rose, a light fog blanketed the battlefield, and like the day before, promised to be hot well into the eighties. Lee had been up since sunrise and had eaten breakfast by 5:00 a.m. The well-entrenched Union line took on the shape of a fish hook, with the tip of the hook being Culp's Hill, the Union's right flank. The line arced through Cemetery Hill, and the shaft of the hook shot straight south through Cemetery Ridge until it reached two hills named Little Round Top and Big Round Top—the Union's left flank. The Confederate line was similar, with its left flank across from Culp's Hill, arcing in a northwesterly direction through Gettysburg. The line turned south, running parallel with the Union line about a mile across from Cemetery Ridge along Seminary Ridge.

A confident Lee showed no sign of concern as he sent a small patrol to reconnoiter the area around Little Round Top and Big Round Top, then up Emmitsburg Road leading north to Cemetery Hill and report any additional Union troop movement. A task expected from Lee's cavalry under the command of J. E. B. Stuart, whose whereabouts were unknown to Lee. When the patrol returned, they found Lee meeting with General Longstreet. Their report indicated there were no Union forces south of Cemetery Hill, including Emmitsburg Road. This news allowed Lee to move forward with his battle plan which involved Longstreet attacking Cemetery Hill from the south by advancing northward along Emmitsburg Road and Ewell attacking Cemetery Hill from the north.

With only two divisions available for battle, Longstreet was not enthusiastic. Pickett's division would not arrive until later in the day. Lee temporarily transferred a division from A. P. Hill's command to make up the difference. Still, Longstreet asked Lee for a delay in order to gather his forces, to which Lee reluctantly granted. Ewell, already in position, would wait for the sound of Longstreet's artillery. When Longstreet opened fire from the south of Cemetery Hill, General Ewell would commence his attack. Satisfied, Lee dispatched Longstreet.

Meanwhile, Union commander George Meade was making final preparations of his own for the anticipated battle at Cemetery Hill. Not known to Meade, General Daniel Sickles, Third Corps commander—whom Meade had an intense dislike—decided to extend his position along Cemetery Ridge near Little Round Top, the Union Left flank. Not happy with the ground he was to defend, Sickles saw a better spot to place his artillery. Sickles moved his line from just north of Little Round Top forward toward Emmitsburg Road, creating a salient or bulge in the Union line. This left his men vulnerable to attacks from three sides. Also, Sickles's movement left a gap in the Union line to his right.

When Longstreet reached the point where he would turn north along Emmitsburg Road, he was shocked to find his path blocked by Union soldiers. Union soldiers that were not supposed to be there. Unknown to Longstreet, this was the Union Third Corps under the Command of General Sickles who had just completed repositioning his men. Longstreet's march to Cemetery Hill came to a halt.

As Lee patiently waited for Longstreet to start the attack, morning gave way to noon, and Lee became anxious. When 2:00 p.m. arrived, and still no action from Longstreet, Lee decided to ride out and see for himself what caused the delay. By the time Lee arrived, Longstreet had learned, from a captured Union sergeant, that the soldiers blocking Longstreet's path were indeed from the Union Third Corps. Lee did not view this as a setback. In fact, he thought of it in terms of divine intervention. If Longstreet had not seen the Federals, his flank would have been dangerously exposed and vulnerable to attack.

After a brief meeting on horseback, Lee ordered Longstreet to start the battle there. After word was passed along Longstreet's men and preparations made, he would signal Ewell with cannon fire for the battle to start.

When Meade was informed of the extent that Sickles had moved his men, he became furious. He ordered Sickles to immediately report to him. However, it was too late; by the time Sickles arrived at Meade's headquarters, Confederate artillery fire had begun. An infantry assault was imminent. Meade decided they needed to return to Sickle's position. Upon arrival, Meade found the right of Sickle's line extended to the Peach Orchard and Emmitsburg Road which left a gap to Sickle's right. To the left was Devil's Den, a boulder-strewn landscape at the base of Little Round Top. Meade indeed realized a Confederate infantry assault was imminent, and it was too late to pull the men back. Instead he decided the best course of action was to move in reinforcements.

Still, Meade had one more problem to deal with. The advisor who informed Meade of Sickles's troop movements, Brigadier General Gouverneur K. Warren, chief engineer, suggested to Meade he inspect the hill known as Little Round Top. With that advice, Meade sent Warren to Little Round Top and ascertain what needed to be done if anything. While Big Round Top was higher than Little Round Top, the latter had more strategic value because its west face, clear of trees, provided an incredible view of the battlefield.

When Warren arrived at the summit of Little Round Top, the Signal Corps (whose mission it was to communicate the movements of the enemy with the rest of the army by use of flags) were the only ones occupying the hill's summit. Warren was amazed as he looked out and saw most of Lee's army. The Signal Corps was preparing to leave. Realizing the importance of the hill, Warren ordered them to stay and immediately sent for reinforcements. The reinforcements did not arrive a moment too soon. Within minutes of their arrival, Confederates launched the first of many attacks attempting to take the hill.

At 4:00 p.m., advancing Confederate infantry under the command of General John Bell Hood, tasked by Longstreet to take

Little Round Top, came under Union artillery fire. The quiet and otherwise serene countryside, complete with squirrels frolicking on the scattered boulders of Devil's Den and birds gathering in trees, erupted into a maelstrom of deafening noise created by the discharge of cannons and thousands of muskets.

Along with the noise came choking smoke that overtook the battlefield. The random beauty of nature gave way to chaos and carnage. Shortly after the battle got under way, Confederate General Hood was wounded in the right arm by shrapnel from an exploding shell and taken from the field of battle. This inflamed an already chaotic situation, as Longstreet's forces attempted to fight their way through the Devil's Den, the Wheatfield, and the Peach Orchard, making their way up to the summit of Little Round Top and Cemetery Ridge.

After repeated charges and desperate fighting, the Confederates nearly succeeded in taking both Little Round Top and Cemetery Ridge. Union forces held firm during the battle which included a daring bayonet charge by the Twentieth Maine while defending Little Round Top, the far left of the Union line, thus thwarting the Confederates' last serious attempt to take the hill. Longstreet would say, after the battle, that it was the best three hours of fighting ever on any battlefield. He may well have been right, but it was of little comfort to Lee. For at the end of the day, Longstreet failed to take Cemetery Ridge or Little Round Top. After all the fighting and carnage, Longstreet was still in the same position he was in at the start of the day.

During the heavy fighting, General Sickles, like Confederate General Hood earlier, would be wounded and taken from the battle. His leg was amputated, and later, Sickles would donate it to the Army Medical Museum in Washington, DC, which later became the National Museum of Health and Medicine where it is still on display.

When General Ewell, the other half of Lee's pincer, heard Longstreet's artillery, he prepared his corps for the assault on Cemetery Hill and Culp's Hill. Ewell tasked General Jubal Early to take Cemetery Hill and Major General Edward "Allegheny" Johnson to take Culp's Hill. Like Longstreet to the south, Ewell would call on artillery to soften the Union position before sending in infantry. Artillery battalion commander, Lieutenant Colonel Richard S. Andrews, was wounded during the battle for Winchester. This left nineteen-year-old Major Joseph Latimer, the highest-ranking officer, to direct the fire of the battalion's fourteen guns. Latimer earned the respect of Ewell during the Battle of Fredericksburg the previous December, calling him Young Napoleon. Those under his command also respected him in spite of his young age and small size, referring to him as the Boy Major.

While Latimer's artillery fire was accurate, it proved mostly ineffective. Union artillery, however, caused considerable misery for Latimer, forcing him to abandon his position on Benner's Hill, a little more than a thousand yards from Cemetery and Culp's Hills respectively. While directing fire, Latimer would be severely wounded by an exploding artillery shell, killing his horse and costing him his right arm. A month later, he would die from his wound after gangrene set in.

The Union soldiers tasked with defending Cemetery Hill watched Latimer withdraw. Because of the lateness of the evening, after 6:00 p.m., they thought the fighting was over. They soon learned otherwise, as the Union defenders of Cemetery Hill observed Confederate lines under the command of General Jubal Early forming for attack. Ewell ordered Early to make the assault and take possession of Cemetery Hill as Lee had initially planned.

The steep eastern face of Cemetery Hill dropped into a ravine that was defended by a small force of a thousand federals. The steepness of the grade prevented the Union gunners on top of Cemetery Hill from sufficiently lowering the barrels of their cannons, making them useless for infantry support. The advancing Confederates used this to their advantage.

The Union line at the base of Cemetery Hill was quickly overwhelmed by a superior force of rebels in a bloody melee which broke into hand-to-hand combat. Men used their muskets as clubs and stabbed one another with bayonets. Anything at hand became a weapon, some even hurling rocks from a wall along which the Union line formed.

As the Union line broke, the rebels charged to the top of Cemetery Hill, seizing a cannon. The Confederate success was short-lived, however, as Union reinforcements emerged from the west side of Cemetery Hill and forced the Confederates to make a hasty retreat.

Around 7:30 p.m., as the fortunes of General Early trying to take Cemetery Hill turned, the other half of Ewell's command—Major General Edward "Allegheny" Johnson's division—commenced its attack on Culp's Hill. The hill, comprised of two peaks: a north peak and a south peak, was being defended by a minimal force of about 1,300 men under the command of Colonel George S. Greene. Meade pulled a significant portion of Greene's command earlier to fill the gap created by Sickles on Cemetery Ridge.

Anticipating a full-scale Confederate attack, Colonel Greene ordered the men to cut trees and form an abatis. Greene gave meticulous instructions to the men who were cutting trees as to their placement on the east face of Culp's Hill. Upon finishing their work, the men heard the distant booms of Longstreet's artillery, reminding them, like their commander, their effort was not in vain.

The breastworks prepared by the Union forces defending Culp's Hill would prove their value. Johnson's vastly superior force was hindered by the fallen trees and the steep hillside. Even with more than four thousand men at his disposal, Johnson was not able to dislodge the Union line only one-third its size. As daylight was dwindling and the Confederates became low on ammunition, they suspended their attack with little to show for their sacrifice except for possession of the south peak of Culp's Hill.

After two days of bloody fighting, the casualty count for both sides combined rose to over thirty-seven thousand killed, wounded, or missing. Now, Gettysburg was the bloodiest battle of the Civil War with one more day of fighting.

Possibly rattled by the carnage and the closeness of Confederate victories during the days fighting, Meade summoned his generals and held a war counsel that night. If Meade was entertaining a retreat to his original Pipe Creek position, he was met with disappointment. After advising Meade of the fighting status of their corps and casualties, the generals present advised Meade to stay and fight. They wanted no more retreats. Meade got the message; then he advised that when Lee attacked the next day, it would be upon the Union center. The generals departed and began preparations for battle the following day.

That evening, as the generals on both sides prepared for battle, the cries of the wounded filled the air. Enlisted men carrying lanterns through the Devil's Den and the Peach Orchard, which by the end of the day became known as the Valley of Death, sought to comfort the wounded left among the dead on the battlefield.

July 3, 1863

On the morning of July 3, Lee realized he had failed to achieve any of his objectives. After all the fighting on July 2, Lee's only success was that General Edward "Allegheny" Johnson had possession of the south peak of Culp's Hill, and Longstreet held the Devil's Den. These, however, were insignificant. Morning essentially found the Union line in the same position they held at the end of July 1.

The failure of both Longstreet and Ewell to achieve Lee's objective, however, did not shake the confidence Lee had in the Army of Northern Virginia. Unlike Meade the previous evening, Lee did not hold a war counsel with his generals. He knew what he intended to do, which was to continue the attack he had initiated the previous day. Adding to his confidence was the arrival of General J. E. B. Stuart—his wayward cavalry commander—and even more important, General George Pickett and more than five thousand fresh soldiers, the latter arriving that morning.

July 3 promised to be another hot and humid day. Lee met with Longstreet early in the woods along Seminary Ridge and altered his plan. Instead of continuing the previous days' attacks, Lee decided to have Longstreet attack the Union center. Longstreet was even less enthusiastic about this plan than Lee's battleplan of the previous day. Again, Longstreet mustered all the appropriate courtesy required when challenging a commander of Lee's stature to allow him move his corps around the Union left. Lee was unmoved as he pointed to

Union's position on Cemetery Ridge about a mile away and told Longstreet, "The enemy is there, and we shall attack."

Longstreet, who believed that such an attack would fail, stated with blunt language, "I have been a soldier all my life. I have been engaged in fights by couples, by squads, companies, regiments, divisions, and armies. And it is my opinion that no fifteen thousand men ever arrayed for battle can take that position." Lee, still unmoved, explained that Pickett's division would be joined by Generals Isaac Trimble's and Johnston Pettigrew's divisions for a total of fifteen thousand men. Longstreet would have at his disposal around 150 cannons to take out the Union batteries. The attack on the Union center was to move forward. Lee left the details of the attack to Longstreet.

The silence of the morning was broken by the sound of Union batteries firing on Major General Edward "Allegheny" Johnson's men who were defending the south peak of Culp's Hill. The artillery barrage was followed by several hours of fierce fighting in which Johnson ordered four infantry charges on Culp's Hill's northern peak. All these assaults failed. By 11:00 a.m., the Union line on Culp's Hill was as strong if not stronger than the previous day.

Meanwhile, the attack from Longstreet did not start as planned. This time, the delay was caused by the late arrival of General George Pickett's division. While Pickett met with Longstreet around seven, his division would not arrive until later that morning. Meanwhile, Longstreet prepared his artillery.

Meade became unsure the Confederate attack would be on his center. Perhaps the inactivity from his left and center and the fighting that was taking place at Culp's Hill caused him some doubt. He also may have been nursing a desire to pull back to Pipe Creek. By noon, the battle for Culp's Hill had died down, and an eerie silence fell over the battlefield. Like Meade, the men along Cemetery Ridge, looking across the shallow valley into the wood line along Seminary Ridge, were not sure what was going to happen next. Some busied themselves by preparing lunch, and others sat nervously waiting.

By noon, Confederate artillery, more than 150 cannons, were ready and waiting for word that Pickett's division was in place. Around 1:00 p.m., Pickett was ready, and Longstreet sent word to commence the artillery barrage. The silence was broken by the largest artillery barrage of the Civil War, and the largest ever on the North American continent. The Confederate infantry, more than twelve thousand men, waited anxiously in the woods along Seminary Ridge as Confederate cannons opened fire on the Union line.

Opposite the Confederate line, arrayed on Cemetery Ridge, stood little more than ten thousand Union soldiers under the command of Major General Winfield S. Hancock. Still, Meade continued to contemplate Lee's intentions. The Confederate artillery barrage emanating from Seminary Ridge upon the Union line, as big as it was, still left Meade second-guessing himself. Did Lee intend to attack his center as he anticipated?

For more than an hour, fire from Confederate cannons directed by Colonel James Walton and Colonel Porter Alexander attempted to disable Union artillery. The noise created by their concentrated artillery fire could be heard as far as one hundred miles. Most of the fire overshot their targets, having relatively little effect. Shrapnel from some shells that found their targets brought death to man and horse. Even Meade and some of his staff were hit by pieces of shrapnel, causing them no serious harm.

Union artillery commander Brigadier General Henry J. Hunt did not want to engage in an artillery duel, preferring instead to use artillery on the anticipated infantry assault. After heated demands from General Hancock, he returned fire using his cannons sparingly. Toward the end, he ordered his artillerymen to draw down their fire gradually to give the Confederates the impression they were out of ammunition.

Along with the lull in Union artillery fire, Colonel Porter Alexander observed Union batteries limbering up and leaving. He sent a note to Pickett that read: "For God's sake, come quick. The eighteen guns are gone. Come quickly, or my ammunition won't let me support you properly."

After getting a tepid approval from Longstreet in the form of a nod, Pickett commenced the attack. Pickett's division emerged from the woods into the sun and sweltering heat. Along with Pickett came divisions commanded by Major General Isaac Trimble and Brigadier

General Johnston Pettigrew who formed on the left of Pickett. Altogether they formed a line of 12,500 men, elbow to elbow, a mile wide. Their destination: a clump of trees on Cemetery Ridge a mile away.

The guns Alexander thought were gone reappeared. As soon as the Confederates presented themselves, they came under horrendous artillery fire. Exploding shells fell among the men as they marched, unwavering at a normal pace. The explosions ripped holes in the line, sending those unfortunate to be nearby hurtling into the air. Still, the advancing Confederate infantry maintained discipline. Those infantrymen not hit by the exploding artillery rounds would fill the gaps by closing ranks with mechanical precision.

The soldiers had no control over their lives as they marched toward the Union line, into the teeth of merciless artillery fire produced from scores of cannons. Still too far away to return fire, they continued to close ranks as one shell landed after another and those around them became casualties. Only fate would determine the survival of one man or another. In spite of the exploding shells raining down upon them, the Confederate march remained orderly. Most of the regimental officers chose to march with their men, saber in hand, on foot. Still, without breaking and in order, they marched forward with their eyes on their point of convergence: a clump of trees—the Union center.

Shouts of "Here they come. Here comes the infantry!" erupted along Cemetery Ridge from excited Union soldiers observing, with admiration, the Confederate advance from Seminary Ridge. Bayonets glistened and regimental flags fluttered in the sun along the Confederate line. Union General Hancock could be seen riding up and down his line along Cemetery Ridge, giving encouragement to his men. Meade could now see Lee's attack was indeed on his center. He ordered reinforcements to Hancock's line. In Gettysburg, steeples and rooftops were filled with townspeople anxious to see the unfolding drama.

Halfway, the Confederate march was halted by a fence along Emmitsburg Road. Union artillery showed no mercy as they went over the fence and reformed, reducing their numbers further. Still, they marched on.

When they came to within three hundred yards of Cemetery Ridge, they were in range of Union musket fire. Union artillery commander Brigadier General Henry J. Hunt ordered his batteries to switch to canister. The cannons became giant shotguns and, with each round containing hundreds of steel balls, would be aimed into the advancing line of Confederate infantry. One well-placed shot could take out ten men. The Union soldiers remembered their humiliation and bloody defeat at Fredericksburg after a similar charge they made, and mocked the advancing Confederates shouting, "Fredericksburg, Fredericksburg," as the slow march turned into a desperate charge.

A brigade led by General Lewis Armistead would be the first to reach the point of convergence: a spot where two stone walls met and formed a ninety-degree angle and referred to as the Angle. The line of Confederates, a mile wide at the start of the march, was now less than half a mile wide. Only half of the 12,500 Confederates made it, and fighting broke into hand-to-hand combat. Union reinforcements overwhelmed the Confederates and forced them to retreat. Armistead would be mortally wounded while trying to turn a captured Union cannon.

A short distance away, his good friend General Winfield S. Hancock (commander of the Union center), would be wounded. Unlike Armistead, however, Hancock would survive the war. After the war, he would supervise the execution of Lincoln's assassins. In 1880, he would run for president and, after gaining the nomination of the Democrat party, would lose to James A. Garfield.

Pickett's division barely made it back to Seminary Ridge, suffering 50 percent casualties. Of the five thousand men Pickett led into battle, five hundred were killed; nearly 1,500 wounded; and a little more than eight hundred captured. Lee accepted responsibility for the failed charge.

When Lee asked Pickett to rally his division, Pickett reportedly replied, "Sir, I have no division." Pickett, grief-stricken, would never forgive Lee. The divisions of Pettigrew and Trimble suffered similar casualty rates. For the first time, a Union commander—Meade—

out-guessed Lee and thus handed him his greatest defeat. Lee held his army in place for a day in the hope he would draw Meade into an attack of his own. A hope that would not materialize. Lee retreated back across the Potomac to Virginia.

To make matters worse for Jefferson Davis, president of the Confederacy, on July 4, the brutal siege of Vicksburg drew to a close. After more than forty days of shelling day and night from more than two hundred Union land-based cannons and gunboats from the Mississippi River, Confederate General John C. Pemberton surrendered to Major General Ulysses S. Grant. Thus, handing the South another defeat, and Grant his greatest victory to that point. Nevertheless, the war would continue for nearly two more years, but after the losses at Gettysburg and Vicksburg, the South lost all hope of victory.

The battle of Gettysburg was the bloodiest battle of the Civil War. Total Confederate casualties for the three-day battle were approximately 3,900 killed; 18,700 wounded; and 5,400 captured. Union casualties were approximately 3,150 killed; 14,500 wounded; and 5,300 captured or missing.

After the battle, hastily dug graves often left bodies exposed. As a result, the bodies of men and horses putrefied in the hot sun, and the stench of death enveloped Gettysburg. It was decided that those who died should have a proper place of burial. The bodies of the soldiers were dug up and reinterred in a new burial ground. On November 19, 1863, following a two-hour oration by Edward Everett—a politician, educator, and pastor from Massachusetts—Lincoln officially dedicated the National Cemetery at Gettysburg. Lincoln's brief remarks, only 272 words referred to as the "Gettysburg Address," is considered by many as the greatest single speech in American history.

Lincoln may have been ill when he delivered the speech. The following day, Everett sent word to Lincoln, "I should be glad if I could flatter myself that I came as near to the central idea of the occasion in two hours as you did in two minutes."

CHAPTER 17

The Gettysburg Address

Buster's Change of Heart

Buster listened to the teacher's lecture and was captivated by the courage and honor of men like his father who fought and those who gave their lives. The women, as well, were at the front and risked their lives to help the wounded. People who set a high premium on honor and commitment and were willing to make the ultimate sacrifice.

Miss Weatherby glanced at Buster sitting quietly on the stool, humiliated. The bleeding had stopped, and his eyes were blackening, and his nose was swollen. She questioned what she had done and if she had gone too far. Indeed, she broke Buster, and for the boy's benefit, it had to be done. Buster was worth saving, for she felt there was good in everyone. Now it was time for her to bring him back. To let him know he belonged with the rest of the students. He should learn to turn his efforts to do good and become a positive leader and role model.

The teacher rifled through the drawers of her desk and found the paper she was looking for. She took it to Buster and said, "Read this to the class." Buster took the paper, and he stepped to the front of the class.

DAVID R. KOSAK

The Gettysburg Address

Four score and seven years ago our fathers brought forth on this continent, a new nation, conceived in Liberty, and dedicated to the proposition that all men are created equal.

Now we are engaged in a great civil war, testing whether that nation, or any nation so conceived and so dedicated, can long endure. We are met on a great battle-field of that war. We have come to dedicate a portion of that field, as a final resting place for those who here gave their lives that that nation might live. It is altogether fitting and proper that we should do this.

But, in a larger sense, we cannot dedicate—we cannot consecrate—we cannot hallow—this ground. The brave men, living and dead, who struggled here, have consecrated it, far above our poor power to add or detract. The world will little note, nor long remember what we say here, but it can never forget what they did here. It is for us the living, rather, to be dedicated here to the unfinished work which they who fought here have thus far so nobly advanced. It is rather for us to be here dedicated to the great task remaining before us—that from these honored dead we take increased devotion to that cause for which they gave the last full measure of devotion—that we here highly resolve that these dead shall not have died in vain—that this nation, under God, shall have a new birth of freedom—and that government of the people, by the people, for the people, shall not perish from the earth.

After reading the Gettysburg Address, Buster stood silent and motionless. He looked at Lil' Bill and thought of his actions earlier in the day. He thought of his encounter with Mary, and his treatment of Anna Mae and her horse. Reading the Gettysburg Address and Miss Weatherby's lecture on the battle affected the self-centered boy. He thought of his father who fought at Gettysburg, and an intense shame rolled over him. He thought of his mother, of whom he only had vague memories. He thought of honor and courage, traits he was unsure he could ever obtain. He took inventory of himself and found he only tried to hurt a defenseless horse and bullied younger children. He found nothing good, and he had no honor. He wondered if he could be like those he had just learned of.

Miss Weatherby said, "You can take your seat now."

Buster approached Miss Weatherby. "Did you know my father fought at Gettysburg?"

"Yes, I did. Did you know your mother was there too?" replied Miss Weatherby.

This was the first time anyone ever mentioned his mother. "No. No one ever told me about her," said Buster, wishing to learn of her.

"She helped take care of the wounded. Your mother was a fine Christian woman," said Miss Weatherby.

"Can you tell me about her, Miss Weatherby? I never knew her. She died when I was young," said Buster.

"Yes, I can. But I know someone who knows her better than anyone," said Miss Weatherby.

"Who?" asked Buster.

Miss Weatherby realized she was reaching the boy and said, "Mary Abbott. The little girl with the horse you chased off is her mamaw."

"How did she know my mother?" asked Buster.

"Your mother and Mary were the best of friends. They grew up together. After the battle, they volunteered to help the wounded," said Miss Weatherby.

Buster thought of his encounter with Mary. He felt the shame grow for what he had done and what he was trying to do to her horse. He knew he would have to face the small old woman. He said, "Thanks. I know what I got to do. Can I sit down?"

"Yes, Buster, you can take your seat. One other thing though," said Miss Weatherby.

"What's that?" asked Buster.

The teacher took on a soft tone. "Buster, you have a lot of good in you. Instead of bullying the weaker kids, maybe you can look after them. That would be one way you could gain honor and use your strength for good."

"You think so, Miss Weatherby?" asked Buster.

"I know so," said the teacher. "Now take your seat." She stood up, and as Buster took his seat, she said, "Boys, before we'll call it a day, I have one other matter to go over."

Buster dropped into the seat next to his old friend and said, "Sorry, Lil' Bill. Can you forgive me?"

Lil' Bill looked at the battered and humbled boy and was grateful for the change that came over him, and said yes, and held out his hand. "No hard feelings. We're still friends." Buster smiled, reached over, and shook Lil' Bill's hand.

Miss Weatherby paced in front of the class. "I think it's time to talk about the last fight at Gettysburg."

Lil' Bill whispered to Buster, "I don't understand. She already talked about Pickett's charge."

"Yes, Lil' Bill, I did talk about Pickett's charge, but that was not the last fight at Gettysburg. We are going to discuss a very special fight. It was the last action to take place at Gettysburg on July 3. It was a Union cavalry charge referred to as the Farnsworth Charge. You're going to hear about Elon Farnsworth, his friend John Abbott, and a special horse. His name is Buckshot."

Lil' Bill said, "Buster. That's Slop Jar."

Miss Weatherby stepped next to Buster and said, "Lil' Bill's correct, Buster. The horse you saw with the little girl was at Gettysburg too. Then, his name wasn't Buckshot. It was Jim, and he would be the last horse shot at Gettysburg."

CHAPTER 18

Anna Mae's Turn

Mary stopped knitting, turned to Katherine, and said, "Child, ya hear that? What's all that snorting? Surely can't be Buckshot."

Katherine leaned forward in her rocker and watched. She saw Anna Mae walking with Buckshot close behind. "It's Anna Mae, Mom. She's back from school. She's got Buckshot. Not been gone thirty minutes. I wonder what happened," replied Katherine.

Mary stood up and saw Anna Mae and Buckshot moving slowly toward them. Mary said, "By thunder, yir right, child. Looks like she's a totin' considerable worry." The two women watched Anna Mae walk Buckshot through the open gate. After closing it, Anna Mae stood under the shade of one of the many oaks, rubbing the horse's neck. Mary reclaimed her rocker and said, "Land sakes, ya better git down tharr. Looks like someone dropped an anvil on 'er head."

Buckshot let out a deep fluttering sigh followed by a friendly nicker when Katherine met them. The familiar surroundings had a calming effect on the horse. His ear was erect and turning about, and his eye was calmly blinking. "Hey, ole boy, it's all right now," said Katherine in soft tones as she ran her fingers through Anna Mae's hair. She looked at her and asked, "What's wrong?"

Anna Mae ignored her mother and continued to rub Buckshot's neck quietly. Katherine said, "You know, when I was upset, your mamaw would say, 'A joy shared is a joy made double, and a sorrow shared is but half a trouble.'"

Anna Mae thought of the horror Buckshot was forced to endure at the hands of the children. A gnawing pain twisted in her stomach. The pain was made worse as she confronted her actions. It pushed aside her hate for the animal. No longer did she see the horse as a decrepit animal worthy of contempt. The contempt was replaced by pity.

Anna Mae saw it as a living being with a heart and remembered how Lil' Bill said he wasn't such a bad horse. Her sudden realization, however, could not erase her behavior. She was forced to face her own actions. She did not understand the forces that drove her to such hatred and anger. She knew only Buckshot was unworthy of the torment heaped upon him by her and the others. She wondered if Buckshot felt the horror of the encounter, as did she.

The real horror, and something she could not erase from her mind, was that in the children, she saw herself. She saw reflected back on her the very things she thought and did to the innocent animal. The image brought to bear a burden that wrenched forth, from the depths of her soul, every regret and every wrong she had committed, no matter how trivial. They were now in the open like a jagged wound. Her conscience became a crushing weight that came down on her with no mercy. She tried but could not reconcile her behavior. The weight of the burden left her trapped and helpless, with no way for her to get from under it.

Anna Mae looked at the horse that wore the scars of man's worst offerings. Scars she did not understand and began to yield to her emotion. Unable to contain the trickle of tears that opened into a torrent, she turned away from Buckshot and threw her arms around her mother. In a voice that was strained with emotion and through halting gasps, she said, "Mom, I have been awful to Buckshot. All he wanted was for me to love him, and I didn't. Why did I do those horrible things to him? He's a good horse. He must hate me. God must hate me."

Although troubled by her daughter's torment, Katherine found relief in Anna Mae's tears. She saw compassion that only a short time ago eluded the child. Seeking a treat, Buckshot looked upon, then moved his muzzle between the child and her mother while snorting. The gentle horse pressed his nose into the child as Anna Mae purged her emotion, trying to ease her personal anguish. Katherine stroked her hair and said, "See, just look at Buckshot. He still loves you. Goodness, we've all done things we regret."

Anna Mae, inconsolable, cried out to her mother, "I said I hated him. I said I wished he were dead. I threw rocks at him like the others."

Katherine replied, "Yes, that was mean, but it's never too late to do the right thing. Do you love Buckshot?"

"Yes, Mom, I love Buckshot. I want him to be my horse. I don't care what he looks like. I just want Buckshot. I want to ride him and brush his mane and take care of him," said Anna Mae.

Katherine looked into her daughter's eyes as she rubbed Buckshot's neck and said, "Why don't you just tell Buckshot how you feel? Tell him you're sorry and you love him. He'll understand. Then ask God to forgive you."

"You think so, Mom?" asked Ana Mae.

Katherine rubbed her daughter on the head and answered, "Sure. Try it."

Mary watched the scene unfold from the porch. She never had any doubts. She knew, through her faith in Jesus, that God's plan was bearing fruit before her eyes and marveled at its beauty.

Anne Mae threw her arms around Buckshot's neck and said, "Please forgive me, Buckshot. I love you. I'll never be mean to you again. You belong to me, and I'll never ever let you go." Then she said, "Thank you, Jesus, for Buckshot. Please forgive me. I'll live a better life." Buckshot's nicker released the child from the burden. Her hatred for the horse was replaced with a newfound love.

Katherine said, "That's all you have to do, is leave it with God. Let's go see Mamaw."

Katherine and Anna Mae made their way to the house, leaving Buckshot staring from the fence. The tears and anguish on Anna Mae's face were replaced with smiles as she left her mother and bolted to her grandmother. "Mamaw, Mamaw," Anna Mae cried out.

From her rocker, Mary said, "What's all the fuss, child? Come over here and tell me all about it."

Anna Mae sat on her mamaw's lap and, as she gave her a big hug, said, "Thank you for Buckshot, Mamaw."

"Why, yir welcome," replied Mary.

"Mamaw?" said Anna Mae.

"What, child? What's on yir mind?" asked Mary.

Anna Mae dropped her chin in shame. She said, "At first I didn't want Buckshot. I hated him."

Katherine stepped onto the porch with Mary looking her way. Mary said, "I knowed all along, child. I knowed ya hated Buckshot."

A look of relief overcame Anna Mae. She asked, "You did?"

"I sure did," answered Mary. "I knowed from the moment ya first laid eyes on ole Buckshot ya hated him."

Anna Mae asked, "Why didn't you get upset?"

Mary laughed. "Child, ya can't make someone love. Love is a gift from God. A gift ya have to find on yir own. Love comes from the heart. Now ya see Buckshot with yir heart."

"You're not mad," said Anna Mae.

Mary exclaimed, "Of course not. In all my born days, I never was upset. Buckshot ain't upset none neither. Why, that horse seen much worse than that. Jist let it go, child. What's done is done. Ya jist need to love him from now on, that's all, an' keep Jesus in yir heart. Everythin'll work out."

Katherine said, "Mom, do you think Anna Mae's ready?"

Anna Mae asked, "Ready for what, Mamaw?"

"I declare she is," replied Mary as she looked at Katherine.

"Ready for what?" asked Anna Mae.

"Child, we was a waitin' fer ya to be ready to tell ya 'bout ole Buckshot. Ya wasn't ready. The Lord was a workin' on ya. Had to wait till yir mind was right."

Looking at her mother Anna Mae asked, "Tell me what, Mom?"

Mary got up from her rocker and said, "I'll be back in a minute. Jist ya wait here now." Mary went into the house and returned with a leather binder and handed it to Anna Mae. Mary said, "I think it's best to let yir papaw tell ya."

Anna looked at the binder, and on the cover, it read, "July 3, 1863, John Abbott."

Katherine said, "I was about your age when I read that."

Anna Mae opened the binder, and a daguerreotype fell to the floor. She picked it up and studied the image of two men dressed in Union blue and a dapple-gray horse. Anna Mae asked, "Is this Papaw?"

Katherine answered, "Yes, and his horse, Jim. But you know the horse as Buckshot. The other fella is your uncle Zeb."

Anna Mae replied, "Mom, Uncle Zeb was so handsome."

Mary let out a laugh and said, "Yes, he was, an' so was yir papaw. Why, I think they was the two handsomest men that ever went to war. They come home on furlough when their pa died. Why, jist look at 'em. They was ready to whup the whole Reb army. Their ma spent a whole dollar on that picture."

"And Buckshot. He was a pretty horse then," said Anna Mae.

Mary replied, "Yes, child, that was before they got shot up." Mary pointed to the horizon. "Yir papaw lost his leg jist over them hills. I reckon it's buried out tharr somewharr with legs an' arms an' the dead of all them who fell or got shot. It was bad. I could hear those guns an' all the fightin', a wonderin' if'n yir papaw was a goin' a come home. Him a fightin' not even a day's ride away. I never prayed so much as I did then. I remember when Zeb returned from Sharpsburg after he got all shot up. It was bad too. I said, 'Jesus, ya git 'im home to me. I don't care what happens. Jist git 'im home.' I tell ya, I waited but jist couldn't take it. I decided to find 'im. Yir ma was little, so I left her with her mamaw, an' me an' Zeb went to find 'im. I was plumb afeared, I tell ya. When we got tharr, tharr was wounded men all about a needin' help. So I sent Zeb to find my John, an' I went to helpin' the doctors." Mary sat in her rocker and continued.

"Wouldn't ya know it, I come upon Buster's ma. She was a huntin' her husband, Elijah. We both got busy helpin'. Two weeks went by, and I finally found yir papaw. He looked bad, near dead, he was. That was 'bout the happiest day of my life. Then I heard all them soldiers a talkin' about Buckshot, the hero horse. Ya coulda knocked me over with a feather when I found out they was a talkin' about Jim.

Ya see, when yir papaw left, his horse was *Jim*. Right purty horse, but when he come back, his name was *Buckshot*. All shot up, that horse was. Those two were a sight, I tell ya. Don't rightly know which one looked worse. Then as soon as yir papaw was well enough, he sat hisself down an' writ down the goin's on that day. He said, "Mary, I want to make sure my young'uns an their young'uns know what happened that day."

"Mamaw, was Papaw a hero?" asked Anna Mae.

Mary wore a prideful grin and said, "Yes, he was, but so was Buckshot. Yir papaw said if it wasn't fer ole Buckshot, he'd a been still out on that field. He sure loved that horse. Spoilt Buckshot rotten he did. We both thank Jesus ever' day for that ole horse. I believe it was all part of God's plan."

Mary pointed to the binder and said, "It's all in tharr, child. Ya jist read it." Anna Mae looked at Buckshot as the horse stood looking at the women. She left with the binder under her arm, walked through the gate, and settled under a tree as Buckshot grazed nearby. She opened it to the first page, "Written in these pages are the facts of my last engagement, July 3, 1863, and are put down to my best recollection. John Abbott."

CHAPTER 19

July 3, 1863

Farnsworth's Charge

When the battle for Culp's Hill—the Confederate left flank and Union right flank—commenced that morning, General Meade ordered an attack from the Union left flank on the Confederate right flank. This order was ultimately given to division commander General Judson Kilpatrick, commanding officer of the Third Division of the Cavalry Corps. The purpose of the attack, the southernmost part of the line near Big Round Top, was to create a diversion. The diversion was intended to hold a portion of Lee's infantry in place and reduce the strength of Lee's anticipated attack on the Union center. Kilpatrick, who earned the nickname "Kill-Cavalry" because those serving under his command felt he had a reckless disregard for his men, wasted little time in carrying out Meade's order.

Kilpatrick would employ the First Brigade under the command of Elon Farnsworth who, on June 29, 1863, was nominated by President Lincoln to be Brigadier General. The promotion, however, was not confirmed by the Senate. Farnsworth's brigade was comprised of the First West Virginia, Fifth New York, Eighteenth Pennsylvania, and the First Vermont cavalry regiments.

The first to attack, in the form of a cavalry charge, was the First West Virginia Regiment. The charge would commence from the base of a small wooded hill called Bushman's Hill. As they emerged from the woods, they found the ground ill-suited for such a cavalry charge. They encountered stone walls, broken ground, fences, and trees. To make matters worse, the Confederate skirmish line, formed by the First Texas Infantry which was supported by artillery, outnumbered the charging Union cavalry. Thus, breaching the skirmish line became a bloody melee. Unable to break through the skirmish line and under withering musket and artillery fire, the charge rapidly fell apart. The First West Virginia Cavalry regiment was cut to pieces. Nearly surrounded, they barely managed to make it back to their line, bravely hacking away with their sabers at the Confederate soldiers.

Quietly, from atop his dapple-gray gelding named Jim, Lieutenant John Abbott, Eighteenth Pennsylvania Cavalry Regiment B Company, watched the First West Virginia Cavalry Regiment struggle back to the safety of their lines. John and Jim were in several engagements, and up to this point, neither had been seriously wounded. Jim was a beautiful and gentle horse with a solid black mane, tail, and blue eyes. Jim's ears slowly rotated, and his eyes darted about indifferent to the ghastly sight. There was no order in the retreat, only chaos as the defeated men returned to Bushman's Hill through a thick shroud of smoke.

A frightened horse emerged through the smoke, catching John's eye. It's left front leg shattered by an artillery round. The animal was frantically hobbling about with the remnants of its lower leg flopping loosely from a strand of sinew. John grew accustomed to the sight, horses killed or wounded, but the frightened horse seeking safety moved him. John had seen the beautiful chestnut mare when a green recruit arrived late June, shortly before the start of the battle.

John chased the poor animal and managed to get the reins of the riderless horse. He looked at the empty saddle and beautiful deep-blue saddlecloth which was embroidered with gold trim and the letters *US* in the corner. He imagined its rider, attired in a crisp blue cavalry uniform with a saber dangling from his belt, mounted proudly on the fine animal for parade and wondered what became of the man. He dismounted Jim and began to calm the frightened horse, its head bobbing frantically against the reins.

John became distracted at the near-perfect heart-shaped white-patch that adorned the horse's forehead and was pulled about struggling to control the screaming horse, her brown eyes wild with panic. Flaring nostrils, wild snorts, and grunts told a story of carnage John had seen often during the bloody war. Confused, frightened, and fighting wildly, the horse tripped and fell to the ground screaming, taking John to the ground with her. Tightly holding the reins, John was dragged a short distance before managing to get the horse to its feet. After considerable effort, he gained control of the terrified horse.

He rubbed the horse's neck and spoke in soothing tones, "*Shh*, ole gal. Relax. Easy, girl, easy." The horse responded. John rubbed and patted her neck and continued, "Attagirl. Easy now. Are you scared? It's all right we're all scared. What's your name? My mamaw had a horse just like you when I was little. She called her Bonnie. Oh, she was a beautiful horse, but you're much prettier."

He stroked her gently and pulled a piece of hardtack from his pocket and held it out for the horse. "You sure are a pretty horse. I wish I knew your name. I think I'll call you Bonnie. Is that all right with you, ole gal?" said John as the horse took the offering and began to chew as it steadied itself on its three good legs. John continued to rub the horse's neck, running his hand through her mane. He looked at the leg dangling grotesquely and queried, "What've we done to you, Bonnie? Don't you worry now. I'm going to take care of you."

He thought of the disregard he had, at times, for life during battle. Both man and horse were expendable commodities. *The cause was more important than life itself*, he thought. But the sight of the beautiful horse restored the humanity within him, suppressed by war, if only for a brief moment. He silently stared at the horse and said, "You know, Bonnie, man has made beautiful things. But you know what?" The horse stared, blinking at John, and continued to chew the hardtack, "Only God can make a horse, especially one a pretty as you."

The innocent animal seemed to forget its predicament. John stroked the horse's jowl and said, "Don't worry, Bonnie. I'll take care of you. I'm goin' to send you to a place where there's no shooting and no exploding shells. There'll be nothing but sunshine and gentle breezes and nice pasture to graze on. Just over those hills."

The horse finished the hardtack, and John pulled his revolver from its holster. He moved the muzzle of the weapon to the side of the horse's head. The war and all the horror about them disappeared. Now there was silence; the only sound he heard was the horse's heavy breathing. He thought to himself how often he had killed men and horses, but this was different. He slowly pulled the hammer back until he heard a distinct click which seemed louder than the discharge of any cannon he had ever heard. He briefly paused to look one last time into the beautiful animal's eyes, and the horse returned the gaze with its ears perked straight up. John knew the animal, only a moment ago terrified, was now trusting.

John said, "Now that's better. No need for you to pin them ears." He closed his eyes and pulled the trigger. The discharge released a deafening sound, and instantly the horse dropped to the ground dead. He gazed upon the lifeless horse bedecked with its saddle and blue saddlecloth and stirrups which hung loosely over the horse's body. These were the silent accoutrements of valor. John saw, in his mind, the trooper preparing Bonnie for the day. He saw him put on the blanket and then the saddle and tighten the cinch. He saw him feed and water her. The very things he did with his horse Jim.

Did this man, that John did not know, feel the same way about her that he felt about Jim? The horse appeared well-cared for. He thought of how he was still on the field, likely dead himself. John looked at the dead horse and said, "Why didn't I ever say hello? I wanted to. I saw you and him several times. I just didn't. I wished I would've." The repressed compassion within John erupted, and he wept bitterly. Wiping the tears away, he said, "You see, Bonnie, I told you I'd take care of you. When I go over them hills, I'll look for you and your master."

A bugle call broke John's trance. He placed his left foot in the stirrup, grabbed the horn, and swung himself into the saddle. The sounds of war resumed, and Lieutenant John Abbott, Eighteenth Pennsylvania B Company, returned. The war, with all its hideousness, reclaimed his thoughts. The found humanity was once again suppressed, buried deep in his soul, to be retrieved for times such as these.

He and Jim would go out there and, hopefully, achieve what the First West Virginia Regiment was not able to. John reached down and patted Jim on the neck and said, "Looks like we're next, ole boy." John nudged Jim with his heels and left to find his friend, General Elon Farnsworth.

Around 2:00 p.m., the Confederate attack on the Union Center, Pickett's Charge, commenced. By 3:00 p.m., the charge had failed. The collapse of Pickett's Charge changed the situation. There was no longer a need for the diversion. Still, Kilpatrick felt he was in a position to run up the Confederate line even after the failed charge by the First West Virginia Cavalry Regiment earlier. Acting on Meade's somewhat open-ended orders, he continued the attack. To that end, Kilpatrick decided to send in the First Vermont Cavalry Regiment and have General Elon J. Farnsworth lead the charge.

John Abbott met Elon Farnsworth in the Utah Territory. They were civilian forage masters. It was there that John formed a brotherly bond with the younger Farnsworth. At the outbreak of the Civil War, Farnsworth joined the Eighth Illinois Cavalry Regiment. It was under the command of his Uncle John F. Farnsworth who also happened to be a US representative. Farnsworth was commissioned a lieutenant and assigned to K Company. It was not long before he made a place for his friend, John Abbott.

Because of Farnsworth's bravery and the genuine concern for his men, John, like the other men under Farnsworth's command, overlooked his youth. Shortly after the Battle of Antietam, and upon the recommendation of Farnsworth, John was transferred to the recently formed Eighteenth Pennsylvania Cavalry Regiment in November 1862, as a lieutenant. When Farnsworth was promoted to Brigadier General, just days before the Battle of Gettysburg, the two were reunited when Eighteenth Pennsylvania fell under the command of Farnsworth.

John found his friend at the base of Bushman's Hill mounted on a beautiful Palomino with a golden coat and a mane and tail that were snow white. He raised his right hand, offered a crisp salute, and said, "Sir, you're a hard man to find."

After returning the salute, General Farnsworth let out a faint laugh and said, "I see you made it. I watched the charge. John, you're goin' to have to be more careful out there."

"Sir, I wasn't out there. We got turned back before we got started. The ground is terrible. I'm sure you heard the artillery," replied John.

"Do tell. I heard it. You're right. I was down there. The ground's terrible, and Longstreet's men are dug in, daring us to attack. No cavalry regiment can turn that line. I doubt that the entire brigade could. We need infantry," replied Farnsworth, shaking his head in the negative.

John paused for a moment, "What're you going to do, sir? Word's out that Lee's attack was repulsed. What purpose does it serve for us to attack? Like you said, they're well dug in. We have no chance. We can't move the enemy from his position."

"Don't know. Makes no sense. Don't see any reason to get our men killed for nothin'," said Farnsworth, and he turned toward the sound of an approaching horse. "It's Kilpatrick. Give me a minute and you'll find out." John wheeled his horse around and took a position in the shade, at a respectable distance. He watched as Kilpatrick joined Farnsworth. From there he watched the two men.

General Farnsworth snapped a salute to his superior that was quickly returned. Kilpatrick said, "The First West Virginia was driven from the field. The Fifth New York and the Eighteenth Pennsylvania didn't even get as far." Farnsworth said nothing. He just looked at Kilpatrick and acknowledged his statement with an affirmative nod. "You still have the First Vermont. I want you to take 'em in."

Farnsworth wondered if Kilpatrick had seen what he had just seen and replied incredulously, "Sir, do you mean that? You want me to run a single regiment over rough ground strewn with boulders and trees, and God only knows what else, only to face an entire brigade of infantry that's well-entrenched and supported by artillery? The other three regiments barely made it back. Hasn't Lee withdrawn his attack in defeat, rendering these attacks useless? Must these good men die in an attack that serves no purpose and will surely not succeed?"

Kilpatrick became angry and said, "Do you refuse? If you're afraid, I'll lead the attack for you."

The assault on his honor could not go unchallenged. Farnsworth turned his horse to face Kilpatrick directly, rose in his stirrups in a rage, and shouted, "Take that back."

Kilpatrick softened and replied, "I didn't mean that. I'll take 'em in."

After a moment of silence Farnsworth said, "Sir, I'll not take responsibility for this charge. If you take responsibility and order me, I'll lead it." Kilpatrick agreed and, as Farnsworth asked, gave him the order. Farnsworth saluted, and Kilpatrick responded likewise; and they parted ways.

Farnsworth met with John. The latter asked rhetorically, "Didn't go well, did it?"

Farnsworth replied, "No, I'm going in with the First Vermont."

John's eyes widened. "I'll ride with you, Elon. You'll need a friend out there."

"You've done enough, John, just sit this one out," replied Farnsworth.

John said, "Sir, I didn't do a lot the last time in. I just watched. I need to earn my pay."

Farnsworth sighed, "I don't mind ordering the men into battle when we have a chance and there's a purpose. But nothing good'll come of this. You've done your share of fighting. You got a family. No need to go out there and get killed."

"Elon, don't be such a pessimist. We'll get through fine," said John.

Farnsworth replied, "That's an order, John."

John grinned and answered, "Sir, I respectfully disobey. Will you have me breaking rocks the rest of my life? Or worse, have me shot?"

Farnsworth sighed and shook his head in the negative. "John, you have nothing to prove. But we've known each other a long time. It couldn't hurt to have another good man out there."

John nodded and said, "Let's go."

"Report to B Company. They need a Lieutenant. See Sergeant Wilcox," said Farnsworth as he wheeled his horse about and departed.

Farnsworth divided the First Vermont Regiment into three parts. Two would make the charge, while one part would remain dismounted and support the other two with covering fire. In all, three hundred men would make the suicidal charge against a force four times their size and supported by artillery. Meanwhile, the Confederates directly under the command of Brigadier General Evander Law were repositioned after the failed charge by the First West Virginia Cavalry Regiment.

Farnsworth would ride in with First Vermont's A Company. He looked back at his men in columns of four abreast and spotted his friend, John Abbott, whom he acknowledged with a nod. He gave the command to the A Company commander who in turn nodded to the bugler who sounded the call to advance. The charge was under way with sabers drawn. They broke from the woods at the base of Bushman's Hill into the open and came under intense fire. Almost immediately, the lead elements of the charge came upon the Confederate skirmish line.

John watched Union troopers frantically flail their way through the skirmish line with sabers flashing brightly in the sun. The Union charge started bunching and becoming a confused mass of men and horses intermingled with the Confederates. They were fighting desperately until breaking free with his friend, Elon Farnsworth, near the front on his beautiful Palomino. When John approached the line, he could see the dead and wounded, man and horse, scattered about from the previous charge. For the first time, he found himself swinging his saber. Jim galloped into the line with Minie balls whistling by.

As with the earlier charge of the First West Virginia, this charge became a chaotic melee. The First Vermonters ran a gauntlet of Confederate infantrymen shooting and stabbing at their horses with bayonets. John gripped the reins and Jim's mane in his left hand while standing in his stirrups. Using his right hand, he swung his saber forcefully and with precision. One unfortunate Confederate officer turned and leveled a revolver toward him, preparing to shoot his horse.

For an instant, they locked eyes. In a flash, John landed a blow with his saber, full measure, just above his left ear, cleaving a portion of his head cleanly at a forty-five degree angle. The blow produced an explosion of blood and sent the soldier's hat, along with the cleaved portion of his head, tumbling through the air.

Without harm, John and his horse broke through the skirmish line. Cannons firing every type of shell and a thousand muskets could not drown out Jim gulping for air. One round of solid shot bounced by, nearly hitting Jim as his hooves clawed into the ground. Sweat drenched the animal as its instincts for survival drove him faster. John lost all concern for the terrain as he pushed Jim for speed to catch up with Farnsworth.

The purpose of the futile charge was beyond the reach of the men, and it became a matter of survival. However, John was committed and continued pushing his horse forward. Fifty yards in front, Elon Farnsworth's Palomino was shot from under him. Farnsworth stopped a trooper, took his horse, and continued the charge. John gave no thought to the beautiful Palomino, now dead, as he went by, closing his gap with Farnsworth to twenty-five yards.

John, and what was left of the first group of cavalrymen, continued to follow Farnsworth, trying to extricate themselves from certain death. Farnsworth turned into the teeth of the Confederate infantry positioned behind a low rock wall in a desperate attempt at escape to Big Round Top. He jumped the wall and was hit by a volley fired from five or more muskets, killing Farnsworth and his horse.

Under intense fire, John wheeled Jim about in an attempt to reach their line. What little order there was at the start of the charge was now complete chaos, and it was every man for himself. John saw a small group from his company attempting a retreat through the line they breeched at the start of the charge. The only chance for his survival was to swing right, avoid the melee, and break through the line and hope not to be hit by either an artillery round or Minie ball.

John spurred his horse, and through the smoke, a cannon appeared, its barrel parallel with the ground. He looked into the opening of the barrel and knew it was loaded with canister and pulled the reins hard to wheel Jim back about.

"FARR!"

The blast sent scores of steel balls that opened into a deadly cone of destruction, in which the horse, with John, was at its center. The steel balls tore into the horse's left side, and a horrifying shudder rose through the animal as it stumbled and screamed. Disoriented, John put his trust in Jim. The horse managed to stay on his feet and broke into a panicked gallop, charging through the blinding smoke.

In the chaos, Jim tripped over the Palomino shot from under Farnsworth and fell to the ground, throwing John a short distance. The frightened horse screamed and rolled to his feet. Instead of running, the horse calmly walked to John who was near death from a wound to his left leg just above the knee.

Fate dropped like a heavy hammer, landing a cruel blow, rendering its verdict on the failed charge. The Confederates fell silent and watched, in amazement, the horse standing over its fallen rider and ceased firing. Like the Confederates, the men along the Union line at the base of Bushman's Hill stopped firing. Everyone stared in awe at the horse that should have died still on its feet. The deafening sounds of one thousand muskets died down to a few pops, and quiet overtook the battlefield. Appearing among the wounded and a battlefield strewn with the dead was the ghostly sight of a solitary horse barely alive, standing over its fallen rider.

Jim blew and snorted, trying to rouse John with his nose. Nudging him; first his chest, then his head. John felt Jim's warm breath in his face, rousing him to consciousness. No noise of battle, just Jim snorting and blowing. He felt his wounded leg and then wrapped his arms around the horse's neck, and Jim pulled John to his feet. The two armies stood opposed in silence, watching the drama unfold. John, weak from blood loss, struggled and managed to get in his saddle. He wrapped his arms around Jim's neck and, with what little strength he had left, held on. Through ghostly wisps of smoke, the horse began to walk toward Bushman's Hill.

The Confederates lowered their muskets and watched. "Hold yir farr, boys!" shouted a rebel private.

Another Confederate looked at a friend and said, "That tharr horse got hit with canister not even fifty yards betwixt 'em. Ain't never seen nothin' like that. They should be dead."

Another said, "Bad powder. I seen it once. Why, I saw a cannon farr, and the ball barely rolled outa the cannon."

The Confederate infantrymen along the skirmish line began to cheer the horse carrying its wounded rider to safety. The men along the Union line joined them in their cheers. The two sides who, only minutes ago were killing each other in a bloodlust, were now unified in their respect for a lone horse. Some removed their hats, and some saluted as the cheering grew louder. The First Texas parted and allowed the horse, with blood streaming from open canister wounds, passage with John slumped over its neck.

After Jim passed through the Confederate line, he continued to walk slowly toward Bushman's Hill through what was only moments ago a no-man's land. When the horse passed through the Union line, he was surrounded by men of the First Vermont and the Eighteenth Pennsylvania Cavalry Regiments. A growing crowd of men followed the determined horse.

A young private by the name of Cooper Powell took the reins and led Jim into the dense woods on a path that led to the top of Bushman's Hill. This was the first action the nineteen-year-old private had seen. He gently coaxed the horse, "This way. There's a doc on top a this hill. You can make it, just a little further."

More men of the First Vermont began to follow in silent admiration of the horse. The private, guiding Jim, looked back and said, "Did ya see that? This horse got hit by canister. Ain't never seen nothing like that. Poor critter got all chewed up. He did. I tell ya, it's a bona fide miracle."

A voice from one of the men of the First Vermont shouted, "Why, that horse is a totin' that lieutenant from the Eighteenth."

Another voice chimed in, "He rode in with us. He don't look none too good neither."

From atop the hill, Union Army surgeon Captain Carl Jenkins just finished with one of the wounded and, wiping blood from his hands, went to check on the commotion. He walked, staring at the horse carrying the wounded soldier followed by a group of men emerging from the wooded hillside. There, as the wounded from the days fighting were lying about, the bloody and exhausted horse collapsed, spilling its wounded rider. Some of the men pulled John, barely conscious, to a tree as others stood looking over the badly wounded horse in amazement.

Private Powell, who had guided the horse, retrieved a canteen and attempted to give John a drink. Captain Jenkins looked at the bloody horse and the small crowd that had gathered and walked over to the tree where John was lying. John took a sip from the canteen and said, "Take care of Jim. For the love of God, whatever you do, take care of Jim," and slumped unconscious.

Captain Jenkins shouted at an orderly, "COME QUICK. I need a tourniquet and a stretcher. Hurry, we gotta stop this bleeding." The orderly sprang into action. Captain Jenkins turned his attention to the private. "What's your name, private?" asked Jenkins.

The private confidently replied, "Cooper. Cooper Powell, but everyone just calls me Coop. I'm with the Eighteenth, sir."

"Eighteenth?" asked Captain Jenkins.

"Pennsylvania. The Eighteenth Pennsylvania, sir. I saw it, sir. It was plumb awful, the awfullest thing I ever saw in all my born days. This is my lieutenant, sir. Can ya save him?" the private shot back.

In a reassuring voice, Captain Jenkins said, "Relax, private. Calm down. I'm taking care of your lieutenant. Who's Jim? I need to find Jim. Where is he?"

Before the private could reply, a gravelly voice from behind the captain answered, "Cap'n, darl'n. Jim's his harse, sarr." The captain turned about, and standing before him was Sergeant Patrick O'Conner of the Eighteenth Pennsylvania Cavalry Regiment Company B. He was a tall thick set man with neatly trimmed red hair that showed much gray. His bright green eyes beaming with pride were deeply set above pocked cheeks, the result of a severe case of chicken pox early in his childhood. His face flushed red when he drank whiskey, and those who knew him could tell with precision how much he drank by the intensifying shade. Otherwise, he presented a handsome figure with a clean-shaven face that highlighted a rugged square jaw and a thin nose. He had a gregarious and confident personality and an intellect which rose well above his limited education. The thirty-eight-year-old O'Conner emigrated to America in 1848 from Ireland at the height of the Irish Potato Famine. He settled in Pennsylvania, and enlisted in the Eighteenth Pennsylvania Cavalry Regiment when it was formed in November 1862 and met Lieutenant John Abbott. Sergeant O'Conner loved his newly adopted country and served with distinction throughout the war.

Captain Jenkins, from Indiana, having never heard such a strong Irish accent, asked, "*Harse?*"

"Yes, sarr. *Harse*," replied O'Conner.

Captain Jenkins paused, looking at the Sergeant and scratching his chin; and it came to him what the Irishmen was saying and replied, "Oh, I got it. *Horse.*"

Annoyed at the captain's confusion, O'Conner retorted, "Aye, Cap'n. Harse. Jim's his harse, sarr."

The orderly arrived with the stretcher bearers. Captain Jenkins turned away from O'Conner and snapped, "Get that tourniquet on his leg before he bleeds to death. Get him ready. That leg has to come off. I'll be there in a minute."

Sergeant O'Conner gesticulated rapidly with his left hand and said, "This way, sarr."

It was now Captain Jenkins's turn to be annoyed. The captain felt Sergeant O'Conner, an enlisted man, was too free with his assumptions. Indifferent to the sergeant's plea, he said, "Sergeant, I don't have time. That man's lost a lot a blood."

Sensing the captain's irritation, Sergeant O'Conner took on a humbler tone and said, "Sarr, please step this way and look." The captain, not over his irritation, stood and stared at the sergeant. "Sarr, please. I'm a beggin'," pleaded Sergeant O'Conner.

Captain Jenkins looked at the young men gathered around the horse and returned his gaze to Sergeant O'Conner, seeing great sincerity in his eyes. It would take a few minutes to prepare Lieutenant Abbott for the amputation. A few minutes that would be well-spent to placate the men and dispose of the matter. Captain Jenkins turned and followed Sergeant O'Conner. Private Powell, who had watched the exchange from under the tree, got up and followed the two men.

Sergeant O'Conner led the captain to Jim and continued his plea, "Sarr, is tharr anything ye can do for this poor critter? He was hit with canister, sarr. After he was hit, that harse carried me lieutenant back to the line."

Private Powell broke in and said, "Sir, I saw the whole thing. Never seen nothin' like it in all my born days. No, sir. That horse got hit with canister, sir. It's a miracle, a bona fide miracle, I tell ya."

Captain Jenkins looked at the horse and assessed the wounds. The horse's left ear was hanging, and his left eye had taken a direct hit from a canister ball. He stopped counting the other canister wounds on the horse's left flank after ten. Lines of dry blood coursed downward from the open wounds. He stooped down and listened to Jim's breathing which was labored and probed a wound with his finger. In his view, the animal was about to die. Captain Jenkins was not about to ruin his reputation by working on a horse. Especially one that was beyond saving. Besides, horses were expendable, and he had wounded soldiers to tend to.

Sergeant O'Conner renewed his plea, "Can ye save the poor critter, sarr?"

As the men looked on, Captain Jenkins stood up and scratched his chin with his left hand. He looked at Sergeant O'Conner, and their eyes locked. After a brief silence, the captain shook his head in the negative and moved his eyes to the sergeant's revolver hanging from his belt. Sergeant O'Conner said nothing. He understood the reality of the situation and knew nothing would be done for the horse. Captain Jenkins broke the silence and calmly said, "Sorry, Sergeant, they'll both likely be dead by morning. There's nothing to be done. I got to tend to the lieutenant. You know what to do."

Sergeant O'Conner gave a nod then a crisp salute, "Aye, sarr." The surgeon returned the salute and left.

Private Powell cried out, "Sarge, ya can't do that. Ya can't just shoot 'im."

Sergeant O'Conner, who felt the same way as the private, turned to him and said, "Lad, that poor critter's goin' to die. Do ya want 'im to suffer?"

The men of the First Vermont formed a circle around the dying horse. The men of the Eighteenth Pennsylvania joined them, and they stood defiantly, shoulder to shoulder. A voice rang out from among them, "Sarge, ya ain't gonna shoot Jim."

Another soldier of the First Vermont stepped forward and said, "The lieutenant's not one of us, and neither's General Farnsworth. But they rode in with us anyway. The lieutenant asked us to save his horse. The horse may suffer and die, but we aim to honor his request."

Sergeant O'Conner stood and looked at the men. He remembered when he had a horse shot from under him and replayed in his mind how Jim saved the lieutenant just moments ago. He found himself in a dilemma with no way out. Private Powell broke the silence and, with a smug look, said, "Sarge, the cap'n didn't order ya to shoot the horse now, did he?"

The men laughed with relief at the loophole, and a devilish grin overtook the sergeant. And he said, "No, lad, I suppose not."

CHAPTER 20

The Experiment

July 4, 1863

Snorts, grunts, and heavy breathing roused Captain Jenkins from a deep sleep. Tired from the previous day's work, he lifted himself on his elbow and looked about, and the sounds stopped. The sun was beginning to show, and he fell back to the cot, surrendering to his exhaustion. Again the captain was awakened by more snorting, and he swung his legs over the side of his cot, resting his elbows on his knees and his face buried in his hands. He glanced up and noticed the flaps of his tent gently flexing inward and then relaxing, as if pushed by a ghostly hand, followed by more snorts and heavy breathing. The racket made it impossible to sleep.

Angry, Captain Jenkins arose from his cot and stormed out to find the soldier who was responsible for the loose horse. His rage turned to wonder when he emerged from his tent and locked eyes with Jim, the horse that should have been shot.

Zzz, shh, zzz, shh.

Captain Jenkin's looked toward the source of the snoring and found Private Cooper Powell propped on a tree sleeping, and his rifle also propped against the tree. The surgeon, who seldom observed military rituals or discipline, made his way to the sleeping private. He briefly studied the young private who was lost in slumber. Captain Jenkins returned his gaze to his tent and Jim, causing his anger to rise.

"On your feet, private," shouted Captain Jenkins. Startled from his sleep, Private Powell knocked over his rifle while searching for his hat. Growing angrier, Captain Jenkins again shouted, "On your feet, private, now."

A disheveled Private Powell stumbled to his feet and stood at attention. A guilty smile came across his face as he saw Jim standing by the captain's tent. Like a child caught stealing a cookie, he said, "How'd Jim get over there? Why, he was lying here next to me last night. Ya said he was goin' a die sir. Must be a miracle. Bona fide miracle, I tell ya."

"Quiet, private," snapped Captain Jenkins. Private Powell became quiet and stood at attention, staring ahead. "Private. Where's your sergeant?"

"Sleepin' sir."

Captain Jenkins glared into the private's eyes and said, "Sleeping, you say."

"Yes, sir. He's sleepin'."

"Well, Private Powell, I want you to go fetch your sergeant and bring him back here."

"Can't do that, sir. Sergeant O'Conner told me not to wake 'im. He's tired. He'll get upset."

No longer able to contain his anger, Captain Jenkins flew into a rage and shouted, "I don't care if he gets upset, private. You go and get 'im here on the double."

"Yes, sir," said Private Powell, and he ran off to fetch Sergeant O'Conner.

Fully awake, Captain Jenkins was over his initial anger. He looked at the wounded horse standing by his tent and chuckled. He walked over to Jim and examined the wounds on the left side of the horse. A random pattern of silver dollar-sized holes covered the entirety of the horses left flank. Trails of dry blood that ran from the wounds matted the horse's dapple-gray coat. He pushed his finger gently into the wounded eye and smelled it and determined no gangrene had set in. He checked several of the other wounds and came to the same conclusion.

He replayed in his mind the grit of the men, no more than boys, determined to honor the lieutenant's dying wishes. The calmness of the animal hid the horrors of the previous day. *This horse should be dead*, he thought. A change of heart came over the young captain, and he decided to try to save the horse.

Captain Jenkins recalled an article he had read in a medical journal after entering the army. The paper discussed a new theory concerning the cause of infections and sepsis. In it, the idea of small animals that could only be viewed with a microscope, called bacteria or germs, were the cause of infection. He also recalled how food could be preserved for long periods of time in cans that were heated to a high temperature. Is it possible to reduce or even eliminate infection by killing these germs and cleaning the wounds? If so, how would he kill these small animals? Captain Jenkins's reluctance turned to excitement at the challenge before him. After completing the examination, a plan began to formulate, and he said to the horse, "Jim, let's give this a try."

As the plan came together, he walked over to check on his patients, one of whom was Lieutenant John Abbott. Lieutenant Abbott, unconscious, was clinging to life; but there was little he could do for him now, as was the case with the others. He gathered his surgical instruments and approached an orderly sitting on a stool, reading a paper, and said, "Corporal Cravits, you're comin' with me."

The startled corporal threw down his paper, snapped to his feet, and said, "Yes, sir." Captain Jenkins left with the corporal and returned to Jim where he found Private Powell and Sergeant O'Conner standing.

"Sergeant O'Conner, I trust you slept well," said Captain Jenkins with a sarcastic smile.

"Aye, sarr, I did indeed," replied Sergeant O'Conner.

Captain Jenkins followed up his sarcasm with a terse admonishment. He pointed to Jim and said, "I thought I told you to shoot this animal."

"Aye, ye did, sarr," said Sergeant O'Conner, offering no further explanation as Private Powell and the corporal listened.

Private Powell turned to the corporal and said, "Ya shoulda seen it. That horse saved our lieutenant. A bona fide miracle, I say. What's your name?"

"My name is Lee Roy. Lee Roy Cravits, but everyone calls me Lee. What's your name?" said the corporal.

"Cooper Powell. But my friends call me Coop," replied the private to his new friend as they turned their attention to the sergeant.

After a brief pause and wishing to force the sergeant into a grand admission, Captain Jenkins asked, "Well, sergeant, why didn't you do as I asked?"

"Ye see, Cap'n, darl'n, ye didn't arder me to, sarr. An' the men didn't want me to shoot the poor critter. They be afraid of bein' jinxed," said Sergeant O'Conner. A proud grin at having outwitted the captain washed over his face, which drew a quiet chuckle from Private Powell and the corporal.

Captain Jenkins could not dispute the sergeant. It didn't matter anyway; he had determined to proceed with saving the horse or at least try. He scratched his chin and replied, "True, sergeant, I didn't order you to shoot the horse." He turned to the corporal and said, "Orderly, here are my instruments. Take 'em and get plenty of bandages and suture, then put them in boiling water."

The corporal, shocked at what he had been asked to do, asked, "Boiling water? Ya want me to put all that in boiling water, sir? Bandages too? Where can I find boiling water?"

Irritated, Captain Jenkins said, "You want to save this horse? Goodness, man. I DON'T CARE HOW YOU DO IT. JUST DO IT, AND BE QUICK ABOUT IT."

The corporal replied, "Yes, sir," and left.

Private Powell asked, "Does this mean you're gonna save Jim, sir?"

"Yes, private," said Captain Jenkins as he turned to Sergeant O'Conner and said, "I need you to get a feed bag and some cotton, and by the way, that's an order, sergeant."

"Aye, cap'n," replied Sergeant O'Conner, and he turned around and left.

Captain Jenkins turned to Private Powell and said, "You're in charge of the horse. You're not to let it out of your sight. Not for an instant." The captain looked at an open spot not far from where they were standing and said, "Take 'im over there, and don't move."

"Yes, sir," replied Private Powell. As he gently stroked Jim's neck, he said, "You're goin' a make it, ole boy." Captain Jenkins went into his tent and retrieved from his footlocker two bottles of chloroform he kept in case of supply problems.

As Sergeant O'Conner went to get a feed bag, he passed by a small barn where the worst of the wounded were recovering. He stepped inside to check on Lieutenant Abbott. Upon entering the barn, he found the wounded lying about. The more serious cases were on cots, and others on pallets of hay. Lanterns were suspended from the rafters, and the faint smell of putrefied flesh hung in the air. A nurse approached Sergeant O'Conner and said, "My name's Clara. Is there anything I can do for you?"

"Aye. I be a lookin' for me lieutenant. His name's Abbott, John Abbott. He's with the Eighteenth Pennsylvania," said Sergeant O'Conner.

Clara smiled and said, "Oh yes, I know who you're talkin' about. The soldier that was saved by his horse. Everyone's talkin' about it."

Sergeant O'Conner said, "Aye, lass, indeed he was. Wouldn't a belaved meself had I not a seen it with me own eyes." Clara listened as Sergeant O'Conner continued. "His harse got hit with canister, kept goin', an' everyone jist quit shoot'n. Ole Johnny Reb let that harse walk right through tharr line carryin' the lieutenant. Jist as if he were General Lee hisself."

Clara led Sergeant O'Conner to Lieutenant Abbott's cot. She said, "That's an amazing story." She pointed to a man stretched out on a cot and said, "He's here, Sergeant."

They found Lieutenant Abbott unconscious. His leg was bandaged from the amputation. His face was ashen, and he looked more dead than alive. She looked at Sergeant O'Conner and said, "Your lieutenant's a very sick man. Bless his soul." She swatted flies from the bandaged leg and said, "I'm afraid he's not goin' to make it. He lost a lot of blood."

Sergeant O'Conner looked at the man and said, "Poor lad, he's a good man he is. Been together since last November when we joined Eighteenth." Sergeant O'Conner asked, "Do ye have some bandages? Cap'n Jenkins is needin' 'em."

"Yes, come this way, Sergeant. Does the captain need help?" asked Clara as she retrieved the bandages.

"Aye, he may indeed," replied Sergeant O'Conner without divulging the doctor's intentions.

As Sergeant O'Conner left, Clara said, "Tell the captain I'll be out directly."

Sergeant O'Conner grabbed a feed bag hanging outside of the barn and returned to find Private Powell and the captain standing with Jim. Private Powell asked, "Sarge, did ya see the lieutenant? Is he alive?"

"Aye, lad. Praise the saints he's still among us," replied Sergeant O'Conner. "Here's ye things, Cap'n. The narse said she's comin' to help ye, sarr," said the Sergeant holding the feed bag in the air.

"Good work, sergeant," said Captain Jenkins. He looked toward the barn from where Sergeant O'Conner came and, to his relief, saw a familiar form headed his way.

Clarissa "Clara" Fellows Jones, a grammar school teacher, was from Germantown, Pennsylvania. After the war started, and when school was out and compelled by a deeper purpose, she would rush to the front and help tend to the wounded soldiers. In 1862, she would nearly succumb to typhoid fever while serving at a hospital in Alexandria, Virginia. After her recovery, she selflessly continued her service. As the school year came to a close in 1863, she traveled to Gettysburg.

Captain Jenkins greeted the comely petite thirty-year-old. "Hello, Clara."

She looked at Jim and asked rhetorically, "Captain Jenkins, is that the horse I been hearin' about?"

Private Powell broke in. "That's him, ma'am. His name's Jim. Saw the whole thing. He got hit with a blast of canister. Stayed on his feet. Bona fide miracle. He saved Lieutenant Abbott. Should be dead. Now the cap'n goin' a save 'im," proclaimed Private Powell with a degree of pride.

Clara walked to the horse and looked at his wounded eye, and she looked at the wounds on his left side. She gently stroked the horse's good side and said, "Poor fella. Is that true, Captain? Is this why ya need the bandages?"

"I'm afraid it is. I may regret this," said Captain Jenkins with a degree of uncertainty in his voice.

Clara looked at the horse, grazing, and said, "What're you gonna do?"

Private Powell took a step closer so he could hear them. The captain replied, "I can't explain it fully, but we're goin' to try an experiment."

Corporal Cravits appeared and said, "I done as ya asked, Cap'n. Got a big kettle an' dumped everythin' in. Bandages too, and it's a boilin' like ya wanted."

Clara asked, "What're you boilin', Lee?"

The corporal replied, "Cap'n told me to dump all his stuff in boilin' water. Bandages too. Thought it was a might queer, but I did as he asked."

In an effort to glean as much information as possible, Sergeant O'Conner quietly joined Private Powell and took a position next to the corporal. Clara looked at Captain Jenkins and asked, "Why are you boiling everything?"

"Like I said. We're goin' to try something. A scientific experiment," said the captain.

"Do tell," replied Clara.

Private Powell whispered to the corporal, "Hey, Lee, ya reckon the cap'n knows what he's a doin'?"

Corporal Cravits cocked his head back and boastfully replied, "I been with the cap'n since Fredericksburg. Ain't nary a better doc in the whole Union Army."

Captain Jenkins looked at Clara and said, "Got everything I need except whiskey." Upon hearing the word *whiskey* fall from the captain's lips, an ominous feeling grew within the pit of Sergeant

O'Conner's gut. He began a discreet retreat before anything else could be said.

Private Powell exclaimed, "Whiskey. Sergeant O'Conner has a bottle he's not opened. Says he's a savin' it for a special occasion." His escape thwarted, Sergeant O'Conner stopped in his tracks, turned around, and imaginary daggers flew from his eyes into the private's heart. The look did not go unnoticed by Clara.

She took on a more formal tone and asked, "Captain, what's the whiskey for?"

"Cap'n, darl'n, are ye goin' to have that harse drink me whiskey, sarr?" asked the sergeant as he nervously fidgeted and beads of sweat broke out on his face.

The captain laughed and said, "Don't be foolish. Of course not, sergeant. But I do need your whiskey."

Sergeant O'Conner replied, "Sarr, why do ye need me whiskey?"

Captain Jenkins said, "To clean the horse's wounds."

Clara's curiosity was piqued and asked, "How'll that help?"

The captain replied, "If there are germs, I believe it'll kill 'em."

"Germs? What're germs?" asked Clara as a look of dread came over the sergeant.

"Yes, germs. They're little animals that get into an open wound and cause it to fester. I have never heard of whiskey spoiling, so I figure they can't live in whiskey. It's a long shot, but we've nothing to lose," replied the captain.

Corporal Cravits looked at Private Powell and whispered, "I tell ya, the cap'n is a smart man."

Sergeant O'Conner asked, "*Jarms*, sarr? Are ye sayin' wee crittars are a inside the harse's wounds?"

"Yes, sergeant. That's what I'm saying," replied the captain. "They're so small a hundred could sit on the head of a pin. I'm gonna kill 'em with your whiskey."

The sergeant's jaw dropped in disbelief, his eyes became larger than silver dollars, and he asked, "Sarr, do ye have to use me whiskey? Can't ye jist drown the little buggars with water?" The look of dread in the sergeant's face at the thought of sacrificing his greatest treasure drew an adoring laugh from Clara.

Captain Jenkins replied, "Sorry, sergeant, I'm afraid not."

Sergeant O'Conner swallowed and looked at each member of the ad hoc band of good Samaritans. A sympathetic smile from Clara provided little relief from the shame Corporal Cravits and Private Powell were staring into the sergeant's heart. Captain Jenkins laughed and said, "Sergeant, if you would have done what I asked yesterday, we wouldn't be here."

The sergeant looked at Jim. The wounded horse, like the others, stared shame into the sergeant's heart. Begrudgingly, Sergeant O'Conner replied, "Aye, Cap'n."

Captain Jenkins said, "Sorry, sergeant, life's not fair."

Dejected and resigned to his sacrifice, Sergeant O'Conner said, "I'll git me whiskey," and left.

Word spread as Captain Jenkins prepared to work on Jim, and men gathered around, wanting to get a glimpse of the hero horse that defied the odds. Among them were the walking wounded and soldiers of the Fifth New York, the First Vermont, and the Eighteenth Pennsylvania. As they thought among themselves, some said prayers, some were curious, but all were anxious for a miracle. The miracle was not if the horse would survive, but that the surgeon placed enough value on its life that he would try to save it. They wanted to see it for themselves. After the carnage they witnessed, would *their* lives have value?

CHAPTER 21

Buckshot

Sergeant O'Conner returned, whiskey in hand. After making his way through a throng of soldiers, he found Clara, Captain Jenkins, Private Powell, and Corporal Cravits waiting with Jim. "Harrs me whiskey, sarr," said the sergeant.

Captain Jenkins took the bottle from the sergeant and looked it over and said, "120 proof. Good whiskey, sergeant. This'll do fine."

"Aye, sarr. Tis indeed," replied the sergeant. "Sarr, I was thinkin'. This bein' a special occasion." Captain Jenkins looked at the sergeant and flashed a skeptical smile. "I was a wonderin', could I have a wee nip, sarr?" asked Sergeant O'Conner.

The captain glanced at Clara who smiled and returned an approving nod. "I don't see why you can't, sergeant," said Captain Jenkins as he surrendered the bottle to Sergeant O'Conner.

Sergeant O'Conner twisted the cap and raised the bottle in the air and said, "Harrs to the lieutenant and his harse, Jim," after taking a generous swallow. "*Ahh*, that be good whiskey," then he returned the bottle.

Captain Jenkins glanced at the crowd of soldiers and said, "I need one more favor before I get started, sergeant."

"Well, sarr, can't ask me for nothing warse. What else can I do for ye?" said the sergeant.

"Once I get started, I can't be disturbed," said the captain.

"Aye, Cap'n, darl'n. Jist ye leave it to me, sarr. Can ye sparr the private?" asked the sergeant.

Captain Jenkins looked at Clara and Corporal Cravits and said, "Yes, I can. Clara and the corporal will be able to help me."

Sergeant O'Conner looked at Private Powell and said, "Come with me, lad."

Captain Jenkins pushed cotton to the bottom of the feed bag and handed it and two bottles of chloroform to Clara and said, "You know what to do." Captain Jenkins, along with Clara and Corporal Cravits, walked Jim to an open flat area and prepared the horse for surgery.

Clara poured a generous amount of chloroform into the feed bag. She said, "I hope I didn't give this poor critter too much." And she slipped the feed bag over the horse's muzzle. She looked at Corporal Cravits and admonished him. "Lee, when he starts to go under, push hard so he falls on his right side."

"Yes, ma'am," replied the corporal.

Seconds later the horse came under the chloroform's effect and began to wobble. Corporal Cravits pushed with all his might but was not able to control the huge animal's inertia and cried out, "HELP."

One soldier heard the plea and shouted, "QUICK, LET'S GIVE 'IM A HAND." Several soldiers ran to help Corporal Cravits, pushing the horse until it fell to the ground unconscious with a loud thump.

Sergeant O'Conner and Private Powell waded into the crowd shouting, "GIVE THE CAP'N SOME ROOM. STEP BACK NOW! STEP BACK."

"What are ya goin' to do, Sarge?" asked Private Powell as he looked over the crowd.

"We're goin' to form a picket," said the sergeant.

"A picket here?" asked the private.

"Yes, lad, here," said the sergeant, and shouted out to the crowd of soldiers, "I need ten volunteers for picket duty."

Some of the men, dreading picket duty, lost interest and began to leave. A voice rang out, "We don't have our rifles."

"Ya won't be a needin' yarr rifles, lads." After pointing to the horse, Sergeant O'Conner said, "We're goin' to form a picket 'round this harse. Come now, lads. The cap'n needs us." A wave of

ANNA MAE'S BUCKSHOT

relief came over the men, and they began to step forward. Sergeant O'Conner pointed out several men, "You, you, and you." The men chosen stepped forward, and soon a wave of excitement came over the crowd. Men began to volunteer in order to have a part in saving the horse.

"Sarge. Pick me," said a private of the First Vermont. Then came more from others, and soon there were more than enough men ready to serve picket duty.

The sergeant, along with his new picket detail, started to form a circle around the unconscious horse. Captain Jenkins and Corporal Cravits were standing over Clara as she administered the chloroform. The captain poured a small amount of whiskey on his hands and rubbed them together. The sight drew a vain complaint from Sergeant O'Conner. "Sarr, it's bad enough to give that harse a bath, but do ye have to wash yir hands with me whiskey? Me dear ole father, God rest his soul, is a rawlin' in his grave."

Captain Jenkins said with a mischievous smile, "Those germs'll die happy, sergeant."

The soldiers laughed as Sergeant O'Conner shook his head in disbelief. Sergeant O'Conner said, "Now, boys, quiet. We need to form a circle around this harse."

As Sergeant O'Conner started to position men around Jim, an unknown soldier of the First Vermont stepped up to Private Powel and whispered, "This here is the queerest picket I've ever seen."

Private Powell replied, "That's 'cause it's an experiment."

"'SPAR-A-MENT? What kinda 'SPAR-A-MENT?" replied the Unknown Soldier.

Exasperated, Private Powell snapped, "Why, it's a scientific experiment. What other kind is there? Now just do as Sarge tells ya.

The Unknown Soldier's eyes flew wide open with astonishment. "Man alive, Ma'll have a conniption fit when I tell her I was in a scientifical 'spar-a-ment."

Private Powell turned to Sergeant O'Conner and asked, "Sarge, what's the password?"

Sergeant O'Conner looked at the horse with Clara at its head. He glanced at Captain Jenkins and Corporal Cravits as they prepared for surgery. Jim showed life as his side lifted and lowered with each breath. "I don't know," said Sergeant O'Conner as he scratched his chin.

The Unknown Soldier exclaimed, "Poor critter. Looks like he was hit with a blast a buckshot."

Relieved, Sergeant O'Conner smiled. "That's it, private."

"What's it, Sarge?" asked Private Powell.

"Buckshot, laddie. The password. Buckshot." Sergeant O'Conner turned on his heel and informed the men of the password and made minor adjustments to the picket line. When he finished, there was a wall of men, forty in all, shoulder to shoulder making a tight circle around the horse.

One of the men laughed and asked, "What're we a lookin' fer, Sarge? Johnny Reb?"

"Ye jist not need to let anyone by," replied Sergeant O'Conner. "Tharr may be spies and saboteurs a skulking about."

One of the men exclaimed, "Spies and saboteurs? Here?"

"Yes, that's what I said. Now ye jist do as yarr told," said Sergeant O'Conner.

Captain Jenkins, with Corporal Cravits close behind, began. He removed the left ear which was loosely held by a strand of cartilage. He wiped whiskey over the wound, then bandaged it and moved to the horse's wounded left eye. The doctor removed what remained of the eye and the steel canister round imbedded in the socket. He cleaned the socket with whiskey, trimmed the eyelids with a scalpel, and sutured them together. Captain Jenkins moved from one wound to the next, working his way back to the horse's rump. He probed each wound, removed the canister round and dropped it in a metal bowl held by Corporal Cravits. He cleaned them with whiskey, then sutured and bandaged them.

Just below the horse's back, Captain Jenkins removed a piece of lead that protruded from the skin. He examined it carefully, astonished. He looked at Clara and said, "This isn't from canister. It's a Minie ball." Clara looked at the mangled projectile and smiled. After a brief pause, he looked at the wound and said, "I believe this is the round that got the lieutenant's leg. It passed through his leg, then the saddle, and stopped here." Captain Jenkins turned his attention to Corporal Cravits and said, "Corporal, don't lose this," and dropped it into the metal pan.

Clara asked, "Is the horse going to make it, sir?"

Captain Jenkins, wiping his brow, said, "He's lucky. I don't know why, but these canister rounds didn't go very deep. His eye looks to be the most troubling. If we can keep it from becoming gangrenous, I think he'll make it."

The Unknown Soldier turned to Private Powell and asked, "Do ya think Jim'll make it?"

Private Powell did not return an answer. He was fixated on an officer talking to some of the men gathered near the barn. After several men pointed their way, the officer—a short skinny man—made a beeline toward him and the Unknown Soldier. Private Powell said, "Don't rightly know, but we're in a fix. The old man is headed our way, and he's as mad as a March hare."

"Who's the old man?" asked the Unknown Soldier.

"Our colonel, that's who. The orneriest man alive. I declare I never seen a man that could deal out misery like the old man," said Private Powell.

"What should we do?" asked the Unknown Soldier.

Private Powell searched for Sergeant O'Conner and saw him at the far end of the picket. "We do as the sergeant told us. That's what we do." Private Powell fixed his gaze on the colonel, whose pace quickened.

"SERGEANT O'CONNER. SARGE, COME HERE QUICK." Sergeant O'Conner saw the colonel and made his way to Private Powell.

The colonel walked up to the Unknown Soldier and asked, "What's goin' on here, private?" The color drained from the youthful boy's face as he contemplated his reply. "Out with it. What's goin' on here?" snapped the Colonel.

"Well, sir. It's—it's a 'spar-a-ment,'" replied the Unknown Soldier. Private Powell watched the colonel step closer and glare into the Unknown Soldier's young eyes.

"What kind of experiment, private?" demanded the colonel.

Rattled and confused, the Unknown Soldier glanced at Private Powell, silently asking for help with his eyes. Private Powell faced the Unknown Soldier and mouthed *scientific*.

The Unknown Soldier instantly regained his composure and said smugly, "Umm, a scientific 'spar-a-ment. There ain't no other kind, sir."

The colonel saw Captain Jenkins working on the horse and said, "Let me by, soldier."

"What's the password, sir?" asked the Unknown Soldier, unable to hide his trembling.

The colonel's anger increased. "BALDERDASH, PRIVATE. The password is, you'll be breaking rocks the rest of your life if you don't let me by."

To the relief of the Unknown Soldier and Private Powell, Sergeant O'Conner entered the discussion and, after snapping off a crisp salute, said, "Karnel, sarr, what can I do for ye?"

"You can start by explaining this lunacy, sergeant," said the colonel.

Sergeant O'Conner said, "Sarr, this here's a picket, and ye got to know the password."

"Poppycock, sergeant. A picket behind our line. No rifles. Lee is retreating to Virginia. This is the most ridiculous picket I've ever seen. I demand an explanation, sergeant. Why do you need a picket here?" asked the colonel.

"Spies, sarr. Spies and saboteurs. No tellin' where they be," said Sergeant O'Conner.

The colonel pointed to Clara and asked, "Is that woman giving that horse chloroform?"

"Indeed she is, sarr," replied the sergeant.

"With all the wounded men, why is that surgeon wasting chloroform on a horse?" asked the colonel.

"Sarr, it's an experiment," said the sergeant.

"Sergeant, everyone keeps talking about some kind of experiment. Just what kind of experiment?" asked the angry colonel.

The sergeant became solemn then looked directly into the colonel's eyes and said, "Sarr, the cap'n believes there be wee crittars git'n in the wounds, causing a fuss, an' he has to kill 'em. He calls 'em *jarms*."

Incredulous, the colonel said, "Little critters? *Jarms?* Have you all gone mad? I don't see any critters."

Sergeant O'Conner said, "Like I said, Karnel, darlin', they be wee crittars. So small ye can't see 'em."

Private Powell said, "Yes, sir, a hundred can dance on the head of a pin, sir."

The colonel fixed a skeptical gaze upon the sergeant and asked, "Just where do these jarms come from?"

Sergeant O'Conner glanced skyward and said, "Sarr, the cap'n says they be in the air."

"Little critters flying about in the air. This is utter lunacy," said the colonel.

The small crowd, mostly wounded men strong enough to walk, was growing, and the men talked among themselves about the experiment. Each man moved about in an attempt to find a good spot to see the horse. Some were even perched in trees. Private Powell, relieved, glanced at the Unknown Soldier and smiled. The colonel, never having encountered a situation like this, craned his neck in an attempt to see what the trio was doing to the horse.

All fell silent and watched the figure of a tall, big-boned man with thick black hair and a drooping mustache, attired in the immaculately clean uniform of a colonel, make his way into the crowd. A deep, stern, fatherly voice said, "Step aside. What's going on here?" He reached for the colonel, who was distracted and unaware of his presence and gently tapped him on the shoulder.

"Sir, may I ask who you are?" asked the arriving colonel.

The skinny colonel turned, and standing before him was, like himself, a colonel. He knew the officer was a surgeon. "Are you in charge here, sir?" asked the diminutive colonel.

"Yes, sir, I am. I'm Colonel Anthony Stone. I still don't know who you are, my good man," said Colonel Stone.

After adjusting his hat, the smaller colonel said, "I am Colonel Otis Smith." Colonel Smith pointed to the horse and Captain Jenkins and said, "Colonel, maybe you can explain this lunacy."

Colonel Stone replied, "Sir, this seems odd. I'm in the dark as much as you are."

Incredulous, Colonel Smith asked, "Are you telling me you're unaware of what your officers are doing? Do you employ horse doctors to treat my wounded men?"

Colonel Stone furrowed his brow, his eyes became big, and snapped, "My good fellow, I'll have you know Captain Jenkins is my finest surgeon. I would entrust him with my own life."

Colonel Smith said, "Everyone is talking about experiments, tiny critters flying in the air. I think everyone's gone mad."

Colonel Stone said, "I've known the captain for some time. He comes from a good family. I can assure you, my good fellow, he is of sound mind. Let's see what he has to say."

Captain Jenkins finished with the horse's last wound. "Clara, I'm done here. You and Corporal Cravits can finish up." He stood, saw the two colonels, wiped his hands on his apron, and walked over to join them.

The Unknown Soldier, Private Powell and Sergeant O'Conner, listened as Colonel Stone greeted Captain Jenkins. "Good morning, Captain. We're talking about you. The colonel seems to be questioning your ability to reason. Says you're talking about flying animals and experiments." The strong smell of whiskey hung like a shroud over the gathering.

The smell confirmed Colonel Smith's suspicions and intensified his determination to end the proceedings. "This explains it," said Colonel Smith.

"Explains what?" asked Colonel Stone.

Colonel Smith said, "The lunacy, sir. Your captain's drunk."

Sergeant O'Conner said, "Sarr, if I may be so bold as to step in?"

"Go ahead, sergeant," said Colonel Stone.

Sergeant O'Conner said, "Sarr, I swarr on me dear old mother's soul, the cap'n has not been drink'n."

"Do tell. I would love to hear this," said Colonel Smith cynically.

Sergeant O'Conner said, "Well, ye see, sarr, the cap'n needed me whiskey to kill them jarms. He said water wouldn't wark."

Colonel Smith lost his temper and shouted, "THIS MADNESS HAS GONE ON LONG ENOUGH. SERGEANT, I WANT YOU TO SHOOT THAT HORSE AND PUT THE POOR ANIMAL OUT OF ITS MISERY."

"Stay that order, sergeant," snapped Colonel Stone.

Sergeant O'Conner said, "Sarr, Colonel Smith's me commanding officer, an' I has to do what he arders me to, sarr."

"That may be, sergeant, but the horse and all these wounded men are under my care and are, therefore, my responsibility. So no one is going to shoot the horse," replied Colonel Stone. A relieved smile came over Private Powell and the Unknown Soldier.

"Captain Jenkins, it's time for you to explain what you're up to," said Colonel Stone.

The captain said, "I'll do my best, sir," and continued. "Sir, during a cavalry charge that cost the lives of scores of men, including General Farnsworth who led the final assault, the horse you see sustained a direct hit of canister. Somehow after being hit, the horse managed to get its rider, a Lieutenant John Abbott, and carry him back to our line. The Confederates, overcome with wonder, quit shooting and allowed the horse to pass through their skirmish line unmolested. Private Powell brought the horse and the lieutenant here. He was near death after being hit with a Minie ball. I removed his leg and now, while he's still alive, will likely die. His dying wish was to save his horse." Captain Jenkins paused to gather his thoughts.

Colonel Stone asked Sergeant O'Conner, "Did you see this, sergeant?"

"Aye, sarr. I did. With me own eyes," replied Sergeant O'Conner.

Private Powell said, "I saw it too, sir. A miracle. A bona fide miracle."

Colonel Stone said, "Captain Jenkins, continue."

"Well, sir, when I first saw the horse, like the colonel, I suggested it be shot. But the men viewed what had happened as a divine sign of sorts and, wishing to honor the lieutenant's dying wish, refused to shoot it."

"Aya, Karnel, I was goin' to shoot the poor critter meself, but like the cap'n said, the men saw it as a sign from God. They wouldn't let me shoot it," said Sergeant O'Conner.

Captain Jenkins continued, "I thought the horse would surely die, sir, but this morning, to my astonishment, the horse was standing outside my tent."

Colonel Stone asked, "So what's all this I hear about an experiment?"

Captain Jenkins said, "Sir, some time ago, I read an article about a new theory. The article discussed the idea of tiny animals called *germs* getting into a wound, causing infection and gangrene. I allowed that if I could kill these tiny animals, maybe I could save this horse and, in the future, save countless men from dying."

"What does the whiskey have to do with it?" asked Colonel Stone.

Captain Jenkins said, "I don't know for sure, but the way I figure it, whatever causes food to rot likely causes gangrene. Whiskey never spoils, so I'm guessing maybe it'll kill the germs."

Colonel Stone thought for a moment, looking at the horse as Clara and Corporal Cravits were gently stroking the unconscious animal. He looked at the crowd of men and saw great compassion. He turned Colonel Smith, "It seems to me I've read something on that. Colonel Smith, the captain's finished. I don't see any harm. We've come this far. Let it be."

Colonel Smith said, "Sir, you mean to tell me you are going to continue this madness?"

"Colonel, with all due respect, it may be madness, but it'll be good for the men. They were put through a rough patch, and maybe this will bring morale up," said Colonel Stone.

The men on the picket line, sensing the trouble had passed, began to chant "BUCKSHOT, BUCKSHOT, BUCKSHOT." The chant grew louder through the crowd of soldiers. Colonel Smith, realizing there was no more to be done, turned on his heel and departed.

Private Powell looked at the Unknown Soldier and said, "Bona fide miracle. This is the Lord's work, I tell ya."

The Unknown Soldier replied, "Praise Jesus."

CHAPTER 22

Bona Fide Miracle

The next morning, Captain Jenkins awoke contemplating the previous day. Staring at the top of the tent, he had misgivings. He thought, *Colonel Smith was right to object. Did I go too far? Did I chase a fool's errand which would end in ridicule? What good would come from saving a horse?* His mind assessed the positive. *Colonel Stone, my friend and commanding officer, didn't object. Why worry? What is done is done, no matter the outcome. No real harm would come of it. After all, my actions didn't kill anyone, just a horse that was goin' to die anyway."

Captain Jenkin's contemplations were interrupted by a familiar voice, "Sir, come quick."

"Who's there?" asked Captain Jenkins.

"Coop, sir."

"Coop?" asked Captain Jenkins.

"Private Powell, sir. Cooper Powell. Come quick."

"Give me a minute," Captain Jenkins jumped from his cot, throwing on his shirt and boots. "What's goin' on, private?" said the captain.

"It's Buckshot, sir."

"Buckshot?" asked Captain Jenkins as he emerged from the tent, finding Private Powell smiling, anxious to share good news.

"Sorry, cap'n, sir. I mean Jim. The men took to callin' him Buckshot," said Private Powell.

"What's wrong? Is he dead?" asked Captain Jenkins.

Private Powell said, "No, sir. Ya got a see 'im. He is up and about, walking around like nothin' happened. Come quick, cap'n."

Captain Jenkins, excited, followed the private, and to his amazement, he found Jim grazing surrounded by a small group of joyful soldiers. The Unknown Soldier standing next to Corporal Cravits said, "Can ya believe it, sir?"

Corporal Cravits said, "We decided to change his name to Buckshot on account of him bein' hit with canister and all."

"Yes, I heard," said Captain Jenkins.

The men, many of whom served picket duty around the horse the previous day, parted to allow the surgeon to examine Buckshot. The horse, unimpressed by the surgeon or his role in saving him and Lieutenant Abbott, did not acknowledge the captain's presence and continued to graze. Captain Jenkins scanned the horse with his hand. He looked at the ear and the eye and found no drainage or other signs of infection and carefully examined the other wounds and found them to be in good shape. "I can't believe what I'm seeing. This is incredible," said Captain Jenkins.

"Why, ya can barely tell he was hurt, sir," said Corporal Cravits.

Captain Jenkins ran his hand through Buckshot's mane and thought, *I should have tried it on Lieutenant Abbott*, and said, "Buckshot, it is ole boy. Time for me to check on your lieutenant." The captain made his way to the barn.

"Hello, captain," said Clara, "Did you see Buckshot? That's what everyone is callin' 'im now."

"Yes, I did. Reckon Buckshot's a fitting name," said Captain Jenkins with a laugh.

Clara said, "I've never seen wounds look so good. You may be onto something, sir."

"Maybe. How's Lieutenant Abbott?" asked the captain.

"See for yourself. Sergeant O'Conner's with him now," said Clara, pointing to Lieutenant Abbott who was propped up on pillows talking to Sergeant O'Conner.

Sergeant O'Conner greeted the captain. "Good marning, sarr. Praise the Lord. Me lieutenant is goin' a make it."

ANNA MAE'S BUCKSHOT

Captain Jenkins, greatly relieved, said, "How are you doin'? Your horse created quite a stir. Do you remember any of it, lieutenant?"

Lieutenant Abbott said, "I'm in pain, sir, but it beats bein' dead. The last thing I remember is seein' the cannon aimed at me, and someone hollered, 'FIRE.' The blast hit me and Jim. Then I woke up here. That's all, sir. Thanks for saving me."

Sergeant O'Conner said, "Lieutenant, darl'n, that harse saved ye. The whole Reb army stopped shootin' an' let Buckshot—I mean, Jim through with ya hangin' on."

"Buckshot?" asked Lieutenant Abbott.

"Aye, sarr. The men changed his name to Buckshot," said Sergeant O'Conner.

Lieutenant Abbott looked at Captain Jenkins and said, "My sergeant says you saved Jim."

"Aye, he did, sarr," said Sergeant O'Conner.

Clara flashed an affectionate smile toward the sergeant and said, "Let's not forget the sergeant's whiskey." She stepped up to the sergeant and gently kissed him on the cheek, causing his cheeks to take on a red hue.

Sergeant O'Conner said, "Truth be told, lieutenant, I still have another bottle."

Captain Jenkins laughed. "I'd like to see the quartermaster's face when I put in a request for five cases of Irish whiskey."

Lieutenant Abbott asked, "Whiskey?"

Clara said, "Just something the captain cooked up."

Captain Jenkins handed the deformed Minie ball to Lieutenant Abbott and said, "I want you to have this. It's the round that took your leg. I pulled it out of your horse."

Lieutenant Abbott scrutinized the piece of metal and said, "Buckshot. I like that. It's a fine name."

"You have a special horse, lieutenant," said Clara.

"He is indeed, sarr," added Sergeant O'Conner.

Captain Jenkins smiled at Sergeant O'Conner and said, "The men who saw what happened think it's a miracle from God. I'm thinkin' they may be right. It took a lot to pull you through, lieutenant. Even Johnny Reb had a hand in it. If what I hear is true, it may well have been part of God's plan."

Sergeant O'Conner said, "It was indeed, cap'n. Never seen anythin' like it."

Captain Jenkins replied, "A miracle. A bona fide miracle."

CHAPTER 23

Buster Redeemed

"Anna Mae. Anna Mae," said Lil' Bill. Anna Mae stopped reading, looked up, and found Lil' Bill standing over her. Lil' Bill, eager to impart his newly discovered news about Anna Mae's horse, said, "Buckshot's a hero."

Anna Mae replied, "He saved Papaw's life at Gettysburg. It's all in this book. I've been reading about it."

Lil' Bill looked at the old decrepit horse napping in the shade. "Yes, Miss Weatherby told us about Buckshot. She told us about Gettysburg and even made Buster read the Gettysburg Address in front of us. I never seen Buster like that. She went after him on account of how he treated you and Buckshot. Remember, I told ya she could be mean. Whupped him, she did. She even broke his nose. He's up talking to your mamaw. I think he's goin' to apologize."

Anna Mae closed the binder. She rose to her feet and looked at the gentle horse stretched out on the ground, snoring. The horse was content, and so was she. She studied the wounds of July 3, 1863. The small discolored scars etched into the horse's coat were evidence of the canister blast that nearly killed the horse and her grandfather. The eye and ear Captain Jenkins fixed presented Anna Mae with the horror of war. Through the horse, the clash of hundreds of men killing each other came to life. Their lives were cut short in their prime, and they would never know the joy she took for granted. Anna Mae wondered if Buckshot had memories of that day. Did the horse remember the horror? Was a horse capable of understanding such horror?

In the scars, she also saw the tangible manifestation of God's greatness and the hope of man. The Confederate soldiers that allowed Buckshot to pass and men standing guard over Buckshot, honoring a soldier's dying wish and refusing to shoot the animal. Private Powell, Clara, the Unknown Soldier, and Sergeant O'Conner came to life as well.

Through her grandfather's writing, the worst of man and the best of man filled her imagination. Buckshot, the old useless horse she once thought of as ugly, became a thing of beauty. The horse showed that underneath whatever horror that was contrived by man, love was waiting to be unleashed. She realized God was love, and for the first time, God was more than a passage in the Bible. Like her grandmother, she was able to see God's presence. And like her grandmother, she understood that Buckshot was a part of a greater plan. She did not need to understand the plan—only that it was God's plan. God used Buckshot to teach her love.

Anna Mae turned to Lil' Bill, holding the ledger so he could see it, and said, "I know all about it. Buckshot got shot by a cannon, and Papaw lost his leg. When he was well, he wrote it all down." She turned her gaze to Buster, who tormented her and Buckshot earlier that morning, making his way to the porch as her mother and grandmother looked on.

Like Buckshot with Lil' Bill the previous week, Miss Weatherby stripped away the barrier to Buster's soul and exposed the cruelty within. A cruelty that buried his conscience which now was set free. He saw within himself what Anna Mae and Lil' Bill saw within themselves, and like them, it was a tremendous burden to bear.

Mary said, "Hello, child. Ya look troubled. Been hopin' ya would come around."

Shame drove Buster's eyes to his feet. As with Anna Mae, every misdeed, no matter how trivial, wreaked torment on him with no way to get from under it. He said, "Miss Mary, you're right. I'm troubled. I've done some bad things to you and Buckshot. Other things too." Watching her mother, Katherine rocked and remained quiet.

Mary saw a change in the boy. She said, "Yes, ya have."

"You won't have no more problems from me," said Buster.

Mary said, "Is that so?"

Buster looked Mary in the eye and said, "Yes, ma'am, no more problems. I know I was mean. I apologize."

Seeking to test Buster's sincerity, Mary asked, "Do ya mean it, child?"

"Yes, will ya forgive me?" asked Buster.

"Yes, Buster. I forgive ya. Let's hear no more of it." Mary paused for a moment. "Ya lost yir ma when ya was young. Yir pa did good a providin' fer ya, but sometimes ya need a lil' more."

Buster, thinking of their previous encounter, was relieved but confused at Mary's response. He said, "You forgive me. You don't hate me? Don't matter what I done? I don't understand."

"Of course, I don't hate you. Why, Jesus suffered far worse than me or ole Buckshot. They drove nails through him, beat him, and left 'im a hangin' on that cross to suffer an' die, an' he's God's Son. He fergive us of all that. An' all the bad things we done. Then he arose from bein' dead. Child, ya need Jesus in yir life. I think Jesus wants in yir heart and is usin' ole Buckshot to git in. All part of the plan, ya see."

Buster asked, "Miss Weatherby said you knew my mother. What was she like?"

Mary said, "Yes, I did. We was friends, an' a fine Christian woman was she. An' loved ya dearly. I remember when ya was born."

"Were you and her at Gettysburg?" asked Buster.

"Yes, we was. It was powerful bad. The dead an' wounded everywharr. She was a huntin' yir pa, an' I was looking fer John," replied Mary.

"Why did she have to die, Miss Mary? I don't understand."

"I don't know," said Mary. "I do know she died with the saving grace of Jesus." She realized the boy was struggling to cope, not knowing his mother, and not able to grieve. Mary felt she had found the root of Buster's anguish, and time was at hand. A time Mary longed for. "Ya know, child, even if'n we live a full life, it's only a small speck on a flea. It don't really matter if'n ya have ten years or a hundred. What matters is how ya live 'em. Yir ma lived a good life, and I believe she's a lookin' down on ya now. God took my John an' Anna Mae's pa. They died in the savin' grace of Jesus. I'll be with 'em in heaven when I die."

"Will I see my mother in heaven?" asked Buster.

"Child, yir on the way. Yir a different boy now than ya was this mornin'. I think the Spirit is a movin' on ya," said Mary.

"But, Miss Mary, I'm awful," said Buster.

Mary said, "Ya *was* awful. I can plainly see ya ain't the boy I knowed last week or even this mornin'. He's gone. The real boy's here now, the good one. None of that other stuff don't matter from here on. Ya see, it's never too late to do what's right. She's a waitin' on ya, and you'll see her again in heaven. But ya gotta believe. Ya gotta have faith."

"I don't understand. What do I got to do, Miss Mary?"

"Ya gotta repent yir ways. That means to turn from yir sin. Then accept Jesus as yir Lord an' savior. I did a long time ago even before I met John. Then ya jist leave all yir sin with Jesus. He paid the price fer ya on that ole cross."

"You were a sinner too, Miss Mary?" asked Buster.

Mary said, "Yes, still am. We all are. Only Jesus's perfect. You'll never stop sinnin'. But the more ya trust in Jesus, the easier it'll be to fight sin."

Buster said, "I never got to see my mother."

Mary held the boy and ran her hands through the child's hair. "Now, child, I'll help ya, but first I want you to git Anna Mae and Lil' Bill and bring 'em to the tack room. Make sure they bring Buckshot."

Buster turned from Mary, and as he left to get Buckshot, he said, "I'll get 'im, Miss Mary."

Mary saw the dread lift from Buster then looked at Katherine and said, "I been a prayin' fer this."

CHAPTER 24

Buster Faces His Demons

Buster found Anna Mae and Lil' Bill petting Buckshot. He stopped short and gazed at the horse that only hours ago was the focal point of his lust for hate. He looked into the one eye, much as Lil' Bill had a week earlier. The horse, like then, showed neither anger nor curiosity. Instead the horse mirrored back to Buster the very hate he heaped upon those he mercilessly tormented. The young boy had reached his lowest ebb.

He replayed the lesson Miss Weatherby taught of the bloody battle, of heroism, and the honor of those who took part in the war. But most of all, the heroism of a horse that had more honor than he had. He thought of what Mary had said to him moments ago. It was never too late to do the right thing. The words ignited a strong desire to change. He was ready to reconcile.

Lil' Bill and Anna Mae watched Buster as he approached the horse with reverence. Buster felt a need to touch the wounds that caused the contempt he had for the horse. He ran his hand over the animal's bad eye, then worked his way to the knob of flesh that was once an ear. A friendly nicker eased Buster's burden and indicated forgiveness to the boy. Buster said nothing to the horse and stepped toward Anna Mae.

"Hello. I'm Buster," said the troubled boy in low and determined tones as he gazed upon the horse not ready to face Anna Mae.

Anna Mae stared at Buster's blackened eyes and, considering her own behavior toward the horse, replied, "My name is Anna Mae." Lil' Bill, having made amends with his friend, said nothing.

"Sorry about this morning," said Buster, wishing to dispose of the matter at hand, and added, "should not have treated you that way." He turned to face the beautiful girl.

"It's all right, Buster. I haven't been kind either," said Anna Mae.

"Miss Weatherby told us about your Papaw and Buckshot. They're heroes," said Buster.

"I know. I just got done reading about it," said Anna Mae, holding the binder to her chest.

"I talked to your Mamaw. I was kinda mean before you even got here. She forgave me," Buster ran his hand through his hair as he looked at her feet, "Can ya forgive me?"

Anna Mae was ready to move forward as well. She wanted her actions to be put behind her and bury them in a deep pit. She replied, "Yes. I forgive you." Her affirmation removed the heavy chains of despair that, until moments ago, he was unaware existed. He felt as though he were closing the door on a dank, dimly lit dungeon and was walking into a vast expanse of never-ending beauty.

Buster said, "We can be friends now."

Anna Mae replied, "Yes. We're friends."

Buster said, "Thanks. Your mamaw wants us to take Buckshot to the tack room." The three left and headed for the barn with Buckshot following.

CHAPTER 25

Love

Katherine and Mary found the three children with Buckshot waiting by the tack room. "Done as ya asked, Miss Mary," said Buster.

"Good," said Mary. "I got somethin' special fer y'all to see."

Mary removed a burlap sheet, kicking up a small cloud of dust and exposing a McClellan saddle. Katherine made her way to a trunk and retrieved a saddle blanket along with a Union saddlecloth. Katherine said, "Anna Mae, bring Buckshot a little closer."

The children curiously watched Katherine position the saddle blanket on the patient horse. After making minor adjustments, she said, "Mom, this is in as good a shape as the last time we did this."

"Did what, Mamaw?" asked Anna Mae.

"You'll see, child," said Mary.

Katherine draped the blue Union Cavalry saddlecloth, trimmed with two gold accent stripes, along the edge, and the letters *US* embroidered in the corner over the saddle blanket. After making more adjustments, Katherine said, "We're ready for the saddle."

Mary turned to Buster and asked, "Buster, can ya help us with the saddle?"

"Sure, Miss Mary," said Buster. Eager to please Mary, he grabbed the saddle and threw it over Buckshot's swayed back. After tightening the cinch, Buster stepped back.

The old horse stood motionless, proudly adorned as he was during the Battle of Gettysburg. "Mamaw, Buckshot's a handsome horse," said Anna Mae feeling a sense of newly found pride in the animal.

Mary said, "He sure is a handsome horse. This here's the very saddle, blanket, and cloth that was on Buckshot the day he went into battle and got shot."

Lil' Bill asked, "Can we ride him?"

Mary reached into her apron pocket and pulled out a deformed mass of lead and said, "Of course, ya can, child. But first, I'm a needin' to show ya somethin." The stoic war-torn horse stood patiently, accustomed to the ritual Mary was about to perform.

Mary handed the mass to Anna Mae and said, "That ole hunk of lead was the Minie ball that cost yir papaw his leg."

"Can I see it?" asked Buster.

"Yes," replied Anna Mae handing it to Buster.

Buster turned his gaze back at the shapeless mass he was holding, once a perfectly formed conical Minie ball. He studied it and ran his fingers over it repeatedly, as if it were a precious gem. The chaotic scene of men fighting a desperate battle came to life. A Confederate infantryman frantically tore open the cartridge with his teeth and poured powder into the barrel. After ramming the Minie ball down the barrel, he placed the percussion cap, pulled the hammer back, and shouldered the musket. He took aim through the dense smoke and pulled the trigger. The blast sent the Minie ball into John Abbott's leg, shattering his femur just above the knee. The story Miss Weatherby recounted now had three dimensions. Buster wondered if the soldier who fired the Minie ball was still alive. If he was, he likely had no idea how special his shot was.

He looked into himself and vowed, in the name of Jesus, to change and become a better person. Mary studied Buster and saw the sincerity in his face as he looked at the mass, quietly stroking it with his thumb. It was as if he was looking into a portal that had opened into the past. But more importantly than that, it was as if the past was reaching out to Buster. She knew what Buster was thinking because she had the same thoughts when she held it in her hand.

Mary said, "Now let me show ya somethin' special." She pointed to a small hole in the skirt of the saddle. Mary lifted the skirt which exposed a hole in the saddlecloth. Next she lifted the saddlecloth and said, "Look at this scar on Buckshot. See how it lines up perfectly with the hole in the saddlecloth and saddle." Mary lifted and lowered the skirt and saddlecloth several times to show the children. "That doctor found it pokin' out of ole Buckshot's hide," she said.

Lil' Bill said, "It lines up. Look, Anna Mae, that's the saddle your papaw was on when he got shot."

Katherine said, "Yes, Lil' Bill, it is."

Mary turned to Buster and said, "Hand me that ole Minie ball." Mary placed the Minie ball over the scar and rotated it until the uniquely deformed mass matched the pattern of the scar. "See how it fits? That army doctor pulled it from Buckshot. This very spot and give it to yir papaw, an' he kept it with that ledger." Mary returned the Minie ball to Anna Mae. "Child, I want ya to keep it and the book. I want ya to have it."

Anna Mae walked over to Buckshot and asked, "Thank you, Mamaw. Can I still have Buckshot? Is he my horse?"

"Sure, child," said Mary. Then she turned her attention to Buster.

Mary prayed for a change in the troubled boy. Now her prayer was answered, and it was time to bring the Lord to the boy. She said, "Buster, I got somethin fer ya in my pocket." Mary handed Buster a Bible. "John carried this here Bible when he was in the army. He had it at Gettysburg an' up until the day he died. I want ya to have it."

Buster took the Bible and flipped through the pages. Its worn leather cover and pencil-marked pages gave to the boy an indication of the strength of the owner's faith. He immediately felt the power of the Holy Spirit lift the burden of his ungodly behavior and replace it with hope. He saw himself as a new person, and this moment would forever be etched into his memory. "Thank you, Miss Mary. Was it with him when Buckshot got shot?" asked Buster.

"Yes, it was. Now, child, if'n ya read it, you'll understand what God expects of ya. Read it ever' day, and remember what we talked about. It'll help ya become a better person," said Mary.

"I'll read it, Miss Mary. I promise," said Buster.

"Buckshot's ready to ride. You care if I ride your horse, Anna Mae?" asked Lil' Bill.

With pride, Anna Mae said, "Yes."

Lil' Bill put his left foot in the stirrup and grabbed the horn, then swung into the saddle. He rubbed the top of the horse's head and wondered of the moment when he was hit with canister. Buckshot responded to a gentle tug on the reins and wheeled about. After a gentle nudge with his heel, Buckshot began to walk forward. "He sure is easy to ride," said Lil' Bill.

"I'm next," said Buster, following Lil' Bill and Buckshot out of the barn.

Anna Mae ran to her Mamaw and threw her arms around her. "Thanks, Mamaw. Buckshot's the most beautiful horse I've ever seen." Katherine watched her mother hold Anna Mae and saw happiness overtake the deep despair that, only a short time ago, was within the child.

"You're welcome, child," said Mary as she stroked Anna Mae's hair.

EPILOGUE

Mary stopped knitting and looked at Anna Mae riding Buckshot. Buster and Lil' Bill were walking beside her on either side. Caesar was darting back and forth underneath the horse, seeking the attention of the children. She marveled at the beauty of the scene and the rapid change she witnessed in the children. After giving quiet praise to Jesus, she resumed knitting, sneaking in short glances. Katherine stepped onto the porch, settled next to her mother, and said, "Those young'uns been riding that horse to school all week."

"Yes, child, thick as thieves they are," replied Mary as she let out a faint chuckle.

"You were right, Mom. I never seen such a change. I was beginning to wonder if I would ever see Anna Mae this happy."

Mary said, "Never give up on the Lord."

Drawn by the sound of trotting hooves, Katherine cast her gaze down the road. A shiny black carriage pulled by two Appaloosas was moving at a brisk pace and kicking up a small cloud of dust. A folding black top was open, protecting the riders from the sun. A single seat upholstered with hand-tooled leather provided ample room for two large men. Behind the seat was stacked several pieces of luggage.

Driving the carriage was her uncle Zeb, but she did not recognize the neatly dressed man at his side. She said, "Look, Mom, Uncle Zeb's headed this way, and he's with someone. I wonder who it is." Mary got up from her rocker; leaned on the railing; and straining to see, she immediately recognized her son, Nicklaus. Scarcely able to contain her joy, she gave Katherine no indication of her knowledge.

"Not sure who it is. Ain't seen a fancy rig like that in a long time," said Mary.

Katherine said, "Whoever's with Zeb's must be pretty high on the totem pole."

"Woah," said Zeb as he gently pulled on the reins, bringing the carriage to a quick stop just short of the children.

Nicklaus jumped from the carriage, removed a slouch hat, and tossed it on the seat. The tall handsome man with an athletic build, blond hair, deep-set brown eyes, and a thick drooping mustache made his way to Buckshot. Anna Mae failed to notice his resemblance to her mother. Nicklaus closely inspected Buckshot and recognized the McClellan saddle and the Union Cavalry saddlecloth. He said, "Little girl, where did you find such an ugly beat-up old horse?" Zeb laughed as he climbed down from the carriage.

Indignantly Anna Mae said, "Mister, this horse ain't ugly. He's a hero. Saved my papaw at Gettysburg."

Buster said, "You take that back, mister, or I'll make you eat them words. That horse fought at Gettysburg, got hit with blast of canister, and nearly got killed."

Lil' Bill quietly walked over to Zeb and asked, "Who's this man Mr. Zeb?" Laughing, Zeb ignored the query.

Katherine recognized her brother and a broad smile washed over her face. "Mom, I don't believe it. It's Nick." She ran toward the small gathering paused and turned toward her mother and said, "Come on, Mom. Let's go see 'im."

Feigning surprise, Mary said, "I do declare I believe yir right. Ya jist go on. I'll be down tharr directly child." Mary leaned against the banister and watched her family come together.

Nicklaus gently patted Buckshot on the neck and said, "I know this ole horse. It's Buckshot."

"You've heard a Buckshot?" asked Anna Mae.

"Everyone knows about ole Buckshot. I bet you're Anna Mae," said Nicklaus.

Anna Mae smiled and said, "Yes, I am. Who are you?"

"Young lady, you look just like your mother. I'm your uncle Nick." He looked at Zeb. "Uncle Zeb, hand Anna Mae that paper I brought from St. Louis."

Zeb reached in the carriage and retrieved a folded newspaper and handed it to Anna Mae as she sat on Buckshot. "Tarnation, lil' lady, looks like the whole darn country knows about that ole horse," said Zeb.

Anna Mae looked at the front page. The headline read, "Gettysburg 25 Years Later." Under the headline was a picture of Buckshot standing proudly with Dr. Jenkins, Clara Jones, Cooper Powell, Patrick O'Conner, and Lee Roy Cravits. The caption under the picture read, "Buckshot, the Hero Horse That Saved His Lieutenant, and the Staff That Saved Him," by Dr. Carl Jenkins.

"That's the doctor that saved Papaw's life. He saved Buckshot too," said Anna Mae. "I read all about it in Papaw's book."

"Yes, it is," replied Nicklaus. "Finest doctor in St. Louis. He told the story. It's all in the paper Zeb just gave you."

Katherine threw her arms around her brother and said, "Welcome home, little brother. We give up on ever seein' you again." She looked intently at the carriage. "Looks like you're doin' good."

Nicklaus laughed and said, "Hello, sis. I was livin' just outside of St. Louis. Took me a while to settle my affairs. Then saw that picture of Buckshot, and I figured I made my pile and knew it was time to get home. I'm sorry I wasn't here when James and Dad died. I was just now able to get here. Had that carriage made in Gettysburg. Special order, picked it up yesterday. Figured on takin' Mom to church in it."

"Losin' Dad was hard on Mom, and James was like a son to her. It was hard on me and Anna Mae too. Why didn't you tell Mom you were coming?" asked Katherine.

"I wanted to surprise her. Last night I stayed with Uncle Zeb," said Nicklaus.

Anna Mae climbed from Buckshot and said, "Look, it's Buckshot," then showed the paper to Lil' Bill and Buster.

Zeb said, "Tarnation, thought I saw a ghost when Nick showed up at my door."

Lil' Bill looked at the picture and said, "Look, Buster. Buckshot's famous."

Zeb, Nicklaus, and the children hovered around the gentle old horse, each seeking a spot to touch and pet. Anna Mae showed the gathering the bullet hole in the saddle skirt. Mary watched from the porch as Anna Mae repeatedly lifted the skirt, pointing to the hole in the saddlecloth. Mary studied Anna Mae as she held the mangled mass of lead next to the scar etched in Buckshot's back as Nicklaus, Zeb, and the children looked on. Rising above the din of friendly banter and laughter, Mary repeatedly heard "Buckshot" and marveled at the beauty of the scene before her. Nicklaus looked at his mother and smiled. Their eyes locked, and she smiled back.

Mary's thoughts turned to the war that caused so much carnage. She thought of the account Zeb had told of Willie and his mother, who like so many mothers lost their sons. Willie's mother did not even have a place to visit. No grave to put flowers to honor her son's personal sacrifice as well as hers. Why was it that so many had to endure such a nightmare as this sweet woman?

Not since she became a Christian had Mary's faith been tested in such an overpowering way. She asked herself, *What kind of plan was it that God had, or what purpose could there have been in having such a terrible war that wreaked so much misery and cost so many lives? Why am I so blessed?* She was not accustomed to asking God why. She never questioned God's plan, and tentacles of doubt were attempting to breach her faith and rob her of this special moment. She then fixed her gaze on Buckshot. The sight of the old flea-bitten nag that had endured so much girded her wavering faith. She repeated to herself what she had been saying to Katherine, "Never doubt the Lord's plan. Never give up on the Lord."

Mary thought about it and realized that God did not create the horror of slavery or the ensuing war that came about to end it. God did not kill the thousands of soldiers during the conflict. God did not create hate and sin. God gave man free will, and man used free will to rebel against God. Sin and hate are man's own doing.

Mary remembered the account her husband, John, had told and committed to writing: the moment that Buckshot was hit with a cannon blast and somehow managed to stay on his feet, saving him and John from certain death. Then a thousand guns fell silent and, for a brief moment, pulled back the curtain on man's hate to expose God's love for all to see. She thought of how Dr. Jenkins, Clara Jones, Sergeant O'Conner, Corporal Lee Roy Cravits, Private Cooper Powell, and the Unknown Soldier all came together to save a horse. That was God's plan for Buckshot. A horse that sought the love of a little girl, all the while showing three troubled children how to love. Mary then asked herself, *Who am I to try to ascend to the perch of God?* The sight of Buckshot made her faith stronger, and she thanked God in the name of Jesus.

Mary reminisced about an entire lifetime of little miracles. Miracles that spanned a lifetime, and some that came in flashes so brief they could not be measured in hours, minutes, or even seconds. She gave thought to other miracles that came in the form of Anna Mae and her children. The biggest miracle of all was unfolding in front of her. She watched her whole world before her and remembered what John had told her, "Only God could make a horse." She saw the tangible manifestation of what she already knew.

Buckshot was an instrument of God's plan. A special horse that brought peace taught a little girl to see with her heart and pulled a boy from hate. Nothing troubled Mary; she was at peace. Mary saw the superpower. The superpower that bridled hatred and halted a brutal bloodlust, if only for a brief moment. The superpower that could change history in a single flash. Mary saw the power of love.

AFTERWORD

When I was seventeen years old, I was driving on southbound I-75, entering Cincinnati. It was a late afternoon, and the highway was crowded with cars and trucks traveling at a high rate of speed. I was heading home and fell asleep.

At that very instant, a bird flew into my windshield right in front of my face, and I snapped to. I knew it was a bird because a small feather was stuck to the windshield. I stayed wide awake until I made it home. Oddly enough, I did not give it a lot of thought.

Over the years, however, I got to thinking about it more and more. Not before or since has a bird, or anything, hit my windshield in such a manner. I must have annoyed many close friends over the years as to whether or not a bird had struck their windshields in such a fashion. As of this writing, I have never had an affirmative answer.

What I failed to realize at the time was that I had won the greatest lottery possible. I suspect that, if it could be calculated, the odds of an event like that occurring in such a way are astronomical. In fact, it may be like winning three Powerball lotteries in a row. What's more, it is not the only time an event like that has occurred in my life. It was these events that finally drove this one-time God skeptic to admit there is a God. It was the example of my wife, her family, and of course, reading the Bible that led me to believe that Jesus Christ is the Son of God. That he did indeed come, teach, and die on a redemptive mission of love to save mankind, including me. Then after the brutal crucifixion, he rose from the dead, appeared to his disciples, ascended to heaven, and will one day return.

After I came to that realization, I would contemplate, *Why would God want to save a worthless person like me?* The answer was simple, to me anyway. Had I lost control of the car, a huge pileup and a significant loss of life, including my own, would have likely occurred. Plus, I surmised that among the other travelers, there was likely a future Nobel laureate in their midst. Or a person that would discover a cure for a horrible disease. Maybe even a busload of school children on an outing. Now that makes sense.

In the closing sequence of this story, Mary reminisced, "Miracles that spanned a lifetime, and some that came in flashes so brief they could not be measured in hours, minutes, or even seconds." It was the many odd occurrences, like the one I just described, that caused me to add that line. It was such events that drove me to write this story.

I am sure a skeptic would point out that with the number of cars on the road throughout the world, at any given moment—hundreds of millions—a bird would hit a windshield sooner or later. Maybe, but from my perspective or the perspective of any given individual, the odds are equally astronomical for such a strike. The misfiring of Zeb's prized Henry rifle at a key moment and the little dog chasing off the bear is intended to mirror my incident on the highway so many years ago.

Anna Mae's Buckshot and the characters directly related to Anna Mae and the horse Buckshot are fiction. The climactic Farnsworth Charge, however, did take place on July 3, 1863, and represents the last fighting of the Battle of Gettysburg. I did adapt it to fit my story. I drew from *Gettysburg Heroes Perfect Soldiers Hallowed Ground* by Glenn W. LaFantasie—an excellent book—and several online sources.

However, most of what I wrote regarding the ill-fated charge is true. The heated discussion Farnsworth had with Judson Kilpatrick just before the charge in which the former lost his life likely took place. This exchange was witnessed. I added some dialogue to help emphasize Farnsworth's legitimate concerns over the ineffectiveness of the charge he was eventually ordered to make. The charge would make General Elon J. Farnsworth the highest-ranking Union officer to fall behind enemy lines during the Civil War. When one tours the Gettysburg battlefield, they will notice monuments marking where generals fell, both Union and Confederate. It is quite remarkable that there is no such monument marking where General Farnsworth fell.

I recreated the overview of the Battle of Gettysburg primarily from *Gettysburg: The Last Invasion* by Allen C. Guelzo, a fine book which I highly recommend. Another fine book I drew from was *Destiny of the Republic* by Candice Millard. These authors do outstanding work, for which I am grateful and enjoyed reading. I also utilized *American Battlefield Trust*. It is an excellent online resource staffed by dedicated individuals that do an outstanding job breaking down complex battles in simple terms by using animated battle maps. The American Battlefield Trust and the authors mentioned have no connection to me or my work.

The nurse, Clarissa "Clara" Fellows Jones, not to be confused with Clara Barton, is a real but a lesser-known historical figure. She was a teacher, and when school was out, she would help, unpaid, at the battlefields. She did not arrive at Gettysburg until July 19. Her part in my story, like the rest of the scene that she takes part, is fiction. I put her in my story simply because I wanted to honor this kind person.

The fictional character, the Unknown Soldier, was added to honor all the unknowns that died during the Civil War. The term "Unknown Soldier" was used as a proper noun during the telling of this story. Upon visiting the Gettysburg and Antietam Cemeteries, I was deeply moved by the number of unknowns and wished to draw the attention of the reader to the thousands of soldiers that died unknown.

Another fictional character, Willie, Zeb's younger friend from the Cornfield, died as an unknown. Through the character, Willie, I wanted the reader to see a mother's sacrifice. I could never imagine anything worse than a mother losing her child, but sadly there is. The thousands of mothers, fathers, sisters, brothers, and wives who said their goodbyes to loved ones, never to see them again and not having a place to put down flowers. Their loved ones are, of this world, forever lost.

When they said their goodbyes, they just vanished into the ether without a trace. They are lost in anonymity, buried under stones marked unknown. They are real, and I wanted to point that out to those unfamiliar with the history of this or any war.

Also real is Jesus, the living God. The God that has a plan for all of us. The fictional character Mary Abbott, in this story, clearly understood this. She saw God's plan in everything, not just the fantastic instances like those outlined in this narrative. She saw God's miracles and the love of Jesus in the simplest of things. Her character is a composite of several older people in my life, which includes my mother-in-law and father-in-law.

In the end, Mary briefly contemplates the carnage of war. Like most of us who question and doubt God's method, Mary, too, questions how God would employ war to advance love. She ultimately reminds herself that God did not create war and hate. Those are the constructs of man. God can only love. It was love that caused God to send his son, Jesus, to reconcile us with his Father in heaven.

When I was younger, before I was married, I asked an older person I respected, "Why do you believe in God?"

Her answer was simple: "Too much order, young man."

Then I asked, "Why do you believe in Jesus?"

Again her answer was simple: "Without Jesus, there is no hope." While it all made sense, I tucked it away to be recalled for times like now. I suppose I denied Jesus. Through this writing, I want to acknowledge that I will no longer deny him.

So what about my fictional horse, Buckshot? Buckshot, to me, is the face of all horses in war or any horse tasked with doing our work and, yes, dying for us. There are many stories of special horses and other animals that rallied those who served in the armed forces during battles or other hardships. I have never served in the armed forces, let alone in a war zone, nor am I a horse expert. I was moved by the forgotten valor of these fine animals, and I, therefore, made it a central force in the story. Ultimately, however, Buckshot was an instrument of God's teaching of love.

Could something like what occurred in this story actually have happened? I think so. Humanity is always near the surface, waiting to be unleashed. Take Confederate Sergeant Richard Kirkland who, after the disastrous failed charges by Union forces at the Battle of Fredericksburg, chose to give water and comfort to the wounded Union soldiers lying about suffering. Or on Christmas Eve, 1914, when shortly after the start of World War I, German soldiers along with British and French soldiers along the Western Front chose to stop fighting. Then on Christmas day, they came out of their trenches and met in the middle of no man's land where just hours earlier, they were busy killing each other. They shook hands and celebrated Christmas. They set up Christmas trees and even exchanged presents, stories, and friendly banter. What became known as the Christmas Truce of 1914 was short-lived, and the carnage would resume.

World War I would become one of the deadliest wars in human history. But for a brief moment in time, thousands of guns fell silent. Not because of any official truce, but because of love. In my view, Jesus made his presence known.

I drew from many resources in the telling of this story, like the ones I just mentioned. I also visited the battlefields of Antietam and Gettysburg and spoke with several volunteers who kindly shared their expertise. I stood in the East Woods of Antietam where the unfortunate colonel, who had lost his nerve, ran in panic. Yes, that actually happened. He was not a colonel in the Eighty-Eighth Pennsylvania Infantry Regiment, however. It is a sad story and a reminder of how any of us have breaking points and can succumb to fear. I left him unnamed.

I also visited Burnside's Bridge and Little Round Top among others. All beautiful places that hardly seem locations for such carnage. Also, beautiful places are the cemeteries of these battlefields which I had the honor to visit. They are serene places of honor for those who gave their all. Like President Lincoln said, "From these honored dead we take increased devotion to that cause for which they gave the last full measure of devotion."

In the end, this is a story of love, and love is a force. Unlike gravity, love cannot be measured. There are no basic units of love. Therefore, it cannot be predicted or calculated. Yet it can be seen and felt. It is a power that resides in all of us, ready for those willing to unleash it.

I wrote this story for my granddaughters so they could know my thoughts long after I have passed from this world. Maybe they will have a doubt or be somehow tested. I would like to be able to speak to them and provide guidance. My sermon to them, even though I have no formal theological training. I suppose I am in no moral position to deliver such a sermon, so I created the character Mary Abbott to help drive home my point. I hope they or anyone who reads this will gain some useful insight or help them overcome doubt. If you have made it this far and do not know me, thank you for reading, especially if you do not believe.

Whatever you believe, be courageous enough to listen to someone you disagree with. If you are a nonbeliever, I hope you find Jesus.

CPSIA information can be obtained
at www.ICGtesting.com
Printed in the USA
BVHW070809141222
654207BV00002B/238